The V...

Tracey S   ... Townsend

Wild Pressed Books

For Omid

The first time I saw you
my he_____ned

I saw a man shot,
A woman screaming
And when I intervened,
My arm was broken.

The Vagabond Seekers

Nearing the shore,
I fell out of the boat.
Woke up in hospital.
I asked the nurse where I was
and she replied with a cocked eyebrow
that I was in France.
I had yet to understand
the British sense of humour.

Part I

Sky ink-clear, dark sea rough, we're thrown about.
I have only a small bag. I'm tired, but I'm not scared.
There is nothing to see but I have a feeling
a city is close by.
Somewhere inside me a small hope wavers,
a candle in the dark.

1

Maya

March 2017

Email from: Ned461@gossip.com
To: Maya Joy Galen

Subject: Cool that you're coming to Samos!

Hey Maya,
Or should I say 'Granny Maya' now? Congratulations by the way, Jodie and I are thrilled to bits you reunited with your sons and discovered some bonus grandchildren as well.

Long time no see! How are you? Yeah, Jodie and I are fine, thanks. It's tough emotionally, you know, dealing with some of the things we see here but at least we feel like we're trying to do something to help. It's all you can do, isn't it? In the face of the batshit political situation and lack of support from the effing establishment I mean, well, I won't go into that right now, I can just see you shaking your head at me yeah, don't deny it.

Anyway. I'm glad you're bringing your daughter to Samos with you, I remember you talking about her a lot when we were in Australia together. Speaking of then, did you know Aiden arrived at the camp a week or so ago? He'll be here a month — staying with me and Jodie in our one-bedroom apartment above a garage, he's sleeping on the sofa. He was going to rent a place of his own, but we persuaded him to use his money on things the NGOs are short of instead. He brought a load of basic first aid stuff and over the counter medicines with him. Heads up, you could do the same if you've got any money — painkillers, antiseptics, bandages, you get my drift. Everything helps. Also sleeping bags and tents but you might not have enough room for those.

You probably wonder how we can afford to rent an apartment, me and Jodie, the masters of living on nothing? Well, we stay here free in exchange for shopping and cleaning for the old woman who owns our apartment. She lives in the main part of the house. A few of the other volunteers rent rooms off her and it's them we mainly clean up after, Jodie had a go at one of them for being such a slob. But I reminded her we're here to serve, haha. You know Jodie.

So yeah, the Australia gang will be back together again soon. How cool's that? After more than two years. FYI, Aiden's still single. He was in a relationship with a girl called Katy but they recently broke up. I think that's one reason he came out here. How about your Daisy? I remember you saying you thought Daisy and Aiden would be a match for each other. Just saying. No, no, I won't say anything to Aiden, before you freak out, I can just picture you!

Anyway, I thought I'd pass on some useful skills that're needed in the camp before you arrive, just in case either of you are wondering what you might be expected to do. Remember when I put together that vagabond living guide, haha. Well, this is something similar. A list of suggestions of things people can do at the camp here:

- Teach English, or any other languages you or Daisy might have.

6

- Teach a musical instrument, do you still have the guitar you bought in Sydney? I remember you playing it around the campfire at that beach party we went to when we met up in Bali.

- Help make up CVs. We try to help the refugees prepare for a life ahead of the shit they're having to go through now. Gives them some hope that things'll get better, y'know?

- Use any computer skills you or Daisy might have, e.g. fixing computers and/or teaching a computer class. (Haha, Maya.)

- Driving — especially a van — well, that would be you then. You with your fancy campervan, haha. Can't wait to see it by the way.

- Sewing and teaching others to sew. There's always a huge pile of mending and we sometimes get rolls of fabric donated. A group of women and a couple of men make clothes for the children. I think there's a quilting circle too.

- Lead activities in the Women's Space. Especially useful if you have self-defence skills. Jodie's an expert — you can imagine.

By the way, I assume you'll both be sleeping in your campervan. I found a campsite for you quite near where we're staying (see attached details). You can book online. Also, Daphne our landlady says you can leave your dog with her while you're at the camp. Her dog died recently so she'd welcome the company. Your dog isn't vicious, is she? Anyway, I told Daphne that Alicia (crazy name for a dog if you ask me) is a teddy bear.

Looking forward to seeing you soon Maya!

Love from me and Jodie xxx

And Aiden xx

Everyone can lose their goals,
lose themselves
Each person is like a tree. They can see
the beauty in themselves.
They can grow.

2

Daisy's new diary

Holland, March 2017

Hello. Hello Diary?

   Hmm.

How shall I begin? I hate first pages. The book is so beautiful when it's blank and full of potential, a shame to spoil it, and I'm bound to.

But I'd better start meaningfully instead of waffling, otherwise this will be a waste of time and not much fun to read, for whoever may one day be reading it, that is. Me, maybe, in the future. Or a possible son or daughter of mine when they find it in my things after I'm dead. That gave me a shiver, probably not a good introductory subject for my new diary, especially if it is a child of mine reading it ... Hello, by the way!

But if I don't have a child of my own, who'll read this in the future? My nephew perhaps. Elijah. The little boy I believed I'd be a second mum to, and now I'm not because I'm not there ... I wonder how Lola's getting on with him on her own. Mum and Dad were probably right though, it wasn't a good idea to give up my job and live at home with her and the baby. I can see that now I'm away from them. Lola's the mother, not me.

The two of us really are different for the first time ever. The last few months of Lola's pregnancy she depended on me and I kind of liked it. But becoming a mum has taken her into a new stage of her life and I hope this trip with Mum is going to do the same thing for me. Lola's got the thing I always wanted - I can't help thinking about Dan, and the baby he's having with his new girlfriend. Stop it, Daisy. It's time to be positive.

Okay, so I've waffled on even more.
Hmm.

I'll start this diary properly by describing the van I'm currently living in with Mum. Yeah me, living in a van - Daisy, the steady one - can you believe it?

For anyone who doesn't know my mum (any future metaphorical person reading this diary who might not be a relative) she's an amazing woman. Her amazingness started when she decided to become a backpacker at the age of fifty-four. She kept it up for like two-and-a-half years. She travelled all over the world in places like Australia, Iceland and Spain. Other places too but I forget the locations right now. Before that she was like anyone else's mother - you know, always having the dinner on the table, do your homework, don't forget to brush your teeth and all that.

But she changed when my younger brother Joe went missing. Well, I suppose technically he'd cut off contact with us and we didn't know what had happened to him. The same thing had happened before with my older brother

10

Jamie. I knew Mum'd been sad in the past about Jamie, but she hardly ever let us see that. Then with Joe, it stopped Mum in her tracks. The only thing she felt she could do to understand him was try and live like Joe. She picked up a backpack - she said she could hardly even carry it at first ☺- and followed in his footsteps. See, she had his journal, so she knew where he'd been. Then she enjoyed the lifestyle of a backpacker - a vagabond, she called it - so much that she carried on living that way. She only returned home recently, when she found out Lola was having a baby. When I emailed her and told her, that is.

She found Joe and Jamie by the way, but that's another story.

I'll never get round to describing our van at this rate!

But actually, I'll start with this book. It was Mum who bought it for me. She said Joe's journal (which she gave him at the beginning of his travels) had meant so much to her it gave her the idea to buy a book for me to write in as well. Not that I'm expected to let her read it, of course. She said that would defeat the whole purpose of my journey, both the physical one and the mental one. I'm pretty sure I can trust her not to snoop. She's changed so much since I was a child. Mum says the best thing about her vagabonding years was discovering her most true and basic self (she got that from a film), and she wants me to use this book to try and do the same thing. It chokes me up to even think about that, because I've honestly no idea what my most true and basic self is- it's always been so tied up with Lola. With her needs and demands. With Dan, before that all went downhill, and more recently Elijah too.

Who is Daisy Galen? Really? I'm hoping this book will help me find out.

My diary is a hardback A4 book with creamy pages.

11

Unlined, so I'll have to watch the direction of my handwriting. Maybe I'll do some sketches on these pages, too. I used to draw a lot. The cover is a deep indigo, traced with a silver filigree pattern that stands out from the background. I love the feel of it under my fingers. I spent a long time letting my hands wander over it before I opened the book and began to write. Not that I've said much so far. Mum said I used to write stories when I was little, I'd forgotten that. Lola preferred acting out those nonsense plays we made up as we went along, that was when we weren't dancing or riding ponies, and it was easier to do what she wanted. Then we grew up and read magazines and practised makeup and fancied boys. I think I must've forgotten the creativity inside me. Working as a teacher, which I loved by the way, used up any inspiration for my personal work that I might've had left.

About my job, you should have seen the Head's face when I told her I was leaving to go travelling with my mother. She must've already heard about Mum (she's the sister-in-law of Susannah Metherington, a woman in the village who I'm certain was flirting with Dad at the Christmas party). She said, why would you throw everything you've worked for away, Daisy? I said I wasn't throwing my talents away. I told her I expect to be using them with the children at a refugee camp in Greece. She softened a bit after that and said they'd be lucky to have me, but they'd miss me at school. Then she immediately added that she'd offer my job to Miss Jackson who was covering Miss Redding's maternity leave, due to end at Easter, so she could let me go before my three months' notice finished, if I wanted.

Hmm. Looks like I won't be missed that badly after all.

Sooo, here I am, two-and-a-half months later. We stayed on a municipal campsite in Leffrinckoucke - that's in France - last night. Our pitch was close to the sea, and it felt weird to know that I'd crossed the channel only the day before. It was my second night in the van with Mum and the dog. Everything's unfamiliar, and I didn't sleep much because of the different breathing sounds around me; the sea, Mum snoring sometimes, the dog whimpering in its sleep.

I said I'd describe the van, didn't I? It's white with a blue stripe along the side. Tall enough to stand up in, thank goodness. The driver and passenger seats swivel around to make a small living area with a removeable table between them and the bench seat. The bench seat unfolds to make my bed at night - tidying it away again in the morning's a bit of a palaver to be honest, but it does mean we have slightly more space to move around. My bedding's rolled into a bundle and placed on the end of Mum's bed at the back during the day. I tucked a throw around it to try and keep it free from dog hairs, but they seem to get everywhere. I guess I'll have to adjust my 'standards' as Mum calls them - she gets defensive where Alicia's concerned. I'm glad I brought a clothes brush with me.

I hope my Tink's getting the attention she deserves back at Dad's in England, I think he was starting to like cats by the time I left, so maybe he'll let her stay in his part of the house. A good job because Tink's scared of Lola and seems quite disgusted by the baby ☺.

It's a relief that we have a miniature bathroom for privacy - some of the vans I went to look at with Mum only had a toilet in a box which you placed a cushion on top and used as a seat afterwards. Our toilet can be emptied via a little door on the outside of the van. There's a water tank under the bench seat. You access the tank through another tiny door on the outside of the van.

That's about all for now. My fingers are cramped from

13

so much writing. We've parked in a lay-by next to a field and Mum's just arriving back from her walk with the dog. Perhaps we'll have another cup of tea — I forgot to mention the built-in stove with the sink next to it — before we set off on the road again. We're planning to sleep in a free parking space for camper vans with water and waste facilities provided, somewhere here in Holland tonight. It's just beginning to sink in that I'm in another country from my twin sister and her baby. And it's not only for a short break this time. My new life is just beginning.

There are many ways to think
but not enough time. There's no point
in looking back,
no way to believe
in what lies behind.

3

Daisy

Germany, March 2017

Email from: Daisy_halfcrazy@dmail.com
To: Lola Galen

   Subject: Be happy for me

Hey Lo,
C'mon, don't be mad at me. What was I supposed to do when Mum asked me to go on the biggest adventure of my life? Even Dad encouraged me, he's worried I was turning into a sort of husband for you, especially with Steve not being around too much. I know that's not true but …

   Of course it's not because I want to get away from you and Elijah! I love him, Lola, you know I do. And I love you too, but I need space to live my own life.

   At first, I fantasised that I was kind of Elijah's other mother. But I'm not and getting away makes that easier to accept. I'm sorry. But you know I've always been the one who wanted a baby. I need to find something in my life that makes as much sense, that's all.

Yes, I'm crying. I know you know that without me having to say it anyway. I know you're crying too. I hope Elijah isn't though. I want to hold him so much. Give him a kiss from me. Please.

Let me tell you about my journey so far, I'm sure you'll want to know everything even if you pretend you don't. You know we stopped on a campsite near Canterbury the first night? It rained heavily on the journey down to Dover the next morning. Mum was asleep while I drove us onto the ferry, it felt so cool exchanging land for water via that flimsy-looking ramp.

We had to leave Alicia in the van on the ferry, which Mum wasn't very happy about, but we were starving so we went to the cafeteria, and they don't allow dogs in there. I had eggs and chips, that was always our favourite when we were little, wasn't it? I know you hate eggs now, but remember?

I must admit I had a sleep in the passenger seat when Mum was driving us away from Calais. When I woke up we parked in a lay-by alongside a vivid green field and it turned out we'd crossed into Belgium! Mum wanted to take Alicia for a walk. So, we did, and then I got my first experience of the smell of wet dog in a cramped van. Not pleasant. Anyway, after drying Alicia with her special dog towel, she put her on a folded curtain (the one from our old utility room) at the end of her bed and to the dog's credit she stayed there and didn't move. We had a cup of tea and washed up — the cool thing about a campervan, besides the fact you can use the bathroom and go to bed in it — then we set off again.

I was driving this time. I had to keep reminding myself at roundabouts to 'look out for traffic coming from the left'. It'll take some getting used to. Now we've stopped again for the night, as we're both exhausted. We're already in Germany! We found a 'Park for night' spot in Aachen. It's a wide-open space surrounded by trees on three sides and a river on the other. There are water and waste facilities, and three other

17

vans are parked here. One of them has a little terrier of some sort that Alicia barked at when Mum took her out.

We heated a pan of macaroni cheese for tea, you used to love that.

I'm sitting cross-legged on my bed. You haven't seen how cosy it is when its all made up with the memory foam topper and my bedding. I've got your pillow here too so I can imagine it smells of you. Like, in a way, you're sort of here with me. That's what I like to think.

Mum and the dog are already asleep — both snoring but only quietly.

I'm using my data as a hotspot so I'm going to finish this email here. I know you're not keen on emails Lola but it's an easier way of getting more information across than WhatsApp or Skype and I like to think of you reading this again at other times. Maybe you'll be breastfeeding Elijah or rocking him in his swing seat with your foot. And I'll be doing something else, something new. My sent mail folder will be like another diary for me to look back on, only I'll know I was telling these things only to you. So ... I'm going to keep on doing this even if you don't answer.

Love you, Lola.
I love Elijah too.
Daisy xxxxxxxxxxxxxx

I have to face the future,
I don't see myself as a stranger.
I don't think about death,
I have already died.
I'm looking
to start a new life.

4

Daisy

Samos, March 2017

Daisy's jolted awake by a long, single blast of the ferry's horn. She thinks she's only slept a couple of hours. The dog sits panting at the end of her mother's bed, the whites of its eyes showing. The gap between the curtains shows the sky is light. They had to pay extra for a deck side cabin (pets allowed) but Mum said it would be their last experience of luxury for a while. Maya seems to have no trouble sleeping through the catch and change in the engine's rhythm, the grinding of gears that reverberate through the body of the boat. It sets Daisy's nerves on edge. Her jaw tenses, waiting for the usual chugging tempo to resume.

She picks up her phone from the bedside table and checks the time: nine o'clock. They're due in port really soon.

She has a cold feeling. *I could have been setting up my little day nursery back at The Cottages with Lola.* She rubs her eyes and sits up. The dog, Alicia — she must get used to calling her that — fixes her with a scared gaze, visibly swallowing.

"It's all right." For some reason the dog trusts Daisy. She's never been a dog person. She misses her cat, Tink. Then she laughs because she reminds herself of Lola, who says she isn't a cat person, and she's been landed with a cat.

Tears burn her eyes. She sniffs. "Okay."

Alicia thumps her tail and jumps down into the gap between the beds. She angles herself towards Daisy and shoves her nose into Daisy's hand just as she lowers it to pull back the bedclothes.

"Clever," Daisy strokes the dog's forehead. Alicia has amazing, kohl-rimmed eyes. "I suppose I could get to like you if you carry on being cute like that. Anyway, you'll have to wait here while I go to the bathroom."

She washes her face and pulls her hair back into a ponytail. Applies cream deodorant from the screw-top tin her mother bought her for Christmas. Drawing the oversized shirt she sleeps in up over her head, she replaces it with a stretchy pull-over bra and a fresh t-shirt. She changes her knickers and steps into the loose cotton trousers she bought in Athens. Then she gives her teeth a cursory brush before zipping everything back into her grey canvas hold-all.

The ferry engine chugs in a different funny way. Back in the bedroom the dog follows her across the room towards her bed. She dumps the bag on it, looking around for anything she might have forgotten.

Maya's mouth's fallen open and she sounds like she'll choke on her stuttering snores.

"Mum, wake up!" Daisy shakes her shoulder. She can't believe Maya can sleep through the noise and the way the ferry's rocking as it seems to be turning in a wide ark. "Wake up." She goes to the glass doors and pulls back the curtains. Shivers at the reality of land. A curved shoreline, blue sea below and blue sky above. Cream and white buildings with red roofs stacked on a semicircle of terraces, behind them olive groves on a hillside. She knows the 'Samos Hotspot' is somewhere up there.

Cramp grips her stomach. One of the first independent holidays she and Lola took together was to a Greek island, not this one. The summer they'd turned eighteen. She remembers the sound and feel of their flip-flops slapping on the hot cobbles as they made their way down to the sea, arm in arm. Greek men sitting at cafe tables turned and stared at them as they passed. They were going through one of their identical clothes and hairstyle phases. They'd worn cream broderie anglaise dresses, she remembers.

The light is strong. The sun makes the ferry-churned waves sparkle. She turns and sees her mother sitting up in bed.

"Sorry," Mum says. "I must have dropped off."

"Dropped off?" Daisy laughs. "You were out cold. And snoring. We're nearly there."

Maya rubs her face, runs her hands through her short hair. "I'll have you know I was wide awake between three and five AM. Wasn't I, Alicia?" She stretches, leans forward and encircles her dog with her arms. Alicia pulls away, panting.

"She probably needs to pee," Mum huffs as she extricates her legs from the sheets. Finally, she stands up, stretching again. "Would you mind taking her to the dog exercise area, love?"

"Mum!" Daisy tuts. "I suppose I'll have to since you're not even dressed yet. I did say before we set off for this trip that the dog was your responsibility."

Maya's looking at her funny. They both burst out laughing, but Daisy still feels frustrated. Her mother's now a bit too laid back for her liking. Daisy remembers school days and how organised Maya was with their uniforms and lunchboxes. They were never late for anything. It felt safe and comforting to have a mum who always took care of everything. Now Daisy feels a nervous flutter in her stomach that Mum won't be ready when it's time to get off the ferry. Like Maya's deliberately sticking her nose up at rules and regulations. She doesn't want to be the one bossing her mum around.

She sucks in her breath. "Where's the lead then?"

The dog goes with her willingly to the fenced-off exercise area. There are three other owners with their dogs there, but Alicia ignores the other animals and immediately goes into a corner and squats. Daisy breathes out as she picks up a poo in one of the little bags Maya gave her. She drops it into the lidded bin on the post at the gate and leads Alicia back down the walkway to their cabin, counting the numbers as she goes. 196.

Before entering she takes a moment to breathe salt air deep into her lungs and stare out at the expanse of sea between the ferry and the looming town of Vathy that straggles up the hillside. She peers at the landscape, there's a campsite somewhere — away from the town — where they'll be staying in their van. Mum's friend has even organised some sort of doggy-daycare for Alicia while they're volunteering in the camp. Daisy takes a sharp breath, holds it for a moment. When she lets it out again, she feels shaky. She focuses on the dog. Alicia has her head between the railings and is taking deep sniffs of the scented air, her nose twitching in every direction. Daisy runs her hand down Alicia's white back. Breathes some more. It's too late to turn back from the commitment she's made. What have I done? She pictures her classroom back in Newark, feels a clutch in her stomach at the mental sight of Miss Jackson sitting behind *her* desk.

She closes her eyes and opens them again to the bright sunshine. *But look where I am now.* The olive trees on the swathes of hills, the intensity of the light, everything is different from home. An adventure for her, just like Lola's motherhood has changed her life forever.

Inside the cabin Maya's dressed and packs her remaining things into her everyday rucksack. Daisy studies her. Back in her wife-and-mother days Mum was plump, glossy, one of the 'beautiful people' in their village. Now she's lean and brown-skinned, though less so of both than when she arrived home in the village just before Christmas. The relative inactivity Mum said drove her mad and the rich food of the better-off have marked her as much as her hand-to-mouth years did. But even though she's cut off the dreadlocks she had until recently, no-one who knew their family in the old days would recognise her. It was funny when half the village turned up for the usual Galen Christmas open house. Where's Maya? People kept saying. I thought you said she was coming home. They nearly died of shock when they realised their former cohort member, who used to blend in seamlessly, was now the hippy in the corner. Daisy saw envy in some of their eyes though. During her two years of travelling Maya did things and saw things none of them could imagine.

Daisy feels lucky to be accompanying Mum on this new adventure but scared too. What if she's not up to the job? I'm a teacher, she reminds herself. The most vulnerable minds have relied on me. I can do this.

The ferry horn blasts a long note, and an announcer informs passengers that they will shortly be disembarking at the port of Vathy, and that they should collect their belongings and make their way to the car decks or to the foot passenger meeting points as soon as possible.

Daisy checks her bag one more time and scans their tiny cabin for anything she or Mum might have overlooked. Her hands shake.

Mum approaches her and rubs her arm gently. "I'm proud of you Daisy," She looks into Daisy's eyes. "It's brave of you to give up everything you know for this." As if she's been reading Daisy's mind.

"Well, I have your footsteps to follow in." Daisy waits a half-beat before wriggling out from her mother's grasp. She folds her arms tightly. She catches a glimpse of herself in the mirror on the back of the door, somehow her hair already looks messy, escaping from the ponytail. Her face is tense. She tries to loosen her jaw as she glances back at Mum. "I'm scared, though. Of the situations we're going to see. Scared I'm going to feel useless."

"Daisy," Mum fastens the buckles on her backpack, shrugs it on and picks up Alicia's lead. "So am I, don't think I'm not. I've never done anything like this before either." She clicks her tongue at Alicia to follow her.

"But you've been all over, done all sorts of scary things on your own," Daisy persists. "I've never done anything like that." She follows behind Mum and the dog.

"That's the point though love. I was in charge when I was doing all my adventuring. This time I've got to answer to an organisation and be responsible for the welfare of other people — that's what scares me." She grins. "You're more used to that than me. We'll have a go at this together, eh?"

"You were responsible for us once," says Daisy. "You know how to do it too." A shadow flutters briefly over Mum's face.

The ferry horn blasts again as their three figures make their way out onto the crowded walkway and join the flow making for the staircases.

I was born in the mountains,
my village had only seven homes.
From there you could see
all the way to the sea,
a journey of three hours by car.

5

Daisy

Samos, March 2017

Email from: Daisy_halfcrazy@dmail.com
To: Lola Galen

Subject: First day at the camp

Hey,

I know you haven't answered my first email yet, but I'll forgive you as you must be busy with Elijah. How is he? Tell him his aunty Daisy sends him lots of kisses, won't you?

And how are you, too? We have pretty good WiFi on our campsite so we can videocall one evening and talk about things if you fancy it. I'd love to see your faces, you and Elijah.

Anyway, I'm writing this to tell you about my first day on Samos.

Mum and I slept in a cabin on the ferry (she snored again, and so did the dog). We got into Vathy (that's the port) at about 9.30 this morning. The island is beautiful, did you know that even though it belongs to Greece it's only two kilometres off the coast of Turkey?

When we drove off the ferry we parked in the town and had breakfast in an orange-painted cafe with blue chairs out the front. I had an apricot croissant and a very strong coffee. After that we took Mum's dog to a lady in a house where Mum's friends are staying. You know, those kids she met in Australia when she first started travelling? Their landlady's going to be Alicia's dog-sitter. She's called Daphne and she lives in this three-story white house with curlicued balconies on the upper floors and a luscious garden. She has a kennel and a dog run left over from her Shi tzu, which died recently, but she says Alicia will mainly be staying in the house with her. Funnily enough, Alicia took to her straight away, even though she's usually suspicious of new people. We left her reclining on a rug on Daphne's veranda, gnawing on a boot-shaped chew the old woman gave her.

Then it was time to go sign in at the *Island Volunteers* office. I was so nervous, but it was quite straightforward when it came down to it, as we'd already filled in all the forms online anyway.

Mum's friends arrived there to meet us: Jodie, Ned and Aiden, you must remember her talking about them loads back in 2014. Jodie has red hair and a fierce attitude that goes with it, I'm not sure she liked me very much, I didn't find her very friendly. Ned's her boyfriend, a tall black guy. He grabbed Mum in this great big bear hug and wouldn't let go of her until his friend Aiden pulled him off. Aiden's fair-skinned and has got really sunburned. Apparently, he only arrived a week ago. When both Ned and Aiden came at me with similarly enthusiastic hugs, I managed to subtly let them know I wasn't into demonstrativeness with strangers. That's when I caught Jodie curling her lip at me. She probably thinks I'm a snob. Lots of people do. It's just I need to get to know people before I'm comfortable hugging them. Well, you know that of course.

I wish you were here too,

Yeah, I can mentally hear you saying how could you

28

possibly be, now you've got Elijah. It's weird having this massive difference between us now, isn't it? Look, can't we just share each other's adventures in our emails? Then we'll know how the other one feels.

Back to my day (but please tell me about yours too?)

The guys – that's what Mum calls them, her friends – took us on a tour of the main camp. Oh God, Lola, it was horrible. Worse than I'd ever imagined. There are hardly any toilets and they're so disgusting it made me retch. The overcrowding's horrific — there're like 8,000 refugees in a camp made for 600. Apparently, rats are everywhere. Ugggh! I was wearing sandals, but I think I'll put on my Doc Marten's from now on. Refugees have to construct their own accommodation, so the place is a mishmash of tarpaulin structures over some kind of framework, whatever they can get hold of. They weigh the bottoms down with bricks and stones to try and prevent rats getting in and keep out the draughts. Little children sleep on threadbare mats on the ground. Think of baby Elijah — oh, I can't. Sorry, I shouldn't have brought up that image.

Nobody has enough food to eat. Some of the mothers go without so they can feed their children. I felt sick at the sight of the little kids' big eyes in their grubby faces.

On the way back to the office a small girl ran up to me and took my hand. She skipped along beside me even though the ground was stony, and she had bare feet. Like a ragamuffin from that film we loved, Oliver Twist.

I never thought I'd find myself in such an environment in real life.

No sign of the Artful Dodger though, and no jolly music either.

Actually ... that's not quite true. Towards the end of our tour, we passed a few makeshift buildings clustered together. Some men were crouching outside by a cooking pot on a fire set in a circle of stones. Another sat on an upturned bucket playing an instrument Aiden told me is called an oud. It's like

29

a lute. Apparently, there's an oud-maker on the camp and a volunteer bought him some materials and tools so he can carry on his craft. The volunteer's managed to sell a couple of the man's instruments for him in Athens.

Ned says there's a sixteen-year-old girl on camp who paints amazing Islamic designs on recycled bottles, and he takes orders for her from places in Europe and the USA. They turn them into lamp stands. She's able to buy her family some extra food with the money. I was thinking of us at sixteen, we didn't have a thought for anybody but ourselves, did we?

The last place I was shown was the tarpaulin building they call the school. Oh my word, Lola. In fact, I don't have the words now to describe how little of everything there is. When you think of the classrooms you and I have worked in, and we think we're under-resourced …

Yep. This was the challenge I was looking for; I realise that now.

We're in Mum's van on the campsite, after a late supper with Jodie, Ned and Aiden on the veranda at Daphne's place. Alicia was thrilled to see Mum at the end of a long day, but she seems quite attached to Daphne already. Mum said it's a relief as she was worried about leaving Alicia, but I think she's a little bit jealous as well, lol.

I'm so tired I can't tell you. I wonder if you're sitting up with Elijah right now. How's Dad, has he been much help to you?

I'll describe the 'school' properly and tell you about the children in my next email.

Love you, Lo.
Big kisses to Elijah and say hi to Dad from me.

Daisy xxxxxxxxxxxxx

It only rained in summertime,
when the mountains turned green.
We lived two hours from the main street,
we walked to and from the market
all of us carrying food
on our backs.

6

Lola

Navengore, March 2017

Email from: Lola_palaver@dmail.com
To: Daisy Galen

Subject: Okay I give in

Hey Dais.
All right I give in, I can't stay mad at you anymore. I really, really miss you though. I cried when I read your last email. It was the thought of that grubby little girl skipping along holding your hand, like she really trusted you. You have that effect on children, don't you? Remember Jacob in your class last year? All the other teachers got annoyed with him, but he was a perfect angel for you. I'm sad Elijah's missing out on your influence. We really miss you here. Have I said that enough? Sorry. I know you've got your own life to live.

Yeah, Dad's fine. He's started decorating his rooms downstairs and it's beginning to look like a bachelor apartment now — all greys and blues with a white trim. He's having a grey carpet put down and he's bought a white fluffy rug for the middle and a huge shiny black desk to put in the front alcove. He also got rid of Mum's upholstered suite and he's chosen a black leather sofa with a matching recliner. Mum would hate it.

I'm afraid your cat's moved downstairs into Dad's apartment because he gives her a lot more attention than I do. Never thought Dad'd turn out to be a cat person, did you? He's talking about getting a cat flap put into the middle back door — which of course now leads into his apartment — and another in the old boot room back door so Tink can come and go as she pleases. And yeah, Dad does help with Elijah. He's said he'll babysit one night a week so I can go out, but I haven't felt like it yet since you've gone. Weird I know.

Another weird thing though. Susannah Metherington keeps 'popping' round to see Dad. What the? She even brought him an actual casserole; can you believe it? When the truth is he's been doing proper gourmet cooking of his own since that cookery course he went on. He doesn't need village ladies setting their sights on him. Did you know Sue M's separated from her husband? They're still living in the same house though.

I think Mum's set a trend. I think Dad's in mortal danger.

Steve came and took Elijah out for a whole day. I defrosted some of the excess milk I pumped at the beginning and packed a bag with several bottles for him. I thought Steve and I could stay friends, but it was hard. I asked him to promise he wouldn't take Elijah to his girlfriend's house, but he refused. I spent the morning crying after they'd gone and then I went out on a bike ride. Yeah, me. I was so mad I just wanted to pedal. I've probably lost a load of my baby-weight from that ride alone.

Remember the first time we rode the bikes we got for our twelfth birthday? Mine was pink and yours was purple. We cycled all the way to Bracebridge Heath, remember? Then I got a puncture and we both had to walk all the way home. Dad bought me my new bike after you left because he said he gave you some money and it was only fair. He thought we could go for bike rides together in the summer, it has a baby seat on the back for Elijah. That's if 'Randy Sue' doesn't get her feet well and truly under the table before then.

How's Mum been? It's crazy to think of her hanging out with friends our age. What did you think of that Aiden then? Mum mentioned that she thought he'd be a good match for you. Yeah, it was on a Skype call when she was in Australia — I remember being a bit miffed at the time that she said you and not me. So, what's he like then? Tell all.

Anyway. I don't really know what else to say. I'm okay. More or less. Elijah's brilliant; Dad gets a weird look on his face whenever S. M. happens to pop by, which is quite often. Don't tell Mum.

I'm sending you some photos of our bonny boy, I'm sure he's grown already since you last saw him. I love being a Mum. And yes of course I kissed him for you. I talk to him about you all the time. Oh, and we had a zoom with Jamie, Lejla, Electra and baby Rudi. Jamie's kids are so cute. I can't believe we were out of touch with our big brother so long. Joe turned up at Jamie's before the end of the zoom with a guy called Amar. Amar's his boyfriend and apparently Joe's living with him! Eh, when did that happen? But it turns out we were right about our baby brother after all, Dais.

Dad plans to take me and Elijah to visit the boys in Germany in a posh hired campervan later this year. I wonder if you'll be home by then.

Okay I'm off now, Elijah's just woken up.
Love you, Dais.
Give Mum a kiss from me.

Lola and Elijah xxxxxx

When I was nine, I broke my leg
playing football
on a sloping field.
They treated me at home.
Home is a long way
from here.

7

Daisy

Samos, April 2017

Daisy's struggling to come to terms with everything. Events turn on their heads without warning. Like today. Around 9.15 AM she arrives at reception with her mother, in the van because Maya's brought up some medical supplies from the ferry. Instead of making straight for the school as she normally does, Daisy helps Maya unload the supplies from the van. She pulls out her phone to check her messages (none) and is about to grab Mum's spare rucksack and head down the track to the school when a woman called Sal comes hurrying out the reception building.

"There's a boat coming in on Mykali beach," she yells. "We need as many people as possible down there. Maya, can you follow me in your van? You too, Daisy."

"What?" says Daisy. "But I'm ... " Sal's already hurrying past to her car though.

"Hurry!"

"Come on love. Get your jacket on." Maya rips open the passenger door for Daisy.

Biting her lip, Daisy shrugs her arms one after the other into the NGO tabard and climbs back up into the van, thinking about the lesson she's planned for her small group of children today. Picture flash cards she made with the art supplies she bought in a local store. The cards depict animals with their names written beneath in English. She bought paints, crayons and paper for the school as well, they're all in the rucksack sitting ready in her footwell.

The classroom: that's her safe place in the chaos here.

Daisy shifts the rucksack with her feet. The children will be waiting for her. She hesitates, not fully seated, her hand on the door handle. "Mum . . . I—"

Maya's already at the wheel, starting the engine. "Seatbelt, quick love." She swings the van round as Daisy reluctantly clicks the belt into place. The van bumps over the stones after Sal and another volunteer in Sal's VW. In the wing mirror she sees two men getting into a dark blue jeep, pulling out after them.

The three vehicles race in convoy along one of the more decent roads on the island that Daisy's been on (she took a bus tour). She fastens her eyes on the back of Sal's grey car in front. *There's a boat coming in.* Every day on Samos so far has outwitted Daisy's preconceptions, but this is the first time she'll have witnessed refugees' moment of arrival.

A thirteen-minute drive — she knows because she's still clutching her phone in her hand, she checks the time: 9.45. The van slows and stops. On a ridge of land above the sand and stone beach the volunteers stand in a line. The sea's blinding. Daisy raises her hand to her forehead and squints at the beach.

There it is! Distorted at first by heat haze the shape forms in her vision: an orange dinghy crowded with figures, lurching on the waves. Voices ringing out from the boat, too – women and men wailing and shouting. She hears a child scream.

Shock breaks in her stomach. Other NGOs in different vests are already on the beach and one van arrives immediately after *Island Volunteers*, pulling up behind them. A sense of anticipation falls over Daisy's group, a moment of stillness.

"Come on." Sal jerks into life, gathering ropes of her grey-black hair into a scrunchie and tying it on the top of her head as she swings back towards her car.

"Grab those emergency blankets from the boot, somebody." Daisy lurches forward, but Sal's already blocked the boot with her own body. When she turns again her arms are full. "You grab those flasks there, ducky, will you?" Sal indicates back over her shoulder with her head. "Maya, would you get the water?"

Daisy lifts the two heavy flasks and Maya strains to carry the crate of water bottles. The other volunteer from Sal's car heaves a first aid rucksack from the back seat onto her shoulders. Their colleagues from the blue jeep bring more blankets and water. Together the six of them step carefully down the slope onto the sand.

There must be twenty volunteers from different NGOs or local helpers on the beach. Sal's group move in amongst the others. The atmosphere on the beach stills, a held breath. The overcrowded boat has gone silent. Seconds pace out.

On the quiet air, backgrounded by the sob of waves dissolving on the beach, a thin wail comes from the sea. Then a shout, followed by a new swell of voices, laughing, crying and hollering. The dinghy looms into sharp focus.

Daisy lifts her chin and meets Mum's eyes. Maya presses dry lips together, gives an encouraging nod, but Daisy notices her bone-white knuckles, her hands grasping each other. The crate of water is at her feet.

A man jumps out of the dinghy and stumbles, falling into the water. Another two jump into the sea, one steadying the first and the other taking hold of the boat's rope. He pulls it towards the shore. Several other men and a woman follow suit, the woman throwing her hands up, her voice warbling to the sky. The volunteers start to move forward, reaching towards the sea. Two women from another NGO wade in and grasp the refugee woman's arms, she collapses between them, and they help her onto the beach. Daisy mobilises herself. She lays the flasks on the sand and bends to the crate of water bottles, filling her arms with them. From the corner of her eye, she notices Mum doing the same. Daisy looks to the sea and takes a determined step forward, then another. More refugees spill out of the boat now, falling into the sea with shouts and cries, one older man even breaking into song as he stumbles into the shallows.

Daisy spots a family: a father, mother and four children. One is a boy of possibly twelve years old. The others are girls, the oldest maybe eight or ten, then a four-year-old perhaps, and a toddler in the father's arms. The boy leads his next-down sister by the hand, she presses herself against his side and he lets go of her hand, flinging his arm around her instead, his hand hooked under her opposite arm. Together they lurch out of the surf. The four-year-old starts to shriek, waist-deep in the sea. The mother tries to pick her up, but her arms seem to go limp and Daisy's in there before she's even thought about what she's doing. She takes the skinny child from the mother before the little girl is dropped into the breaking waves.

"It's okay," Daisy murmurs into the child's wet hair. "It's okay, you're all right now. Everything's going to be fine." The child's hands cling to Daisy's clothes like limpets and her small body shivers uncontrollably. The mother hangs on to Daisy's hi-vis vest as they wade out of the foam, Daisy can feel the weight of her. They clear the last wavelets and the woman's legs give way. On damp sand she reaches out for her daughter. Daisy lowers the toddler into her mother's arms.

She looks around for the drinking water, where did she drop it? She can't even remember letting go of the bottles she was carrying. The father and the woman's other children have caught up with her now and the six of them huddle together on the wet sand. Daisy drags over a bundle of emergency blankets, separates them and begins to drape the silver shrouds over their shoulders, first the children. The father meets her eyes, and she feels that cold shock again in her stomach. It's all in his eyes, the family's journey, their horrors. Almost immediately he shuts the story away though. He forces a smile and takes the next blanket from her. He wraps it tightly around his wife and the toddler, before drawing the final blanket around his own shoulders, tucking it around the one-year-old in his arms.

The family crouch together on the damp surface of a land they've risked their lives to reach. Their lips are cracked, bleeding at the corners. Daisy finds water, unscrews bottles and hands them out. The father shakes his head after she has handed him two bottles, he puts up the flat of his hand. Daisy pauses. The father places the bottle first at his youngest daughter's lips and next at the ten-year-old girl's. The mother feeds her toddler a drink from her bottle, then offers the bottle to her son. Finally, the mother and father drink reservedly from the bottles, before passing them amongst their children again.

Daisy fights tears. "Please," she says. "Take more bottles. There are plenty." But the father puts up his hand again and the mother shakes her head.

"Thank you, thank you so much," she stutters. She cuddles her toddler, strokes the hair of her son.

Daisy notices that the ten-year-old is wearing only one shoe, a scuffed black trainer. The sock on her other foot is half-off.

Daisy wants to push the sock properly onto the child's foot, even though it's soaked through. She chokes on a sob. For half a second her head feels sucked empty, she stands on the beach wondering who she even is. Then her thoughts and feelings flood back in again. Her hands and arms tingle. "Wait here," she says pointlessly. "I'll be right back." She stumbles up the sand thinking about the flasks of soup. She trips on a small rock, jarring her ankle, and swears to herself. Calm down, she thinks to her erratically beating heart. She takes some slow, deep breaths and moves forward again, passing other volunteers drawing blankets around clusters of families and single men.

"Miss," says what appears to be a teenage boy leaning against a slick rock at the edge of the sea. She almost missed him. Daisy stops, leans over. *Nobody is helping him.* His teeth knock together so hard he can hardly speak. The boy hunches forward; his arms wrapped around his knees. The lifejacket he's discarded is flat, uninflated, and she wonders if it was ever any good. "I cannot stand up," he keeps his hooded eyes downturned and forces out the words. She notices that his cheeks are hollow, his lips peeling. His dark, freckled skin looks bleached.

"That's okay." Daisy wipes her forearm across her eyes and sniffs hard. Scanning the beach, she can see that there are no volunteers available, except herself. "Wait here, I'll be right back."

She heads for the flasks of soup, but they are not where she left them. There are two remaining bottles of water. She wonders where Mum is. She checks around for more of the insulating blankets, but she can't see any. Tears sting the backs of her eyes again. She grabs the two bottles of water and heads back down the beach. The teenager is still shivering. She fears she can hear his bones rattling. His head rests on his knees and she worries he'll lose consciousness.

She glances over at the family she left before and sees volunteers helping them to their feet. Border guards have appeared, they're herding people into a group. A line of volunteers and refugees makes its way up the beach towards a carpark in the other direction from where Maya's van is parked. There is a bus in the carpark.

She needs to warm this boy up. Daisy lets the bottles of

41

water fall to the sand and slips her arms out of the yellow and blue vest she wears. She pulls her hoody up over her head and replaces the vest over her t-shirt. Dropping to her knees, she wraps the garment around his thin shoulders, tucking the arms in under his chin. Pulls the hood up over his hair, stiff with salt. He doesn't move, apart from the juddering of his bones. She unscrews the lid of a water bottle and places the top of the bottle near his lips. She sees his eyelids flutter.

"Drink," she says. "Please."

Maybe he can smell the water. His eyes open slowly, he leans towards the neck of the bottle. Daisy tilts the bottle. A dry tongue pokes forward to receive the water that drips onto it.

Thank God.

I have one son, and three daughters.
I have a Masters
in Computer Science.
I want to work,
and have a good life.

8

Daisy

Samos, April 2017

Daisy's proud of her small group of children at the school. They've learned to identify the animals on the flash cards she made and will call out the correct names when she holds up the cards. Their English is improving. Each child is given a small backpack, pencils and an exercise book to bring to school on their allotted days.

Class has finished for the day and Daisy's offered to help with a food distribution at the overflow camp in the olive groves. She gets into a jeep with Aiden, Mum's friend. She's shy in his presence. Mum's hinted that Aiden likes her — Daisy doesn't want to mislead him. He's good-looking, polite, he seems kind. He's even made her laugh a few times. But she doesn't feel any spark between them. And anyway, her mind's too full of the enormity of everything she's seeing and doing to have room for romantic attachment. She glances sideways at his profile. That shock of red-gold hair, it's grown already since she met him. Speaking of which, Aiden had only been planning to stay on Samos three weeks, but he's extended his volunteering stint and obtained some sponsorship from the company he works for. His blue eyes focus on the rough road ahead. Her fingers curl on her thighs and she hopes he hasn't noticed. He glances away from the wheel briefly.

"You okay?" That kink at the side of his mouth.

"Yeah fine, thanks. Are you?"

"Yup. You ever done a distribution before?"

"No, this is my first one. How does it go?"

"Jeff'll be in charge. I'm just bringing some of the supplies up. We give out sandwiches and bottled water and stuff. We have some clothes the guys can look through too, but they need to take turns choosing, otherwise it gets too chaotic. We'll be doing a separate distribution for those later, from the back of Jeff's van."

"Are they mostly guys, as in males?" Daisy asks. "Any women or families on the hillside?"

"The families mostly live in the main camp, and even though their accommodation's pathetic it's better than what you get on the hill. A tarp if you're lucky, and a blanket. It's awful, but what can you do without the resources? And yeah, there are women as well as men." She's aware of his Adam's Apple bobbing as Aiden swallows. "Here we are."

He brings the jeep to a halt on a roughly flat area of land at the foot of a slope.

Jeff meets them practically at a run as Daisy hops out. He has straggly black hair and a rounded belly. "Hi you two. Okay so we're taking snacks and water up to the folks on that side of the hill. There aren't many, we've already done a long queue in the olive grove over there." He gestures to the right beyond a stone wall, where a heat haze wavers around the tops of olive trees. Daisy can see silhouetted figures moving beneath them. "Have you brought your rucksacks?"

"Yes," says Daisy. "I'll get them. She feels shaky as she reaches into the cab of the jeep and pulls them down. "Here,

Aiden." She hands one of the green rucksacks to him, quickly withdrawing her fingers as they brush his. Under Jeff's instructions they load the carriers with halal sandwiches from the back of the vehicle, along with fruit and bottled water.

"Take as many blankets as you both can carry as well," Jeff says. "See if you can see if there's anyone who doesn't have one. It's not unusual for some stealing to go on." He raises his hands. "Understandable of course, but still. We must look out for the vulnerable as much as we can."

Daisy glances at Aiden and sees he's watching her. She feels her cheeks redden. There's a flutter in her stomach, too, but that might be nerves at going out into an unknown situation. Working in the school's become routine to her now. She feels safe with routine. But there's no time to think about it, Jeff and Aiden are setting off up the hill on the left-leading path. Aiden looks back over his shoulder and smiles. Daisy's lips twitch in return. She's soon out of breath, climbing the slope with the weight of the rucksack on her back. She has blankets tucked under her arm. She loops both arms around them as if she's carrying a baby.

While she puffs up the hill, she's shocked at the reality of what she makes out under the trees and against an old stone wall. Clusters of people that only become fully visible as her eyes focus on aspects of the rugged landscape. The people stand against the trunks of olive trees, lean against the wall, or lie and sit on the ground, some squatting around a small gas stove. Daisy's heart pounds. Some of the people have constructed shelters out of tarpaulin, cardboard or planks of wood. Many only seem to have a square of blanket to mark out some personal territory.

"You can start over here," Jeff says, coming to a breathless pause. He slides his rucksack to the floor and withdraws a bottle of water which he drinks from. He tucks it back in a side pocket. He fixes his small dark eyes on Daisy while he catches his breath. She looks at the ground and shuffles her foot. Dust rises. "Offer them a sandwich, water and a choice of fruit," Jeff continues. Daisy looks up at him. "Always ask before you enter their personal space. If you're concerned about anything step away. A member of the team is always within earshot if you need to call one of us."

The back of Daisy's neck prickles. "Spend a moment or two chatting, if they speak English," Jeff says. "Especially to single people. There's a high incidence of depression. People feel hopeless, understandably." He scratches his right upper arm, brings the arm up to his face to peer at a bite on it more closely. Then he leans to pick up the loaded rucksack and blankets he'd dropped on the ground. "All right then. So, you're going that way, Daisy. You can take the next terrace up, Aiden. I'll go on up to the highest level. That okay?"

"Yes, that's okay," says Daisy. She swallows nervously.

"Fine," Aiden adjusts his rucksack on his back. "Need any help, Daisy?"

"No thanks," she stumbles as she steps forward again, but quickly realigns herself. Her heart pounds a bit too hard and she realises she's been holding her breath. *Let it go.* She thinks about her mother, saying she could hardly lift her backpack off the hotel floor when she first packed it in order to begin her travels. And yet look where that backpack took her. Daisy lifts her chin and walks.

"Give us a shout if you need anything." Aiden waits for a moment, but Daisy doesn't respond, so he moves ahead and veers up the slope to the next terrace. Glancing up, Daisy feels a spark of irritation. She should love his niceness, but she doesn't. Dan comes into her mind, her ex-boyfriend. He wasn't nice at all. Not really. But she was mad about him. She has a flashback to the time she stalked him and his new girlfriend to a restaurant in Newark, and he spotted her peering in at the window. His rage, the way he knocked his wineglass off the table and pushed past a waiter while making for the door. She ran. He reported her to the police! Heat pounds in her head now.

She wipes sweat off her forehead with her sleeve.

Coming into the shade under a cluster of olive trees, Daisy locates a pair of young men lounging on a dirty blanket, their heads resting on bags. Empty plastic bottles litter the ground around them. One of them pushes himself up on his elbow, and then into a sitting position. She leans down to greet them. The other doesn't move. He remains on his back, his arm over his eyes.

"Hi," Daisy says.

"Hi." The sitting man responds without interest. He pushes a stick into the dirt at the edge of the blanket. He glances up at her, his eyes dark and watchful.

Daisy hesitates. "Do you mind if I . . . ?" He shakes his head imperceptibly, his face blank. She wonders what feelings he's restraining. The stick pushes harder in the dry earth.

Daisy almost overbalances, lowering herself into a squatting position. She should have slid the rucksack off her shoulders first. It bumps to the ground, and she swings it around to her front.

"I have sandwiches," she pulls open the top of the bag. "Meat. Halal," she says awkwardly. She pulls two sets of sandwiches out of the rucksack. After a moment the lying down man jerks suddenly upright. He sits, drawing his knees up in front of him. Daisy jumps and the other man nudges him and laughs. Daisy laughs too, though she's uncomfortable. Tousled brown hair falls into the second man's eyes. He points to the bag. His fingers are dirty.

She wishes she could offer them facilities: a bathroom, a clean bed for a rest. Instead, she hands them sandwiches, then offers each a bottle of water. They accept, thanking her. The first man gestures with his hand for her to sit with them on their blanket — he turns his hand side on and crooks the fingers, seeming to indicate she should take a sandwich for herself.

"Thank you," she says. "But I can't. I've got to get on." She hesitates, remembering what Jeff said about chatting. "Is everything all right with you both?" They look at her, uncomprehending. "Do you need anything?" Her ankles are beginning to ache from squatting. What a stupid question! Home, the possibility of escape from this island. Of course, they need something. So many things.

The first man gives her a bitter smile, chewing on his halal meat. The tousle-haired one points at the pile of blankets next to her.

"I need," he says roughly. She hesitates again. Is it all right to give him one? But they do only seem to have one between them. He smiles at last, as she hands him the clean blanket. She notices the similarity between the men then, little more than boys really. They're probably brothers. She swallows a lump in her throat, thinking of Jamie and Joe, lost to the family for so long. When they could have come home any time. She wonders if the mother of these two young men knows where they are.

"My name's Daisy," she says. She points to herself. "How about you two?" She indicates each of them with her hand. The first brother licks meat off the edge of his thumb. Daisy thinks about germs.

"Ibrahim," he says at last, nodding. He points to his brother. "Ahmed."

"Ah, thank you. Ibrahim and Ahmed." She's self-conscious trying to form the hidden 'ch' sound in his name. "It's a pleasure to meet you both." She begins to push herself up from the ground, then remembers the fruit. She pulls out apples and oranges from the bag, tilts her hand at one fruit and then the other.

"Which would you like?"

"Yes, thank you." Ibrahim takes both an apple and an orange and his brother does the same. Ah well, thinks Daisy. And why shouldn't they have both? She laughs as she moves away but she feels hollow at her centre.

The next group of people — all male — sit on blankets in the shade of a wall.

"May I?" she asks, indicating their space with a sweep of her hand.

"Yes, yes. Please," says a man who looks almost elderly, with whitening hair, but is probably only in his forties. He beckons her forward. She asks them their names, although she cannot make out most of them and feels uncomfortable asking them to repeat themselves. But she catches and repeats back two names. 'Hailed' and 'Isaias'. She gives them her name in return.

Each person is polite, and grateful for the food. She distributes two extra blankets, one to the older man and the other to a boy who looks barely in his teens, sitting at the edge of the group. She thinks they might be a family, or perhaps they're a mixed-age group who have formed themselves into one. She asks a middle-aged man in the group where they're from and he tells her they're all from Eritrea. She counts out exactly enough items of fruit for all seven to choose one piece each. She hopes they don't notice that her previous two clients obtained double their share.

"It's lovely to meet you," she tells the by-now-chattering group. I must go now."

The teenage boy stares at her with limpid eyes and she feels guilty turning away.

"Goodbye," Daisy calls, shrugging her arms into the rucksack straps.

I want to give back to this country,
respect all the rules,
do the right thing.

9

Daisy

Samos, April 2017

Daisy wipes her forehead on her three-quarter-length sleeve. A vest-top would have been more suitable, but her skin's so fair and she always burns. Anyway, it's more sensitive to the service-users to cover her shoulders. She hears her own breathing in her head. The rucksack straps dig into her shoulders. She stops to adjust them and glances down the hill. Below her is the town of Vathy, spread out for the tourists as if nothing wrong is happening here on the hillside. At a cafe near the seafront Daisy heard an English woman remark that it was selfish of refugees to land on the tourist beaches in their dinghies. It spoiled peoples' holidays and the discarded life jackets made a mess. Daisy had been having an after-work coffee with Aiden. She opened her mouth to respond but Aiden put his hand on her arm and stopped her. Daisy shook him off.

"Don't you think we should say something?" She sounded more cross than she meant to. But his reasonableness annoyed her as usual, and on top of that she was annoyed at herself for being the kind of person who was troubled by someone's niceness.

Aiden remained reasonable. "I can understand why you want to, Daisy. But we're not going to change that woman's opinion and it's not our place to anyway. Also, Sal at the office said not to engage with anyone's negative opinion. We do what we do, and that's enough." He smiled at her and tilted his head on one side.

"Hmph." Daisy took a savage bite of her flapjack. She couldn't look Aiden in his patient blue eyes, he was too intense.

On the hillside she turns away from the glare of the blue sea in the distance and focuses on the shadows in the glade. A young man sits alone, reading a book. She recognises the cover, a book of wildlife on Samos that she herself borrowed recently from the book exchange at her charity's reception centre. Daisy can't believe her luck, now she'll be able to have a conversation with the reader, they've got something in common.

Everything has a greenish tinge in the shade of the trees. It takes Daisy's eyes a moment to adjust. When they do, she sees that the young man has marked his place in the book with an olive leaf and has closed it and laid the book down on the blanket beside him. He pushes himself to his feet and brushes dust off his hands on the front of his jeans.

His hair is all tumbled black curls. He has a scar under one eye. He checks his right hand, she thinks for cleanliness, before offering it to her to shake.

"Good afternoon, Miss." He clears his throat. "Excuse me, but welcome my humble abode, ha." He makes an encompassing gesture with his left hand, still holding his right towards her.

Daisy hastily rubs her own right hand on the leg of her canvas trousers and takes his. His grip is firm, his hand dry. He stares at her. She flinches, wanting him to look away but at the same time not wanting him to.

"Your eyes very beautiful," he says after what feels like an intense moment. "If you not mind I say."

Daisy coughs in her throat. She swallows. "I don't, thank you for the compliment." She withdraws her hand, not quite knowing what to do or say next. It must be the heat making her dizzy. She unbuckles the waist strap of the rucksack and begins to slide its weight from her shoulders.

"Please," says her new friend, hurrying behind her to catch the rucksack as it falls, "let me."

"Thank you." She feels unbalanced, emotionally as well as physically. Safer to let herself sink into a squat before she topples.

"Yes, we sit together. Please," he smooths a corner of his grey blanket, and she lowers herself fully to the ground, taking as little space as possible. He seats himself on the opposite corner of the blanket and they smile at each other. The pause that follows is comfortable. Daisy could sit here all afternoon. They gaze out from the shade at the sea in the distance. A loud buzzing announces a bee that hovers close to her ear for an unreasonably long moment while she holds still, tense. *That time both Lola and I got stung by two different bees, sitting in the patch of long grass we insisted Dad left unmown for the insects. My sting was on my right arm and Lola's on her left.* When it swings away, she sees it making for the olive branch above her head. The bee is soon contentedly rummaging in one tiny white flower after another.

"It thinks you flower, see," her companion grins crookedly. One of his lower teeth leans in front of another, leaving an uneven gap on its other side.

"Maybe," she smiles at him. "Hmm, would you like some water?" She realises how dry her tongue is. "I'm going to have some myself." She's so thirsty suddenly. She holds a bottle between her knees and unscrews it with one hand whilst handing another to him. After they've both taken a drink, they smile at each other again.

"So—" begins Daisy.

"You walk long way?" Her new friend speaks at the same moment.

"No, no, not far. Just up the hill." She indicates with her hand, thinking of the miles he must have walked to arrive here. She takes another gulp of water. "I have food if you would like some. Sandwiches and fruit."

"Yes, thank you." His hand goes to his stomach. "I have later. Unless you want eat with me?"

"No, thank you. I'm eating with my mother and some friends later." She doesn't want to say too much about the long table on Daphne's veranda, the carefree company that will gather there. It doesn't seem fair. She wishes she could invite him — invite everyone here on the hill. Then she thinks of Aiden, Mum's happy glances between the two of them when they're talking together. Aiden, what does she really think of him? Twisting her neck, she shields her eyes from the sun and scans the level of hillside beyond this line of olive trees. Everything looks wavery. She can't spot Aiden.

Her refugee friend's talking, she turns back.

"Your mother, here on island?"

Daisy wipes water from her mouth with the back of her hand. "Yes, it was her who brought me here."

"She helping too?"

"Yes, she is. Doing lots of driving, you know, supplies. Also taking people to appointments and things."

"You good people. Thank you," says her friend. She knuckles her hand into her chest, it's something about his smile, his dignity.

"No, don't. Don't thank me. I'm hardly doing anything. I'm not good, not like that, honestly." She plays with a buckle on the rucksack. "Hey, look, I forgot to ask your name. I'm Daisy, by the way. Daisy Galen."

His smile widens. "Aha that why bee like you. Your name flower, yes? Like this." He reaches up to an olive branch and picks one of the tiny white and yellow flowers, holding it out on his palm until it flutters off in a faint breeze.

"A bit like that, yes, only a daisy grows on the ground. It's supposed to be a weed, a flower you don't want on your grass," she explains. "Only I would never let my mum or dad cut them because they have the same name as me." She looks at him to see if he's understood. He nods, looks around, and plucks a decorative grass head to show her, miniature pearls of seeds nestled in formation against each other.

"They call this weed, too, but is beautiful, no?" He laughs and shakes the loaded seed head. It makes a dry, tinkling sound. "Me," he says, placing his hand on his chest. "My name Umid, this mean 'hope'. Umid Habibi," he bows his head. "Pleased to meet you, Daisy." He lays the grass stem to one side and shakes her hand again.

"Thank you. I'm happy to meet you too." She shifts on the blanket, feeling the prickle of the dry grass beneath. "I see you are reading 'Wildlife on Samos', Umid." Daisy reaches to lift the book. "I know this book; I borrowed it because I thought I might have time to study the wildlife here. But I haven't seen any. It's good though. I like the pictures."

"Is good book," her friend agrees. "I take it when I go to centre for my volunteer." He pauses as if thinking. "My volunteer*ing*, I mean. I help in kitchen. Give me something to do, you know. Practice English, read book."

"Your English is very good," Daisy says. "And I'm sorry you're stuck here on the hill so much of the time. It must be hard for you."

He makes a dismissive gesture. "Many things hard."

Another pause.

"Have you ever seen any of the wildlife in the book?" Daisy glances into the sunshine outside the circle of trees, half-expecting a parade of animals to materialise from the heat haze.

At this his eyes become animated again. "Yes, yes. I see jackal. Golden jackal, is only on Samos, book say. Used to be on all Greek islands, but now only Samos. Sad. But I see! One evening. Up there." He points to an olive grove further along the hill. "Peep out behind tree. And then it run, that way." He traces a line with his finger. Daisy follows with her eyes, imagining the red coat of the jackal lit gold by the sunset. "Then I not see."

"That's amazing," says Daisy. "A golden jackal." She wants to keep the conversation going. "And do you know what these birds are, these cheeping ones in the trees all around us?"

Tipping back her head she watches the small fawn birds hopping restlessly from branch to branch. They have pale bellies and black markings on their heads. Umid rifles through the book's pages. He investigates the tree, glances at Daisy then studies a page in the book again. His black curls tumble forward as he nods knowledgeably.

"Yes, I see. They called oliv— how you say it? Oliv*aceous*," he repeats the word after Daisy sounds it out for him. "Olivaceous warblers." He nods again, satisfied. "Olivaceous warblers. Now I know these birds."

"Olivaceous warblers," repeats Daisy. "Well now I've learnt something too. Thank you, Umid."

He bows his head and smiles, then half-returns his attention to the book. She notices the edges of the sandwiches she'd handed him beginning to curl in their packet. The scent of the fat orange sitting next to them is strong. She realises how long she's been sitting here.

"Well, Umid, I must go as I have the rest of this food to distribute. Is there anything else you need that I could maybe ask about getting for you?" Unfolding her legs, she helps herself to her feet, grasping an olive branch for balance. "Would you like another blanket?" She asks recklessly, not caring if she gets in trouble from Jeff. She imagines Aiden telling her to play by the rules.

Umid hesitates, nods. "Another blanket very useful; I make tent with it." He uses the discarded grass stalk to mark his page in the book this time and closes it. "I make shelter, other side of hill, over there." She follows the direction of his gaze. "But I gave to young woman with two children. They need it more."

Daisy swallows an ache in her throat. She hands him one of the three folded blankets she has left. "Would I be able to bring you anything else? Next time I mean?"

"Ah," he pauses again, then rushes on. "It very dark at night. I have torch but has run out. I like batteries if you can get. Here," he rummages in a black backpack leant against the tree. Pulling out a palm-sized torch, he unfastens the end and tips out two AA batteries, which he hands to her. "Thank you. If you can, I mean."

"I will," says Daisy. She slips the batteries into the leg pocket of her cargo trousers. "I'll get some. I'll come back as soon as I can, okay?"

"Okay." Umid looks at her from under his black curls. "Goodbye Daisy. I hope we meet again soon."

Daisy drops her eyes from his gaze. "Goodbye for now, Umid. Take care." She doesn't know why her throat hurts so much.

I went to the city,
I thought too much.
Some people can see
all the good things,
some can't.

10

Daisy

Samos, May 2017

Email from: Daisy_halfcrazy@dmail.com
To: Lola Galen

Subject: Falling (help)!

Hey Lo,
How're you and our boy? Oooo, what a squidge he is! Well done for the photo of him sitting up for those few seconds, that's pretty advanced, I think. Maybe you could send me a video next time, hey? His smile is infectious, and I can't believe how quickly he's growing. Tell him I miss him.

And how's Dad, is S.M. still prowling around? I wonder what Dad sees in her, I've always found her annoying. And no, I haven't told Mum. But I hope S.M. isn't spoiling the plans you and Dad have for a trip to Germany to see the boys and their families. I must admit when I think about that I have wobbles, and I feel like giving all this up, then I could join you in Berlin.

But I did promise this thing six months, and I don't want to let Mum down.

Why do I have this tingly feeling on my tongue? Okay, you got me. I'll tell you the truth. It's not just about the promise I made — there's another reason I wouldn't want to leave here yet.

I'm sitting at an outdoor cafe writing this, because I don't want Mum to accidentally see it. We're so cramped together in the van ... but I won't moan about that now. Good job I'm so knackered every day: I sleep like a log at night and don't hear her snoring anymore. I have a view of the harbour from here. The late afternoon sun's painting the tops of the fishing boat masts gold, and it looks beautiful. I'm typing on my iPad 'cause this cafe has WiFi, better make the most of it as the one at the campsite often doesn't work. I always come here 'cause it's the best coffee. I've ordered a piece of *karythopita* too — that's spiced walnut cake to you. Mmm-mmm.

So. Yeah. You sensed I was keeping something back in my last email, didn't you? Well, you were right.

His name is Umid. It's been hard not telling you, but I feel guilty about it. I don't think this should have happened; I know Mum would be disappointed in me for not being 'professional'. But I've fallen for Umid, Lo, I *really* have. I can't stop thinking about him.

Argh. I'm scared of losing myself all over again. Like what happened with Dan. I promise I'm trying to keep a grip on myself this time — for Umid's sake as well as mine, I need to be careful. Oh, I wish you were here to give me one of your withering stares, lol.

I came across Umid when I did my first distribution on the hillside. He was reading a book about the island's wildlife; one I'd borrowed previously myself. We talked about wildlife and about why I'm here, and all sorts of things. And he asked me if I could get some batteries for his torch, so I did.

Oh Lo, you can't imagine what it's like for the people stuck on the hillside with only a mat and a blanket, having to wait to be fed. The indignity of it. Like animals in a zoo, Umid said. They don't know how long they're going to have to stay here, in limbo. After the journeys they've had, the terror they've escaped. Umid's intelligent you see, sensitive and strong. He wants to study and work; there's so much he could do. He's creative: his talents are being wasted. He only wants to be safe, and get on with something useful, not this. He wasn't safe in Iran, where he comes from. You can be killed for demonstrating against the government. His name is on their list. He was lucky he got a warning from the father of someone he was at the demo with, if he hadn't left when he did, he would have been arrested like his friend. They keep you in prison for years. Can you imagine? I know we've never been the demonstrating types ourselves but remember Donna Prior from school? She's heavily involved in *XR* and she got arrested for chaining herself to a train. But she was let out straight away. In Umid's country you can be tortured … I can't bear to think of it.

I've never met anyone like him. I just needed to tell you, but I'll stop for now. It's all feelings on my part, I acknowledge that. I don't know if anything's going to happen. I know what I'm like for over imagining things. I need to keep control of myself this time. Tell me what to do!

Sorry for going on about myself. Tell me something new about the baby. Is he trying to crawl yet? and is he sleeping any better at night?

I'm sorry you're lonely. Maybe you should try the new parent and baby group you said they were starting up in the village. I really think it would help if you mixed with other mums a bit more. You need to be around people who understand you. Has Johanna Harker had her baby yet? I know you and her weren't always the best of friends but at least you'd have something in common now. Sorry if that isn't appropriate. I

62

know there's more to you than being a mum.

Well, I'd better finish my cake and pack up my things. I told Mum I wouldn't be long. She was taking Jodie and Ned over to Pythagoreio — that's right over the other side of the island — to pick up a chest of drawers for their bedroom, and I said I'd meet her at Daphne's place where Jodie and Ned live. It's where Alicia stays during the day as well, Mum's a bit jealous at how much Alicia loves Daphne!

Speaking of pets, how's my Tink? Give her a stroke from me.

Love you Lo,
Kisses for you and Elijah,
Bye for now,
Daisy xxxxxxxxxxxxxxxxxxx

I followed a dream,
that turned into a lie
and I found myself in prison.
From the window I saw
a small part of sky.
and I wished for home,
for Yemen.

11

Daisy

Samos, May 2017

Rasan, a small boy from Iraq, clings to Daisy's arm. In some ways this little boy reminds her of Jacob, a child back in her school in Newark. Like Jacob, Rasan's moods are hard to read. The other teacher, Meg, called him obtuse the other day. Daisy thinks Meg's been at the camp too long and is losing her empathy. She herself feels protective towards the boy with the stretched-looking eyes. She peers at the doorway to see if she can spot Rasan's aunt, who usually walks him back to their section of camp, but there's no sign.

"I have to go now, Rasan." She pries Rasan's fingers delicately from her arm and kneels in front of him. "Me," she taps her chest. "Go," she points to the door. "Rasan goes too. Bye bye." She taps his chest and then points to the door, saying bye bye again. The other children have collected their bags from the pegs and are filing out, as they've been taught. "Rasan must join the line." She clamps her lips shut so as not to give away the emotion she feels. At the same time, she wishes she could wrap him up and take him home. He has no family apart from the reluctant young aunt, traumatised herself, and who must have once had other dreams than to be the sole carer for her brother's only surviving child.

"Come on, Rasan." He's grabbed her arm again, holding on tight with two hands. His face is clenched, determined. A thin sound vibrates from a gap between his lips. If she's not careful he'll start howling. "Come on now." She wants to pick him up, but she's been advised not to. Instead, she leads him at a half-crouch, while he still clings to her arm, towards the pinned-back tarpaulin flaps they call the door, grabbing his bag on the way.

"Look at the sky," Daisy sings under her breath. With the arm he holds she points up into the thick blue, taking his hands with her. "Look at the ground," they stumble on a mess of stones underfoot. She rights him, stroking his hair with her other hand. He's followed the trajectory of her pointing finger, now pre-empts its imminent change of direction with his quick glance, pushing her arm the right way: "Look to the left," (the small building containing the terrible toilets, the ones that make Daisy gag) "—and look to the right." He's already looking and now points, too, letting go with one hand. There's his young aunt, running towards them as best she can in her thin sandals. Her delicate headscarf wafts in the breeze her movements create.

The child releases Daisy and reaches for his aunt, who takes him by both arms. She's younger than Daisy, still in her teens probably. Daisy straightens her shoulders.

"Rasan," the young woman sounds breathless. She speaks to him in their own language and then nods an apology to Daisy. "I'm sorry I'm late, Miss. I had to wait in the food line."

Daisy pushes back her hair. "Please don't apologise, it's fine, honestly."

"I try to teach him to come home by himself, like the other children. But he is too shy."

"I know," Daisy says. "It's difficult for you. I'm sorry it's so difficult." She feels her cheeks burning.

"No, no. It's fine. My name is Farah, by the way. And you're Teacher Daisy, right?"

"Just Daisy," Daisy laughs. "Your English is very good."

"I'm taking lessons. Just like Rasan," Farah adjusts her headscarf. "My lesson is this afternoon, with Teacher Pete. And that's why I must go now. Come on Rasan. I need to feed him and leave him with Grandmother Leila while I go for my lesson," she says the last part in an aside to Daisy. "See you tomorrow, Daisy."

"Wait, your grandmother's here?" Daisy had been under the impression the teenager and child were alone.

"No. not my real grandmother. Is just what everybody call this woman with all the children. I think they're not all her family, but they live with her. She has Rasan for me in the afternoons. Sorry, I must go now. Say goodbye to teacher, Rasan."

"Bye bye, Rasan, see you tomorrow. Bye for now, Farah." Daisy twists the end of her ponytail around her finger while she watches the boy kick up dust, trotting beside his sister.

Daisy missed most of Aiden's leaving party yesterday afternoon. Maya's mouth pursed tightly when she eventually turned up, and Jodie shot her scornful looks throughout dessert. Daisy thinks Jodie doesn't like her because she perceives her as overprivileged, Maya's spoilt princess. Daisy overheard a snippet of conversation between Jodie and Ned to that effect once. Aiden smiled of course, said it was all right that she was late, he was only glad she'd made it at all. The party took place at a restaurant in town. Even Daphne had left her usual late afternoon spot on the veranda to join them, and Alicia lay under the restaurant table the whole time. Daisy hadn't meant to be so late, she couldn't help it, she'd miscalculated the bus times. She's worried though.

Because she's sure Jodie knows what's going on, even if it's only in Daisy's head.

The day before yesterday Jodie had said "It's not your turn for distribution," when Daisy offered to cover for her on the afternoon shift. "You must really like getting hot and sweaty, and lugging heavy bags around. When you don't have to. What's really going on, eh?" Jodie's pink face had clashed with the wisps of red hair escaping from her green hairband, and a trickle of sweat ran down the side of her face, right down into the neckline of her maroon t-shirt. There was no shade on the forecourt where the jeeps were lined up. She scrunched her eyes up at Daisy. "Anyway, I thought you were going on that trip to Tsamadou beach. Your Mum said you were. Said it would do you good. Said you'd been working too hard, poor dear."

Jodie had never been openly hostile to Daisy before (why does Mum even like her?) Daisy hoped Jodie didn't notice her uncomfortable swallow. She shrugged, sweat sliding in her armpits.

"I just thought you'd like to swap, that's all. Mum said Ned was going on that trip and you aren't. I'm only offering to help. It's up to you."

Jodie narrowed her eyes even more suspiciously. She threw a box into the back of the nearest jeep and wiped her hands on the sides of her shorts before bunching them onto her hips and giving Daisy another searching glance.

"Suit yourself. If you really must act like a martyr, I'm not stupid enough to pass up the chance of a swim and a hang-out with *ma boi*. But you don't fool me, lol." Daisy wasn't taken in by her attempt to sound jokey. "I reckon there's more going on than you're letting on. However, you're welcome to my work. Can't promise I'll cover for you when it's officially your turn though. See you!" She untied the shirt from around her waist and slung it over her shoulders before turning and making her way down the hill.

Nobody has specifically told Daisy that forming a

relationship with him is forbidden (Haram, Umid would say) but she's pretty sure it ought to be. The way she allowed – encouraged – Umid to kiss her *must* be wrong. It must be *haram*. Even though he says he's not religious. And what if it puts Umid's position in danger? What if it stops him getting his papers? Oh, she's so selfish. She knows she is, but she can't help it. She loves Umid, doesn't she? But if she truly loved him, wouldn't she let him be? Allow him to concentrate on obtaining permission to leave this stasis he's in. Unable to escape from the island.

He was the one who pulled back from the lingering contact of their lips and regarded her from under his eyelashes. Her pulse bumped in her throat. *So stupid.* But he laughed and brushed stray hair back from her face. "Your lips are sweet, my friend," he'd said. "Thank you for that."

Was that a brush-off or a cultural thing? Was he inviting her to try again? They'd fallen back into their easy conversation, easy on his part anyway. Inside she burned with shame. And yet she can't let it go, that kiss.

She huffs and puffs as she makes her way up the hill. She thought she'd have become fitter by now.

"I never thought it would be like this," Umid has said about his sojourn on the island. "I walk so many miles; I travel in back of lorry. I swim when boat sink, and now they keep me here like prisoner. Stuck here, on hillside."

Afternoon food distribution's finished — Daisy watched them driving back in before she left. Umid will have received his allowance of plain rice and some vegetables, or the packaged sandwiches they have sometimes. He'll have cooked on his tiny stove, eaten, and be sitting on his blanket under the tree reading the latest book she brought him, an English thesaurus. He's going through it, word for word. He already knew some English before he left Iran, his mother is a teacher. He says he wants to practice his English; talk of

69

the things that he'll do in the future. He confessed that his dream is to become a film director.

From a kiss to a discussion of his potential future, without any mention of Daisy in it. Why would she even think there should be? *We're just friends. He called me friend, remember?*

Daisy doesn't know what she's doing, walking up this hill towards him when she should be leaving him alone. She gets a picture in her head of peering in that restaurant window at Danny with his new girlfriend. He'd told their formerly mutual friends she was mad. Her GP asked if she wanted to be referred to a counsellor!

Maybe she's obsessive. Her heart thumps heavily.

It's still warm. Daisy stops and wipes sweat from her forehead with her sleeve. She pulls the elastic from her hair, combs through it with her fingers and refastens it into a neater ponytail. She hesitates, finding that her body's half-turned back but her feet are still pointing up the hill. Her feet say continue — she only wants to check Umid's all right. She'll keep it professional. Her brain says go back down, don't be stupid. Her body says it'll do what it wants to. And it does. She continues up the hill, excuses and reasons to visit him jostling in her head.

After prison,
I worked in Turkey
to fund my escape to Greece.
There I spent two years
on an island
wondering if things
would ever change.

12

Daisy

Samos, June 2017

Email from: Daisy_halfcrazy@dmail.com
To: Lola Galen

Subject: Fallen (too late for help)!

Hey, Lola,
Don't be mad at me. I know you said I shouldn't get myself into a state over someone there's very little chance of a future with, but I couldn't help it. Hmm. I've got so much to tell you, but I don't really know where to start, especially since I'm struggling to work out your reaction to all this. You managed to keep a good poker face, lol, when I talked to you about Umid on that video call. Maybe it was only because Elijah kept trying to grab the phone out of your hand though.

So, I'm going to tell you anyway, Lo.

I can't help myself. I just want to say it, write it, think about it. All the time, I can't concentrate on anything else.

We spent a night together! It was at a bed and breakfast near Kokkari Beach, to celebrate his birthday – but you could say it was for my birthday too since it was our twenty-seventh last month. He's twenty-four, by the way, because I know you'll ask. Yes, he's younger than me, so what? Oh. Lo. It was the best birthday present I ever had …

Oh, I can't stop myself feeling prickly, it's this fear that you're going to judge me. *Please* don't, Lo. All right, I'll say it: I love him! I really love him. So, be kind to me, okay?

I couldn't tell Mum where I was going or who with, she'd have gone mad. Instead, I lied and said I was bunking in with Emmaline for a night, she's a girl who arrived here about the same time as me and Mum. Emmaline and I did go out for a drink together once so Mum didn't have any trouble believing it. Umid and I took a bus up the coast to Kokkari; I booked the room there as it's about five miles away from Vathy. There was no chance of bumping into Mum, lol.

It felt so wonderful sitting next to Umid on the bus, holding hands. So normal, you know? Well, I suppose it's hard for you to imagine what I mean by that, but for Umid, who lives on an actual blanket on a hill under an olive tree, it felt like freedom. And for me the best part of the whole trip was seeing him blossom like a flower in the sun.

We checked into the B&B and the woman who runs it treated us like any normal couple. Umid's got so used to being shunned by townsfolk, you know. But we were just a young couple on their holidays, as far as she was concerned. She made us a quick lunch of bread, this amazing sheep cheese, and grapes. She refused to take any extra money for it. She asked all the usual holiday questions like how long we were staying on the island and started telling us what we should go and see, such as the folk museum or the archaeological museum. She asked so many questions and kept up a running commentary in her quirky English that we were glad to escape to our room, which had a balcony with a sea view. It was twelve o'clock by that time, and I could already feel my

73

hours with Umid slipping away. But once we were in our room with the door shut, Lo, we both did whatever we could to avoid each other's eyes, busying ourselves with unpacking our backpacks and admiring the view. It was like we were strangers suddenly. I locked myself in the bathroom to put my swimsuit on under my clothes, and tried to stop myself shaking, you know those shivers I get when I'm nervous?

When I came out Umid must have noticed my eyes were red; yeah, I'd been crying in there, idiot that I am. I tried to brush past him and roll up my towel ready for the beach, but he grabbed my hand and pulled me towards him. We didn't even say anything, only started kissing. I think I would have been perfectly happy, Lo, if we did nothing but kiss for the rest of our lives. Anyway, we did stop eventually, and by that time I felt completely at home in his arms again. In case you're thinking we jumped straight into bed: no. We only hugged for a long time before laughing a bit, slightly shy with each other again once we drew apart, then grabbed our towels and headed out to make the most of our glorious afternoon together.

We went for a walk on the beach first, and then had a swim in the sea. Later we watched the sunset from the balcony of our room, sitting at the patio table drinking proper Greek lemonade. We've watched the sunset together many times before, but this time it was different, we were together. I wasn't getting ready to leave him alone on the hill. It was like our own little home. We went out again and ate dinner at a seafront restaurant, pricking our fingers on lobster shells and mopping up the buttery juice with olive bread. After a dessert of *loukoumades* (fried honey doughnuts, omygod) we tried drinking with our arms linked together, you know like those German exchange students taught us when we were sixteen, but I spilled red wine on my white top.

I can hear you going so did you ...? Well, the answer is yes! Yes, my dear sister, we did when we got back to the B&B; and it felt like the most natural thing in the world. I won't go into details on this email, but I'll tell you all about it when we next call, if I can get some privacy from Mum, lol.

So, how's everything in Navengore? Is Elijah enjoying his one afternoon a week with the childminder while you study? I think it's great that you're getting qualified, Lola, then you can start small with just a few children to look after in our future day nursery premises while you wait for me to come home. How's the conversion work been going? They must be nearly finished. I'm excited about the future but at the same time I can't imagine leaving here while Umid's still stuck on the island … No, I won't think about that now. I was asking about home. You say Susannah M is hanging around more and more often? Honestly, I really can't think what Dad sees in her! He told me on our last videocall that he's started going to the gym. He does look like he's lost a lot of weight. The last few years have been so weird, Mum and Dad hardly seem like the same people anymore. Still, I suppose none of us are, what with you having a baby and me expanding my horizons here in the refugee camp.

I've gotta go now, just wanted to update you with my news while I had a few moments to spare.

Loads of love to you and Elijah,

Dais xxxxxxxxxxxxxxxxx

Until you have suffered
you cannot know about this.
You cannot understand, unless
you have slept on streets,
gone hungry,
been imprisoned.

13

Daisy,

Samos, early July 2017

At the end of class that morning Rasan gives her a
handkerchief with a paisley pattern embedded in the soft
fabric. He pushes it into her hand while she gazes out for his
aunt, Farah – late again. Daisy considers taking the child by
the hand and hurrying him along the path in the direction
she's seen Farah lead him so many times. She'll turn left at
the rancid toilet block and trot him along the crumbling
track that passes the blue tarpaulin house on the corner, the
one with the falafel stall opposite, and all the time she'll be
fighting the urge to run, let go of his hand, because it
wouldn't be where she wants to go. But instead, she forces
herself to slow her breath and wait with the boy. Her
stomach feels hollow, not only from lack of food (she finds it
difficult to eat now) but with anxious anticipation.

He's not going anywhere. Umid. (She feels guilty every
time this thought creeps into her head. He should be going
somewhere. Months of his life are being stolen from him.

Over the course of the visits she's paid him — always with some gift: a new book, a better torch, a warm jumper she found at a shop in town, which he accepts part-reluctantly and then presses his hand over his heart in the repeated wordless expression he has of gratitude – she's noticed a hardening around the edges of his eyes. Resentment sprinkled in with the gratitude. The softness of hope that his eyes shone with when she first met him is drying up now. All he wishes to do is leave.

She forces herself to swallow the hurt she feels at his lack of mention of their beautiful night in the B&B together. He will still put his arm around her and pull her close against him as they sit under the olive tree taking turns to look through the cheap binoculars that she found for him in a tourist shop. He will still kiss her and touch her hair. Sometimes he still spends long moments searching her eyes with his, but more often now she finds it hard to capture his gaze. And when she slides her hand under his jumper and rests it on his heart, he pulls back. She hears a noise in his throat. He gently removes her hand from the warm hairs on his chest, tugs his jumper down and presses her palm against his cheek instead. He murmurs words in Farsi that she doesn't understand, and he refuses to tell her what they mean.

He's distracted.

She has a vivid recollection of Dan's eyes flickering away from hers when she questioned him towards the end of their relationship. She mustn't harass Umid like that. She needs to be patient. She loves him and she'll wait until he's ready to hear it before she tells him.

She's forgotten Rasan, until she feels the delicate wool and silk of the woven square being forced into her curled palm. She glances down at the boy and her breathing catches in her throat. Smiling distractedly, she raises the gift and shakes open the richly patterned, dark amber fabric. Staring at it, she's uncomprehending at first, her thoughts still on the gifts she always feels compelled to give Umid. Hopeless gestures of compensation for his incarceration, and for her freedom.

She squats down next to Rasan, watches his eyes flicker anxiously over her face.

"This is so lovely, Rasan." He searches her eyes again, checking for truth.

"You like it, Miss?"

"I love it. But you can't give it to me, thank you so much anyway." She folds the handkerchief — scarf maybe — loosely and presses it back into his hands. "Does your aunt know you brought it to school?"

"Yes Miss. She say give it to you," he pushes the scarf away from himself.

"That's kind of her, Rasan. But I don't understand why?" The refugees here have managed to bring so few items with them from their abandoned homes, and many of the things they did bring have been lost or bartered during their journey, or while in camp. Why would Farah part with what looks like a family heirloom? The fabric's worn in places, she rubs it between her finger and thumb, gathers it to her chest and holds it there between both hands. She'll ask Farah about it when she finally arrives, Rasan must have made a mistake. Straightening, she scans the always-moving crowd. "Where is she, anyway, your aunt? She's very late today." She feels an irritating tickle on her arm, uses the corner of the scarf to brush a fly away. It circles and lands on Rasan's head, she shoos it away again. The fly moves off towards the rancid toilet containers.

Rasan taps her arm to regain her attention, stretching up on tip-toe, his eyes gleaming. "I not wait today, Miss. My aunt not come for me. I am walking home alone!" His face splits open in a grin. It's infectious.

"Why, Rasan, that's good news. I'm proud of you and I bet your aunty is too. Off you go then, say hello to Farah for me. And thank her for the scarf, yes?" Rasan's hitched his small blue rucksack onto his shoulders and has already turned away. He looks back over his shoulder once, checking to see she's watching. Daisy waves, swallowing a lump in her throat. *He called their makeshift wood-and tarpaulin shelter home.* Perhaps he's already blocked out the memories of the home he used to have, and his parents.

She tucks the paisley scarf carefully into her back pocket and pulls the flap of the schoolroom door closed behind her. She hopes Umid will be waiting for her at the stone wall by the track at their usual time; they're planning to take their walk over the other side of the hill from usual this afternoon, then they might circle round and finish their time together with a coffee in her favourite café down by the harbour before Mum finishes work and asks too many questions about where Daisy's been. She hasn't said much to Mum about Umid. She imagines Mum would disapprove.

She hopes the spark might have returned to Umid's eyes when she looks into them again.

*I walked from Iran
to Turkey.
Made it by boat
to a Greek island.
I was given a mat
and a blanket,
bread and a bottle of water,
and told to get on with it.*

14

Daisy's diary

Samos, late July 2017

Hmm.

I don't even feel like saying hello. But yeah, you got me, diary. I hate starting writing without some form of greeting so, I suppose I'll have to say it, "hello." Huh.

So how am I? How is life? Well, if you want to know the truth, everything's gone to shit. U's gone, he's just fucking left. I made a complete idiot of myself searching the hillside for him and later the kitchen, where he volunteers. I got a mutual acquaintance, someone we used to hang out with sometimes, to tell me the truth in the end. Apparently, U was given his stamp last week, well, that's what M says anyway. Why would U tell M and not me? And not say goodbye?

Did I imagine everything that went on between U and me? Did I imagine the feelings were as real for him as they were for me? I really thought so, those last weeks.

But it can't have been true. I've made a fool of myself yet again. I feel as though I can't bear it, yet I've got no choice. How can I though? Oh god, how can I?

I never wanted to go through this again. I can't stand the way my whole body is taken over by this misery. Mum commented this morning how pale I was. I had to go into the bathroom quickly, so she didn't see my eyes filling up. Later I said my eyes were sore, it must be some sort of allergy. She just went, oh yes, maybe it's the dryness of the grass. Or something like that. Is she really that blind she can't see how I'm dying inside? Or maybe she notices and just doesn't want to talk about it. I suppose I've always been careful before about telling her how I feel, not wanting to upset her with my upset. She probably thinks I'm a totally together sort of person. Yeah, she always said I was the 'sensible' one. Oh god, she doesn't know me at all! It was better last year and the year before when we were emailing, I could give her snippets of what was happening, then cut off the narrative wherever I felt comfortable. Like with Lola's pregnancy that I wasn't allowed to mention. Or the mess of ending (or not ending) my relationship with Dan. I certainly never told her what happened at the end of that, how I would have got arrested if Dan hadn't asked the police to let me go, right there on the street outside the restaurant. Even feeling as shit as I do now, I still want to curl up into a ball when I think about that time.

Now we're living in each other's faces, Mum and me, and our ability to communicate seems to be drying up. We don't have the fun we had when communicating by email – she was fun then, and kind of exotic. I kind of miss that mum I didn't see very often.

We only seem to talk properly when we're in company, like on Daphne's terrace when we finish work. We don't seem to have any energy left by the time we settle in here for the evening. We sit here reading our separate books or writing in our diaries – yeah, I think Mum's writing one too. Or some sort of travel journal anyway. She got the idea off Joe and that's why she bought me this book too.

Bugger. Alicia's just come up to me and nudged my elbow and now there's a smudge halfway across this page. Damn you, dog. No, you can't jump up on my bed. Oh, apparently you can ...

Hmph. Mum's animated enough when her precious Ned and Jodie are around, and she was positively grief-stricken when Aiden left ... and mad with me for not falling in love with him, that's probably why she can barely bring herself to speak to me ... but she can't seem to notice when I'm falling apart.

U ... Where are you? Apart from being furious at him for not saying goodbye – not even telling me he was going – I'm scared for him too. Scared and sad. My stomach keeps churning just thinking about all the things that happened to him in the past. Wondering what might be happening to him now.

I think I really am falling apart. I just cried so much I was sick. Thank god Mum left me here in the van and walked to the Centre, where she's working today. I'll try and get all my tears out and act normal when she comes back.

I know I'm pathetic. I swore I'd never get myself into this kind of state over a man again, but that was before I met U. The even more pathetic thing is at the beginning I convinced myself it was him who needed me. For once I could be the strong one, someone in control. I should have realised any one of those people in the camp are stronger than me. How could they not be after everything they've been forced to go through? They've lost their homes and families, yet you don't see them collapsing into puddles on the floor like me. U must have thought I'm pathetic too. Why else would he have left without telling me?

Oh, U. When I took him to the B&B for the night on his birthday, we could have been any couple, anywhere. We sat at a window table in the restaurant, looking out at the reflection of the moon on the water. Walked close together around the harbour edge (the feel of his strong fingers linked with mine, oh fuck, I can't bear it) and threw stones into the sea before returning to our bedroom for the night and then ... well, you know what happened there, diary. I know and I will never forget, I promise you that, U.

How could that have been only four weeks ago?

Was he pretending, the things he said, the way he acted? I didn't think so. I didn't feel so. Surely my instincts aren't that far off?

Shit, I must've fallen asleep. What time is it? Still a couple of hours until Mum gets back. I'd better take the dog for a walk; I promised her I would.

Back now. I think the fresh (hot) air's done me some good. We walked up the hill track near here - a different walk to any I've done with Umid, though it was difficult to choose a direction - so it didn't have any memories for me.

I will pull myself together, I will. I had him, what felt like his love, at least for a while. This is nothing like what most of the people here have lost. At least U is on his way now, making his way towards safety. Inshallah as my new friends would say. (But where is he?) Maybe he'll carry a part of me with him on his journey (but where will he have gone?) Our mutual friend M said he had no idea. He only told me that U had been given his stamp. Oh well, I'd better stop writing about that in case it sets me off again. I promised myself on the walk that I'll pull myself together. I mustn't turn back into the kind of person I was when Dan finished with me.

The main thing is that U's finally got off this island. That was what he wanted, so it's something to celebrate. Yay.

(More tears.) I hope he's safe.

Remembering my family
fills my eyes with tears.
My grandfather always told me
to seek and fight
for my dreams.
When I think of my homeland,
I think of food and beaches.
I think of my mother there,
taking care of my children.

Part II

I had never felt more alone.
I found myself a spot on a hill,
made a shelter
from boards.

15

Maya

Athens, August 2017

Email from: Maya_Lifeforce@dmail.com
To: Conrad Galen

   Subject: We're leaving Greece

Hi Con,

I hope things are well with you and Lola and of course with our darling grandson. I can see from the photos Lola sent Daisy how much he's grown! Seven months old, my goodness. Ooh, I wish I could hold him.

   On another note, I'm sorry to hear Bev's left after two years — Lola told Daisy. Why did Bev resign, I mean is she giving up cleaning or something? I suppose it's none of my business anymore, but you might want to try that amazing woman the Kearstons used to have. You could see your reflection in their kitchen worktop after she'd finished. Sorry, I'm sure you can manage your own house and home, I must continue to remind myself it's nothing to do with me anymore. I'm learning to let go a little bit at a time, I promise. I guess it's time for both of us to live our own lives now.

Thanks for being so great about everything, by the way. Yes, the money for my share of the house has finally landed safely in my account — I'm a rich woman, indeed. I agree with you, I shall leave it in my savings for the time being as I accept that one day, I *may* wish to own a home of my own again, though now I'm still enjoying the potential of a life on the road ... I'll let you know how that goes come the winter!

Speaking of a life on the road, I don't know if Daisy's told you, but we've left Samos. I know we were planning a full six months' volunteering, but Daisy hasn't been herself lately. Has she been in touch? She'd started taking half each week off sick, she doesn't seem to have any energy. I tried to persuade her to see a doctor on Samos, but she refused. She says she's just tired, but I wonder if it could be something like glandular fever — remember Jamie's friend Andy was off school with that on and off for a whole term? Mononucleosis I think they call it now.

She's tired and listless and she looks so pale, despite the healthy tan she'd gained, and you know how translucent Daisy's complexion normally is.

Anyway, just keeping you informed. Don't worry too much, she's not *ill* as such. We'll make our way slowly back to the UK, but we thought we'd stop off and see the boys in Berlin before we return. It will be lovely to meet our newest grandchild — Rudi, what a lovely name. I admit I felt envious of you and Lola seeing them last month, but we won't be far behind (that's if they're not fed up with all the visitors by now)! We're lucky that the children we made have multiplied, aren't we Con? (If you see what I mean?)

Just think, only a few months ago we were a fractured family with half of us missing — it's hard to believe now that we didn't know where our two boys were for so long! I could never have pictured my rosy-cheeked baby boy with the mass of black curls — remember that yellow babygro Jamie had? — living in Berlin with a wife and two children one day. It's hard to imagine them as adults when they're babies, isn't it? Perhaps that's all part of living in the moment. If I'd known some of what was to come ... Thank goodness I didn't.

Oh, look at me rambling on, I'll stop being sentimental so you can stop cringing now. Anyway, I must get on with this as Daisy's going to be back soon and we'll have to leave. It's crazily difficult to get a parking space this close to the marina — yes, I'm sitting looking out at the boats — and I feel sure some authority's going to come bristling over with a fine if I overstay my 'welcome'. Not sure how welcome a scruffy camper is next to some of the cars parked around here anyway (I'm next to a shiny silver Mercedes, for example). Daisy's gone shopping by the way. She has this idea of finding a present for Lola in every city we stop in. Yes, she found the energy for that, she seems a little better today. But then she did the day before yesterday as well but took a turn for the worse yesterday. Children, you never stop worrying about them do you, however old they get?

Perhaps it's because Daisy and I are living 'in each other's faces', as she put it to me the other day. I mean I spent more than two years hardly seeing her and now we each have to shut ourselves in my tiny bathroom to gain a few moments of privacy, or go out separately, as Daisy has today.

Right, so. I'm only keeping you updated. Bear in mind I should be delivering Daisy back to Navengore around the beginning of October, I expect, no later than that anyway. Probably earlier, depending on how Daisy is. I'd like us to explore a bit along the way: Serbia, Hungary, Slovakia perhaps. I've always wanted to see those places.

I do worry Daisy will become entrenched in a routine with little chance of getting herself out of it if she moves back in with Lola, which she's determined to do. They've talked about it. Apparently, Lola's delighted. She says Daisy can help her with the baby. I'm sure Daisy will love that for a while but is it really the right thing for her in the long run, Con? We discussed

92

this, didn't we, before we left for Germany in January. Perhaps Daisy could move back to Newark and get a job in a new school. She's gained lots of diverse experience from teaching in the refugee camp, any school would snap her up.   Or Nottingham.   Somewhere different from Navengore but not too far away. What about your mum's house in Grantham? Now your dad's moved back to London. The house is empty. She could pay her granddad some rent, and I could stay with her when I take breaks from my travels. Oh no, that's not fair of me, is it?   I mustn't try to plan Daisy's future in order to accommodate my own.

Daisy's perfectly capable of planning her own future anyway.   Even if that does involve being a substitute 'husband' for Lola. Perhaps I'm misjudging both our girls.

Sorry Con, I'm rambling again. I feel a bit all over the place now, I must admit. As soon as Daisy returns to the van we'll get off and find a park-4-night somewhere up on the hillside. I'll cook our daughter a wholesome meal and hope she gets a better night's sleep than she has been lately.

Kiss our other daughter goodnight from me, (and that delicious baby) and goodnight yourself.

Best,

Maya x

But I gave my home away
to a woman with two children,
she needed it more.

16

Maya

Serbia, August 2017

The van jolted as Maya drove over a large pothole, but Daisy seemed not to have woken. She lay on Maya's bed at the back of the van — illegal, and Maya was terrified of getting stopped, again — but Daisy had gone as white as a sheet earlier and Maya had given in to her pleas to be left alone and allowed to sleep. She'd dithered about finding a doctor, though. Daisy was suffering from an overwhelming lassitude. No temperature or blotchy skin or anything else she could put her finger on. But what if she'd missed something? She felt rusty at motherhood. Awful scenarios sprang into her head — what if Daisy had cancer (don't even think it)! Or had developed ME from the cold she caught not long after they arrived on Samos? Or another of those debilitating conditions. It would explain her complete lack of energy. Visions of Daisy pale and drooping in a wheelchair flashed across her mind. *Stop it, Maya.* Her mother had always called her dramatic.

A moan from the back that Maya could just about hear over the rattle of the road convinced her Daisy was at least alive. What kind of moan had it been? She strained her ears to hear. Daisy but could be in pain — dear lord, she could be about to have a seizure or a brain embolism. Maya raked the surrounding landscape with snatched glances. There was nowhere to pull over and check, and probably no mobile signal either. She daren't stop here anyway, the road was narrow and had steep edges.

"You all right in the back?" She made her voice level.

"Ugh," Daisy groaned again. "I was, until a loud noise woke me up. What happened?"

"Just a pothole, we're fine," Maya breathed a sigh of relief. Alicia glanced sideways at her from the passenger seat, panting. "We'll stop as soon as we can."

She gripped the wheel more tightly with both hands, hoping there was no damage to the van. She must keep a more careful lookout for potholes! What on earth had possessed her to attempt this drive? She'd been warned about the poor quality of some roads in Serbia, and about the dangers of burglary if she decided to wild camp. Jess on Samos had even stressed the need to have handfuls of cash ready in case she needed to bribe anyone at the borders. The idea had sounded to Maya like something that would happen in a movie but then she *had* been stopped on a wooded section of the road to Lescovak. For absolutely no reason.

The police officer had been sitting in a vehicle at the edge of the woods. As she approached, he got out of his car and waved her down. She eased her foot on the brake and rolled to a stop beside him, saying *shit* under her breath to Daisy (this was before Daisy went to lie in the back of the van, thank goodness) asking herself what she might have done wrong.

Both front windows were fully down because of the heat. Maya's elbow clicked as she pulled the handbrake on, and her hands trembled as she lifted them to rest on the steering wheel.

The officer stared gravely at her a moment. "English?" Maya nodded, her jaw tense. The officer cleared his throat, before asking her in his heavy accent to step out of the van and hand over her driver's licence, passport and travel insurance. She did so and stood trembling while he examined them. She tucked her hands under her arms and tried to breathe normally. Alicia uttered a low growl from inside the van, on the bed at that point. The officer looked around at the sound. He glared at Maya and shifted his baseball-style cap higher on his forehead with one finger, still clasping her documents in his other hand. He was young, not much older than Jamie. Maya teetered between fear, hairs raising on the back of her neck, and the threat of hysteria, bubbling up inside her. *I haven't done anything wrong.* She focussed on the feel of her shirt against the upper section of her back, damp from the sweat of the drive. She pressed her hands tighter under her arms.

A faint breeze stirred the nearby trees, invoking the scent of warm pine. She wanted to lift her face, take a break from driving to walk through the woods. She wished she had a pack on her back again. No van to spoil her experience of nature with its noise and pollution. No ailing daughter causing her worry she could not escape from, not like when she'd been miles away from everyone she cared about. It had been easier then. Just Maya and the dog.

Especially, she wished she was not standing by the side of a road at the mercy of a police officer who could ask her for well — anything.

The officer pretended to study her documents again, before glancing up and seeming to fully notice Daisy in the passenger seat, sitting still with her hands in her lap. The police officer and Maya were standing on the right-hand side of the van. Maya followed his gaze through the van's interior. Daisy appeared calm, giving a faraway impression. As they both stared, she lifted a hand and hooked a tendril of dark hair, escaped from her ponytail, behind her ear. The moment seemed to stretch and drag. Maya blinked and hunched her shoulders, then let her hands slide down her sides, unfurling her fingers against her thighs. She wiped sweating palms on her linen trousers. The officer cleared his throat again and handed Maya her papers, indicating that she should get back inside the van. With a curt nod he turned and made his way back to his car. *Phew*. Maya stood strong for a few moments, before feeling as though she was collapsing from her middle downwards. After the stories she'd heard about the corruption of the police, it could have been worse!

With her knees trembling, she managed to climb back into the driver's seat, start the engine and steer the van away with shaking hands.

The landscape surrounding the road was becoming more built-up.

"Where are we?" Daisy called from the back.

"We're coming up to Belgrade now." Maya changed down to third gear. "There's a bloody IKEA up ahead, I'm going to pull into their carpark and stop for a breather. I need coffee, I wonder if they'll have a stall outside. Maybe we could get some cake as well. What do you think, Daisy?"

"Why did you call it 'bloody' IKEA, what's it ever done to you?"

Maya jumped at the feel of Daisy's hand on her shoulder.

"Daisy, what the fuck do you think you're doing, do you want to get us arrested again?" Daisy had planted herself on the edge of the passenger seat next to Alicia, and was unclipping the dog's seatbelt, gently shifting her half-onto her lap.

"We weren't arrested, Mum."

Maya brought the gear down to second, slowing further as she indicated and turned left across the highway once there was a gap in the traffic. Despite the months she'd been in Europe she still had to constantly remind herself of the opposite road rules to those in Britain. "Don't you think we've had enough trouble today already?" She craned her neck, looking for a parking space. "God, I hate IKEA. Can you see a van or anything selling coffee? You wouldn't get me inside that place if you paid me."

"Oh yeah," Daisy laughed slightly, her hand against her stomach. "I remember you having a panic attack in IKEA that time we went to get new desks for me and Lola when we turned twelve."

"It wasn't a panic attack. Ah," circling the car park, Maya spotted a decorated van with a short queue of people lined up in front of it. The smell of coffee and bakery products wafted into the van as she drove past, three times, before she found somewhere to park.

I stayed there
two and a half years,
watching the ferry
sail to the city,
while I waited for permission
to leave.

17

Maya

Campervan stop near Belgrade, August 2017

Maya turned off the highway onto the bypass and pulled in at the campsite she'd pre-booked for one night with an option for a second. The van rolled along a chalk and gravel track past a fenced-off orchard, peaches dangling from the trees, and a low wooden building with a terracotta-tiled veranda. There was a WC and shower sign on a post at its entrance. Daisy turned her head as they trundled past.

Their pitch was partially shaded by trees at the edge of a small area of woodland. There was a two-van space between theirs and any of the others, and Maya hoped nobody else would pull into it. She had little-enough privacy in her life at the moment, without having to try and avoid staring in the windows of any van parked next to theirs. It was always a worry if a campervan neighbour had a dog as well. Alicia didn't take kindly to having her bum sniffed, and other dogs did particularly seem to like her scent. Maya in turn didn't enjoy feeling she had to apologise for Alicia's mild reactive behaviour (usually a growl and a warning charge with bared teeth) in the face of an over enthusiastic admirer. Their owners seemed to take it so personally.

"Thank goodness," Daisy picked up the hem of her floaty skirt (it was nice to see her back in her old style of dress, she'd bought some thin cotton items in Athens, along with a white embroidered blouse for Lola and a cute mob cap for the baby) and wiped her forehead. "I think the heat has made me travel sick." She pushed open the passenger door and jumped down onto the flattened, wheat-coloured grass. "I'm just off to the loo, won't be long."

Alicia nosed her way between the seats from the back, where she'd retreated after their coffee stop earlier. Maya stroked her soft white head.

"That girl's all over the place at the moment," she told her. Alicia propped her head on Maya's lap. "It'll do us all good to have a quiet evening here. We can put the chairs and table outside and unroll the awning. Pretend we live here for the rest of the day. Let's get these seats swivelled round first though, give us a bit more room."

When Alicia gazed deep into her eyes like that, Maya imagined they were thinking along similar lines. How simple their life had been when it was just the two of them, a rucksack and a tarpaulin to sleep under. "But here we are," she said brightly. "I don't even feel like that same person anymore anyway. I bet I could barely lift that rucksack now." She patted the softness of her belly, wondering where the strong, lean woman had gone who had taken over her body for a while. But that life would have worn her down in the end, wouldn't it? Look at the freedom she still had. The freedom to roam, for another couple of years, at least. She swallowed hard, trying not to picture the future looming where it would be all visas and passport stamps again, and limited periods of time in any one place, as it had when she was a teenager and she and her sister Jen had bought inter-rail tickets for the summer. They had once visited

102

Belgrade, when it was part of the former Yugoslavia.

A shudder went through her. *Concentrate on the here and now.* Finished driving for the day, sitting in her own van with her own dog, and a Serbian luxury ready meal for two she and Daisy bought at a supermarket. *Duveč,* a sort of stew that they could pop in the van's tiny microwave. With a *šopska* salad: tomatoes, cucumbers, onions, peppers and white cheese. The wine was actually from neighbouring Macedonia, but neither she nor Daisy had been able to resist its pretty label depicting a woodcut-style folk scene of traditionally dressed musicians in front of a rolling landscape. Or the name on the label, *Tikves Smedererevka Belo.* It was slightly cheaper than the rest of the bottles on display as well. The wine would at least be somewhat cool from their – admittedly underperforming – fridge.

Maya's limbs seemed to vibrate, the back of her neck too. It was a consequence of driving all day. If she wasn't careful, she'd fall asleep while she waited for Daisy to come back. Concentrate on the here and now, she reminded herself again. How lucky she was to be here, *somewhere.* Anywhere she chose to be, for the time being. No longer trapped behind the receptionist counter at the GP surgery in Navengore. Or sitting in a cavernous, empty house waiting for Con to come home from work, late again; her dinner pots washed and put away, his plate covered with one of what seemed several hundred Tupperware lids and containers that filled a massive cupboard. She'd had too many cupboards in that house, too much of everything, and still not been happy. Not even been truly aware of her unhappiness until that day in Australia when she'd shrugged her arms into the oversized rucksack and closed the hotel room door behind her. The first day of her freedom.

Maya got up from the bench seat where she'd been sitting, dislodging Alicia's head from her lap. She sighed and stretched and climbed down from the van to plug in the electric cable at the post by her plot, before unrolling the van's awning and retrieving the fold-up chairs and table from the space at the back under the bed. Alicia jumped out after her, slinking to the hedge behind the van and squatting to relieve herself. Then she flopped onto her stomach in the shade of the awning. Maya brought out a bowl of water for her and she lapped greedily, her head to one side, without moving from her prone position.

Daisy returned with her hair wet and dripping down her back.

"Oh, it's great here, Mum," she bent to throw her arms around Alicia's neck. "I've just had a lovely shower." Alicia squirmed backwards, half under the van, apparently not appreciating the cold droplets falling on her despite the heat of the afternoon.

"You didn't take a towel, did you?" Maya looked up from pouring them each a glass of wine. She pulled one of the folding chairs over for Daisy to sit down. Daisy sank into it, her wet hair hanging over the canvas chair back.

"No, but once I'd used the loo, I had an overwhelming impulse to get in anyway. I shook myself dry, like the dog."

Maya smiled at Daisy's change of mood from that morning. She looked more herself again.

"Oh well, at least you'll feel refreshed I should imagine. I might go over and have a shower myself after I've taken Alicia for a walk. Here's your wine. Do you want to have dinner now or wait for a bit?"

"Now please," Daisy said enthusiastically. "I'm suddenly starving."

Thank goodness, she was back to her old self.

After eating, Maya and Daisy carried their bottle of wine over to an area where tables and benches were laid out in a line under the tiled roof. A couple of young women sat further along from them; Maya noticed they had their hands entwined beneath the table. At the very end an older man sat with a teenaged girl — Maya couldn't decide whether she was his daughter or granddaughter — they were eating what looked like trifle out of chunky ceramic bowls.

"I remember trifle," Daisy placed her wine glass on the table, still half-full. Maya was on her second, she could feel her cheeks flaring. *Better slow down, don't want to leave Daisy in charge of a drunken older woman.* "Why don't we have it anymore?"

"Well, I suppose we only really had it at birthday parties," Maya took a more modest sip of wine this time. Daisy held her glass to her teeth, Maya could see the pink tip of her tongue against the rim. She watched Daisy take a tiny, decisive sip and swallow, screwing up her face afterwards.

"And Christmas," Daisy said. Grannie used to bring a big bowl of trifle at Christmas, remember?"

"That's right." Grannie could be relied upon to bring trifle. And, in Maya's mind, for her judgemental comments about her daughter's parenting choices, any choices she made, in fact. Especially when Jamie disappeared and was out of touch with his family for thirteen years. Of course, it was Maya's fault. Her mother had had a blind spot as far as Con was concerned, it was always "poor Con this," and "poor Con that," and "has Maya made you cook the dinner again, Con?" Her Mum never knew that she had found Jamie again, or about Joe breaking contact too. She hadn't got round to telling her. Contact had been limited since the twins had grown up.

"Con always cooks the lunch on Saturday Mum, you know that," Maya would reply. "I cook it every other day of the week." She'd look to Con to back her up, but instead he'd play along with her mother.

"Yes, she got the whip out," he'd say. "What else could I do?" She was never able to return the smile he shot her. He basked in her mother's adulation, and it hurt because Maya had never felt that from her mum. She rubbed her bare arms, feeling the hairs on them rising.

"Sorry," Daisy said, watching her face. "I know Grannie's a sensitive subject."

"What do you mean?" Maya straightened, picked up her wineglass again. "She isn't, you can talk about her any time you want. You two got on, didn't you?"

"We did from when I was about eighteen." Daisy ran her finger around the top of her wineglass. "Though I didn't see her often. I felt awkward around her when I was younger though. I always felt she preferred Lola to me."

"I'm sure she didn't," Maya started to say, but stopped herself. There was no sense in invalidating Daisy's feelings any more than there had been in Con invalidating hers. "Well, maybe. But I remember you two clicking over a shared love of sewing in the end. Lola wasn't interested in that, was she?"

"No, but Lola was the one who made Grannie laugh." Daisy rubbed her chin on her shoulder. "Mum, Grannie would have loved to meet her great-grandchildren, wouldn't she?"

"Yes, I think she would. Crikey, I have to keep reminding myself that *I'm* a grandmother. It all feels so new, especially since I haven't seen any of them for months and I'd barely had chance to get used to the idea then. Won't it be exciting to see our little Electra again, and meet baby Rudi?"

"I haven't even met Electra either yet, remember." Daisy raised her glass and clicked it against Maya's. She took another sip before setting the glass back on the table.

The sun was lowering behind a line of trees at the edge of the campsite, and from where Maya sat against the wall of the building behind her, Daisy's hair, fresh from washing, flared away from her head in a dark halo with golden tints. For a few moments the whole campsite was lit up orange, and then the sun slipped a little lower. Maya breathed in deeply.

Daisy's face was half in shadow now.

"Mum?"

"Yes, darling?"

"Do you think Jamie and Joe will still like me? Now they've met Lola, I mean."

"Oh, love." Maya leaned across the table and stroked her daughter's arm. "They'll both love you. You're Joe's big sister. Remember how you used to look after him when he was tiny? And you're Jamie's little sister. You were his favourite when you and Lola were both small, but don't tell Lola." Maya smiled, her eyes starting to sting. "You used to attach yourself to him and he always had patience for you." She drew back and touched under her eyes with the sides of her fingers. "You don't have to compare yourself to Lola, love. Neither of you have ever needed to do that. I love you both equally, and so will your brothers." She finished her wine. "Now, I'm going back to the van. I still have to walk Alicia."

On that island
I learned to speak English.
I volunteered, teaching children.

18

Daisy

August 2017, near Belgrade

The small amount of wine she drank the previous evening feels as though it's tingling in her blood. Her heartbeat is irregular. Daisy presses her hand to her chest, where a thin film of perspiration has dampened her cotton nightdress. She's slept for what only feels like a few minutes at a time, and now dawn light is dissipating into her end of the camper van and she's sure she'll never get back to sleep again. She bunches her pillow behind her head and shifts herself higher up the memory foam mattress, drawing her legs up to her stomach. She wraps her arms around them and rests her chin on her knees. From the back of the van, she hears the soft rumble of Mum's snores – or it could be the dog. The two seem to have melded almost into a single being, it's astonishing how tuned to Maya's every mood and movement the dog has become. Daisy recalls a book she and Lola loved in which each character has a "daemon", a familiar spirit in animal form. Her stomach clenches.

Christ, I need to get up, she thinks. Take a walk, clear my mad brain. And bloody hell, I need to pee again (she's been up more than once during the night). She didn't think she'd make it as far as the camp toilets, so she used the van loo. Tiptoeing in fear of waking Mum. She doesn't like the way Mum's been scrutinising her lately, every time she thinks Daisy isn't watching. Daisy just wants to be left alone with her thoughts, the lack of privacy's becoming unbearable. Anyway, Mum never woke once during the night, not that Daisy could tell at least. But she'd felt the dog's eyes on her in the dark, so maybe Maya *had* been noticing her, through the eyes of her familiar spirit.

Oh god, she thinks as she swings herself out of bed and takes the two steps into the space between the kitchen area and the bathroom again. She slides the toilet door open as quietly as possible. *I really am going mad.* She pees and holds down the lever to release the flow into the cartridge below, then presses the flush. After rinsing her hands, she slides the door open again and peers into the dark bed space to her left. The curve of Mum's still form faces away from her. Daisy strains her eyes for the movement of Mum's breathing. This must have been how it felt for Mum as a parent – you want them to stay asleep, but you also want a visible sign that they're still alive.

She doesn't know when this feeling she has of semi-dread started inhabiting her (she does). It was when Moussa first answered her message asking him if he knew where Umid was. He said his friend had gone. Left the island, didn't she know? Shame had flooded her then, embarrassment that she'd made a show of herself again. Frightened another man away. There must be something badly wrong with her to have that affect on people. Nausea swells in her stomach, a familiar sensation since she realised Umid had gone. She fears she's going to be sick. She pauses with her hand on the bathroom door, waits to see if the nausea will invade her throat, but the feeling subsides as rapidly as it rose, and she's left feeling hollow.

Mum sleeps on. The dog's eye remains open and steadily fixed on her, even as it continues to snore.

Daisy turns away abruptly, her scalp tingling. I need to get out of here, she thinks.

She takes a towel and a lightweight blouse and skirt to the shower block, remembering how refreshed she'd felt after her dousing the evening before. There's nobody else around and the cacophony of water hitting tiles on the floor and walls of the cubicle echoes around the high-ceilinged building. She stays under the water a long time, repeatedly pushing the button that keeps it flowing. She turns and turns beneath it, the weight of her soaked hair easing the tingling feeling of dread that has been crawling through her follicles. What did she do wrong? Why did Umid leave without telling her? She knows it's selfish and unreasonable to be even asking herself these questions.

He must have left illegally, despite Moussa's transparent lie about him getting the right stamp, maybe even on a whim. She knows how being trapped on the island was affecting Umid's mental health, the feeling that he would never be able to escape, his real life unlived. There must have been little space in his head left for thoughts of Daisy. Of course, he couldn't have told her. Her knowing would have put his plan at risk. She ought to be happy for him that he's managed to resume his journey.

When she had found Moussa and asked him why he hadn't left with his friend, he'd answered that he was afraid. The journey was dangerous, the border guards brutal. He was prepared to wait as long as it took for his papers to come through, even if that was years.

Are you in touch with Umid now? Daisy had asked. Where is he?

But Moussa had squirmed under her gaze and replied that he didn't know, he couldn't tell her. His eyes flickered in his thin face. Which is it? Daisy had demanded, half hysterical.

You don't know or you can't tell me?

They had been in the morning distribution queue, well Moussa had been, an early bird. Daisy had hiked up from the village, knowing he would be there. The queue snaked out behind them, over a series of small hills and through a copse of olive trees. Daisy felt Jodie's eyes on the back of her neck from the head of the queue, which Moussa had almost reached.

"What are you doing here?" Jodie handed Moussa some stale bread and a wrapped hunk of cheese. "You're not on duty, stop bothering my customers."

Daisy folded her arms tightly. "What's it to you, anyway?"

"You know your mum's worried about you, don't you?" Jodie lowered her voice. Moussa hung back, waiting for Daisy, though he wore an expression of being tortured. The Somalian man next in the queue traced a pattern of dust on a bare patch of ground with his foot, looking away, looking back again, embarrassed. "She told me she thinks you're ill. Look, maybe this kind of work just isn't for you. You're obviously not as tough as your mum. Go back to teaching toddlers, why don't you, Daisy? You've got to admit you're acting mental here, everyone can see it."

Shame burned Daisy's cheeks. She gnawed the inside of her lower lip. She swallowed, forcing herself to not burst into tears, which would only prove Jodie's point. To be fair, Daisy wouldn't have argued with her, if it had been someone else Jodie was discussing. The sun had risen higher in the sky, nibbling away at the patch of shade Jodie's distribution station was in.

"Right, well thanks for that," Daisy turned stiffly away. She stumbled on a rock half-buried in the flattened grass, and Moussa took her arm to steady her. "Thanks," Daisy said to him. She glanced back at Jodie, but she was already handing out provisions to the Somalian guy. "I'm sorry," Daisy said.

"What for?" Moussa adjusted his battered backpack with its tied-on strap as they walked downhill together. Daisy knew the bag contained everything he owned, including a single creased photograph of his wife and one-year-old daughter in Yemen, where they waited patiently for news of the safer life that they hoped he'd one day achieve for them.

"Just for not hating me. For not appearing to hate me, anyway." Moussa didn't answer straight away. She glanced sideways at him. His jaw was set.

"I'm going to be honest with you, Daisy," he said in imperfect English, and after a long pause. "This is not about you. None of this is about you. She," he pointed back over his shoulder at Jodie, "she probably right, you should go back and teach English children in your safe country."

"What?" Daisy felt stung. She'd thought Moussa was her friend.

"I shouldn't have to, what is it? spell out to you," he said. "You can choose to leave any time you want, and I think you will now you know Umid has gone. I can tell your heart in right place Daisy, you care about our problems here, but you don't truly understand." Moussa laid his hand briefly on Daisy's arm as she followed him through a gap in a low stone wall. She stepped down onto a rough track that led towards the village, involuntarily jerked her shoulder away. I'm behaving like a brat, she thought. Soon I'll have no friends left. She didn't answer Moussa.

"What you need understand," he continued, ignoring her sullenness, "is that you do not have influence on Umid's decide to leave. Don't you get that, Daisy?"

She stopped walking, slightly out of breath. Olive trees in the field on the other side of the wall twisted towards the sun. Tiny green beads of their future fruits sat nestled in the brown frills of their spent flowers. That was how Daisy felt, spent and dried. Moussa was saying she'd meant nothing to Umid. She turned to face him where he'd stopped to wait for her.

"You mean he didn't really care about me?"

"Oh, Daisy. You deliberate misunderstand. It not about that. This is his *life*. I'm jealous of his courage for doing what he's done, I wasn't brave enough. I could be stuck here another year or more, while my wife keep send me messages: she asks what I am doing to save our daughter from starvation. We should celebrate that Umid's broken free of this place. I pray he find fins to swim and wings to fly, and that he finds place of safety soon. Inshallah. You should wish that, too."

And the thing is, Moussa was right. Daisy did leave soon after she found out Umid had gone.

Daisy is towelling her hair after pulling on her clothes, when her phone buzzes in her pocket. She tucks the towel in around her head and reaches into the folds of her skirt. A message from Moussa!

> Hi Daisy, I hope you are well. I hear from friend who ran into Umid last night. They together in Serbia.

Then another message:

> Umid not have phone, lost it jumping on train. If you see him don't say I told you anything.

Then a third message comes through:

> Thanks for new backpack and clothes. You should not have but thanks anyway. I no answer you again for saving data. Be well.

When I finally arrived in Athens
things were worse than on the island.
People homeless and hungry,
crammed on the streets, and in the city square.

19

Daisy

August 2017, near Belgrade

With trembling hands Daisy brings up a map of Serbia on her phone. Where will he be? He must be heading for the border to ... *maybe Hungary.* Some quick research tells her a place called Horgoš is where migrants are likely to head. Something like a stone drops heavily in her stomach when she reads accounts by refugee agencies of the possible brutality facing those who try to cross the border. She hunches over, fighting a surge of nausea. *Oh, Umid. I have to find you.* Her mind won't allow her to think any further ahead than their imagined reunion, pushing away uncomfortable thoughts of herself as a would-be 'white saviour'.

For a mad moment Daisy considers hijacking the van, Mum, dog and all, and setting the SatNav on her phone to Horgoš. Only about two hours' drive away. Maybe she could persuade Mum? But she knows Mum would refuse, say their job was not to interfere, only offer support with practicalities like food, clothing and shelter.

Besides, Mum has no idea of the extent of Daisy's involvement with Umid. She clutches her stomach again, blows out a long breath.

It feels as though she's been sitting on the bench outside the shower block forever, but her phone tells her it's still barely 6 am. Unwinding the towel from her head, her hair is almost dry. Traces of mist rise off the grass leading towards the copse of trees, as the sun begins to edge over the treetops. She needs to decide what to do before Mum wakes up, usually around 7 am when Alicia starts to get restless. Daisy shakes loose her hair and combs it with her fingers. She slips her feet into her sandals and gathers up her bag of toiletries. With the damp towel over her arm, she sets off quickly back to the van. She hasn't decided, as such, but she can feel a decision happening inside her. Without acknowledging it, she knows what she's going to do.

Outside the van she hangs her towel on the wing mirror and slips her fingers into the door handle, sliding the door open as quietly as she can. Peering inside she sees that Mum has turned over and now faces the kitchen area. *Damn.* The dog has also changed position, long body flattened alongside the back doors of the van, chin resting on Mum's hip. Both the dog's eyes are open, they stare at her and Daisy freezes, one foot on the top step. She pulls herself up fully into the van, gripping the kitchen worktop for balance. Despite her care the movement can be felt in the van. She checks Mum, still sleeping. The dog makes a grumbling noise but her tail thumps softly against the metal of the doors. Then Mum stirs irritably, rubbing at her nose with the back of her hand. Daisy freezes. But Mum only sighs and drags the sheet more tightly under her chin.

"Shhh," whispers Daisy to the dog, forcing her face away from its magnet gaze. She feels bad sneaking about, but she can't face a conversation with Mum about Umid. *Please don't wake up.* She tiptoes into her bed space and scans around for her backpack. There, under the driver's seat end of the bed. Hesitates a moment – how long will she be away from Mum and the van? *What am I doing?* To stop herself thinking anymore about how crazy her plan (not-plan) is she makes herself act decisively: lifts the door of the over-cab space and grabs a few items of clothing; underwear, shorts and t-shirt, a long-sleeved cotton dress crumpled in the depths of the curved space. Leggings. Socks? May as well. Reaches even further back for her passport, which she slips into the 'secret' concealed zipped compartment near the bottom of the bag. Diary – stupid thing but it feels a part of her now – and purse. Ah, charge wire for her phone and the power bank which must still be almost fully charged, she hasn't used it. She closes the cupboard quietly and grabs her heavy cardigan from the headrest of the inward facing passenger seat. Comfort clothing. What else? Her bathroom essentials are already outside on the grass in their waterproof bag. A dry towel. She winces at the click of the door catch when she opens the linen cupboard above the fridge, casts an anxious glance back at Mum, but Maya barely stirs.

She stuffs a lightweight towel and on second thoughts, a thin facecloth as well, into her bag. Then a thought, unbidden. *Take a scarf.* She feels in the over-cab space again for the soft, pale green cotton shawl she bought from a stall in Athens as a possible gift for Lola. She unfolds the tissue paper covering it as quietly as possible, draws the scarf from the cupboard and feeds it into the neck of the bag. She leaves the cupboard door open to save making more noise. *My fleece blanket.* A cold shock inside as she asks herself again what she's doing. But still, she finds her hands untucking the velvety throw that she's had since she was about fourteen (hers is a deep rose colour and Lola's was blue) from the foot of her makeshift bed, she rolls it as tightly as she can. Into the backpack it goes.

When she turns her body around in the tight space the dog raises her head from her paws, her gaze level on Daisy. Daisy keeps her breath steady. She places a finger to her lips and steps carefully backwards out of the van, holding onto the door frame. She slides the door closed behind her, takes care not to let it slam.

Daisy half-runs down the track to the main road from the campsite. Partly because she's afraid Alicia'll alert Mum to her subterfuge, and Mum'll come blasting after her in the van. Or on foot, in that holey t-shirt she wears as a nightdress. God, the embarrassment. But she soon gets a stone in one of the lightweight slip-on shoes she'd exchanged her sandals for and needs to stop and remove it. Mum'll think she's only gone to the toilets, or for a walk or something, and she'll moan that Daisy ought to have taken Alicia with her. Unless Alicia really can communicate telepathically with Mum, as Daisy's often suspected. Her thoughts churn in her head as she walks. The bag feels heavy already. An image of Mum traipsing across all those countries carrying a rucksack three times the size of this one comes into her mind. She straightens her back and raises her chin. This is the first time she's ever set out in a strange country on her own. *I am Daisy, and I am strong.* A mantra Mum used to encourage her to repeat when she was little, and she had insisted she couldn't do something.

Out on the main road she needs to stop again to repack her backpack. She rests the bag on a bench next to a battered sign – in Serbian, of course. The bench is in a small shelter, it's a bus-stop. An older woman comes jogging towards her, seeming unsettled. She peers up and down the road. Daisy begins to load the backpack onto her shoulders again. The woman moves closer and speaks to Daisy, presumably in Serbian. Daisy raises her hands. "Sorry," she says. "I'm English."

"Ah, Engleski jezik," the woman breathes heavily. "Has bus gone?"

"Uhm, I haven't seen a bus."

"Bus to Horgoš?" the woman adds hopefully, straining to see further down the road.

"Bus to Horgoš?" Daisy feels a swell of relief. She hasn't

119

been looking forward to hitchhiking in a foreign country. *All the way to Horgoš, that's amazing.*

"What time?" she asks the woman, tapping her bare wrist.

"Six-thirty but think missed it." The woman gestures to her watch. Daisy checks her phone, 6.37. the relief morphs into disappointment.

"I haven't seen a bus though. Maybe it's late." Just as Daisy finishes speaking a bus rounds the same corner the woman appeared from. "Oh, is this it?" Daisy reopens the rucksack and fumbles for her purse. She'll go as far as the bus will take her. Mum won't catch up with her now. She's really on her own.

I'd had no idea what it would be like
when I set out from home.
Nobody does.
But I have made the best of it.

20

Daisy

Border of Serbia and Hungary, August 2017

Daisy comes to with a jolt as the rumbling bus engine belches to a stop and there's a shout from the driver. Bleary-eyed, Daisy glances around. Most of the bus seats are empty, any remaining passengers getting to their feet now and filling the aisle with bustle and chatter. The woman from the bus stop, who had squeezed onto the seat next to her and instigated a rather awkward conversation in stilted English, along the lines, Daisy thinks, of whether the water tastes better in the UK or in Serbia, has gone. Daisy didn't notice when she left. She must have slept most of the journey. She takes out her phone and checks the time: 9 am. Ignores the notifications of messages: *Mum, Mum, Mum, Mum.* The driver calls out again, Daisy jumps. She's the last person on the bus. She stretches in her seat and hauls her backpack up from between her feet, moving into the aisle and shrugging it onto her back. The driver watches her in the rear-view mirror as she approaches, his face impassive.

"Thank you," she says as she grips the handrail and takes the steps down to the tarmac. Turning her head, she sees him nod curtly, before starting up the engine again and backing the bus out of the parking space.

She's in a bus station. Her stomach rumbles and her eyes scan her surroundings to see if there's anywhere that she can get some food. A kiosk advertises something in Serbian, which she knows from their stop yesterday means coffee and croissants. *That'll do, pig.* A sudden wrench in her chest remembering their baby brother's giggles when she and Lola kept repeating that phrase after watching the film *Babe* on video, countless times. Will she get to Germany to see Joe now? All grown up and in a relationship with a boyfriend. Not to mention her big brother Jamie and his family.

Dizziness causes her to stumble. She grabs onto a telegraph post to stop herself falling and stands for a moment, getting her bearings, checking no-one's noticed. But it's quiet and the few people around mind their own business, hurrying across the concourse or checking the departure boards. She asks herself what on earth she'd planned to do. Go to Horgoš. Right, well you made it here, clever clogs, she mutters under her breath. What now? Umid might not even be here, there must be other places on the border with Hungary he could have gone to. She suppresses a sob. It hurts physically to imagine him struggling through barbed wire or falling from a high fence. Being shot at or beaten up. No. Where are you? Standing in an almost-deserted bus station in a town she doesn't know, with no idea what to do next, she feels like crying. Roaring. At the same time acutely aware of her foolishness. She sucks in her breath and straightens her back, the bag weighing heavy on her shoulders. *Get some coffee and a croissant, you'll feel better when you've eaten.* Something she's said to Lola so many times in the past and it's almost as if Lola's voice is inside her, guiding her now.

Seated on a metal chair at a rickety table, breathing in

exhaust fumes, she packs the bottle of water she bought and a pair of packaged cheese sandwiches into her bag, then sips her coffee and tears strips off a bedraggled-looking croissant. *Plan, Daisy. You've started this and now you need to follow it through. At the very least, try to speak to Umid, if you can find him. See if there's anything he needs.* I'll try not to interfere, she promises herself, no more than I have already. If she could only have one last conversation with him. Put a proper end to the relationship that so obviously meant so much more to her than it did to him. *This is not the same as Dan, it's not. I won't keep on stalking him. I promise I'll let Umid go once I've seen him one last time.*

She takes her phone out again. Mum must be frantic. She'll have checked Daisy's things and realised she's gone. She didn't even leave a note! A quick scan through the messages confirms Mum's concern and fear. *Sorry, Mum.* Shame prickles Daisy's skin, the back of her neck and under her arms. Her thumb hovers over Mum's name on the screen, ready to press, but she can't speak to her, not yet. Instead, she types a message:

> I'm sorry for worrying you. I'm fine, I just had to go and meet someone.

She presses send. Thinking the message inadequate, she sends another:

> I'll be in touch later, don't worry. Try and relax at the campsite.

She adds three kisses. Then she switches off her phone and tucks it into the inner pocket of her bag.

The obvious place to go is 'the border' but when she painstakingly enquires at the ticket office with the aid of a translation app, the ticket officer regards her disdainfully. "You want to go to Röszke, Madam?" he says in accented English.

Daisy feels herself turning hot. Sweat prickles under her arms again. "I, err, I want to go to the border."

124

"What for, Madam?" the thin-faced man with a bushy moustache rubs his chin as he stares at her.

Daisy falters, then draws herself up. "I have an appointment, if you want to know. Now, can I get a bus there or not?" she feels sick, and hopes she isn't going to throw up all over the counter.

"You must mean you want to catch the bus to Horgoš Customs, then, Madam. Stop H-SB. The bus is in thirty minutes." He hands over a ticket in exchange for a tap of her credit card, his dark eyes looking her up and down. She turns away swiftly, not trusting herself to hold back the vomit pushing its way into her throat. Beads of sweat have broken out on her forehead, and she feels dizzy. Through blurred vision she manages to locate the toilets and makes it into a cubicle barely in time to throw up the coffee and the few bites of croissant she just had.

At the mottled mirror she splashes water onto her face and pats it dry with a paper towel, takes a few deep breathes to test the state of the nausea now. It's been plaguing her often lately. *Since Umid left.* That's all it is. She was the same after the ending of her relationship with Dan. *Well, this time I'm going to finish things properly and then get on with my own life. I only want to say goodbye, that's all.* The nausea seems to have subsided. Glad I didn't eat much, she thinks.

Her second bus journey of the day lasts only fifteen minutes. Alighting from the bus to curious stares from the driver and some of the other passengers, she twists her ankle slightly when she steps down onto a kerb. Limping away from the bus onto a broad stretch of paving, she bends to rub it, trying not to see the injury as a bad omen. Straightening again, she watches a young couple mount the steps and settle into the seat she's just vacated. A girl in a long skirt and a boy with long hair, they look like tourists, like her. What am I doing? she thinks again. But she's set herself on a course now, no going back. The bus rolls away and angles itself into a queue in one of many lanes stretching towards rows of booths dividing to road into, she assumes, territory belonging to Serbia and Hungary. The queueing vehicles puff exhaust fumes into the air, the traffic crawls slowly forward. Daisy is left on the path, feeling abandoned. Feeling stupid.

Oh well, I'm here now. She tries to look as though she knows where she's going. Modelling confidence, she turns and walks back a bit the way the bus has come, testing her sore ankle. The pain is fading already. She wishes she'd thought to take out her walking boots from the storage space under the floor in the van. That would have woken Mum up though, she's sure of it. Instead, she only wears the canvas slip-ons she'd grabbed from under the van before she left. She turns away from the toll booths and the gasping lines of traffic. She must look conspicuous walking alone here, she's going, presumably, in the wrong direction too. If she continues walking in full sight of the road she's bound to be stopped and asked what she's doing. Her stomach churns. She needs to find somewhere off the main road to sit for a while, think and take stock. On her left is a low metal barrier. She steps over it, gathering up her skirt, finding herself on a strip of scrubland bordered by another low barrier and beyond that, fields. Of course. It's not as if refugees are going to be queueing up at customs along with the traffic, is it?

She steps over the second barrier. A car horn honks at her as the vehicle passes. She adjusts the rucksack straps on her shoulders and turns her back to the road. She'll head for that hedge across the field, parallel to the road and sit, drink some water. There's a tree there, too. She longs for the shade. Her ankle aches. Her hair is heavy on the back of her neck. She wishes she'd worn a hat.

The field is stubbly from a recently reaped crop, scratching her bare legs as she walks. Daisy pants as she stomps over the hard land, taking care not to stumble on the mounds and ruts left by the tracks of farm machinery. She presses a hand to her stomach, feeling a combination of hunger and nausea. Maybe she should eat the sandwich she bought at the bus station, when she finally gets to sit down. She hadn't realised it was this far. What is she doing here in the middle of a field in Serbia, with no plan? *Don't think about it, Daisy.* Everything is hazy, unreal. Maybe in reality she's still asleep in her bed in the van, tossing and turning in a ridiculous dream. She'll wake to the dog's tail in her face and the smell of coffee on the stove. Her scalp tingles. A bird chatters overhead. Though she's alone in the middle of a field it feels as though many eyes are watching her. She rubs her arms and blows out a breath. *Keep going.* Yes, she could retrace her steps and return to stop H-SB if she wanted to, catch a bus into the centre of Horgoš and wait for another to take her back to the campsite. There's always that option. She imagines telling Mum she'd met up with the friend she mentioned in her text. Pretend it was Emmaline, that girl who'd arrived on Samos at a similar time as they had, then left to go backpacking with a friend from Germany. But she knows she isn't going to.

She ploughs on. Her skirt catches on an overlong stalk and when she bends to detangle the swirling cotton, she receives a sharp scratch on the back of her hand. She straightens and sucks blood from the scrape. Picks a scrap of straw from her lip. The sun has risen higher and burns hotter on the top of her head. Daisy remembers the shawl in her backpack. Recalling how her friend Farah from the camp on Samos wore her headscarf, Daisy shakes out the soft, pale green cotton rectangle and drapes it loosely over her head. She throws one end over her shoulder and tucks the other into the neckline of her embroidered blouse, where she can feel the skin of her chest has burnt. *Better.* She feels protected in more ways than from the sun.

Stepping forward again Daisy experiences a surge of longing for Mum. A kind of second-hand nostalgia for Mum's days of lonely travelling with a backpack. She was a complete novice when she started her trip three years or so ago. She'd been just 'Mum' before that, someone you could ask where things were, and she'd always know. The one who'd make you a hot water bottle and a mug of hot chocolate when you were feeling down. But Daisy had never really considered who Mum was as a person in her own right, not before she astonished them all by giving up every ounce of security she had and going it alone. Then they had to think about her, what she wanted. I could be more like Mum, like Maya, Daisy corrects herself as she continues to put one foot in front of the other. Maybe I could 'find myself' this way too. It feels as though I could. The idea is tempting, to start again from nothing, from a low point in her life like Mum did. She knows she's got to sort herself out.

That's why this goodbye is important, Daisy reminds herself. I need to finish one thing off before I can start another. She doesn't let herself consider that she might not be able to find Umid. Her quest is the only motivation to continue walking, otherwise she'd allow herself to collapse in the middle of the field. That tree by the hedge, it's looming closer now. She'll settle down in its shade, take a drink of water, nibble her sandwich, and maybe close her eyes for a while. Everything will seem clearer when she opens them again.

I lost my parents when I was five,
grew up in my uncle's house
until I was seventeen.
In my country,
my people had been made stateless
by our own king.

21

Daisy

Border of Serbia and Hungary, August 2017

Daisy's mouth is parched. The fingers of her right hand are cramped. When she looks down, she sees the water bottle gripped in her hand, its lid still on. She must have fallen asleep before she could open it. She unscrews the bottle and tips her head back to take a long gulp. It seems quite dark, she can't have slept that long, surely? But it's only that the scarf has slipped partially over her eyes. She pushes it back from her face and the sun is still burning in the sky, bleached now to near-whiteness. She swallows another sip of water, more carefully this time. She should have bought two bottles, or more.

A nugget of fear in her stomach, along with a gnawing hunger. This must be how it feels to sit on that hillside on the island, knowing you will only have access to a small amount of food, and when it's gone . . . She reaches into her backpack, propped next to her in the roots of the broad tree she rests her back against, pulls out the wrapped sandwiches. The tail of her spine has gone numb, she shifts position, unlocking her crossed legs and curling them up to one side. Taking a bite of sandwich, she gazes around her. Although traffic noise is a steady rumble; the road is far away, she feels in the middle of nowhere. But the sensation lingers of being watched by someone or something unseen. Birds chirrup in the branches above her and there's a rustle in the undergrowth behind. She stretches her shoulders and moves her head from side to side to loosen the knot in her neck.

Taking in her immediate environment she can see that not far off to her right, partly obscured by the hedge and more trees, a high fence ranges out from both sides of the vehicular border crossing. The nugget of fear expands into a rock in her stomach. She takes one more bite of bread, chews it carefully, and rewraps the sandwiches, pressing them back into her bag. One more sip of water, then she puts the bottle away too.

She needs to pee. Despite the appearance of desertedness, she pushes her way into the hedge behind the tree and squats furtively, glancing around her as she splashes onto the twigs and grass at her feet. She can't bear not to dry so she reaches for some squares of tissue from her pocket, then realises she can't just leave it in the field. She'll need to use the plastic bag from the sandwiches and water for storing waste. Grabbing some dock leaves from the hedgerow she uses these to wipe her hands afterwards, thinking how Lola wouldn't be able to bear this, she'd want to sacrifice some of the water from the bottle.

Daisy reflects that Mum lived this way for more than two years, in several countries, and she's amazed all over again. Mum might have become a bit of a *know all* since she first returned from her travels, but Daisy's admiration for her is growing by the second. She recalls the emails Mum used to send her in the early days, her descriptions of how she set up camp under hedges such as these, how frightened she was to be on her own the first few nights.

With a shock, Daisy realises that unless she makes her way across the field again the way she came and catches a bus back to somewhere she can spend the night in a room with a bed, she's going to end up sleeping rough, too.

It occurs to her that she could send Mum an email just as Mum used to send them to her. She can make it light-hearted and fun the way Mum did, despite how scared she later confessed to Daisy that she'd been. She'll be honest about her intent. She wants to make Mum proud of her, even though she's behaved stupidly in rushing to leave without any preparation. But she wants to do what Mum did. After all, Mum set off in search of someone she loved, just as Daisy is.

Daisy has hiked for what feels like miles parallel to the fence that straddles the fields. She has stayed back from the fence, sheltered by trees and hedgerows where possible. She doesn't know what she was expecting – to meet friendly refugees and ask the way? She's seen no-one, though beyond the distant fence an occasional patrol vehicle with coloured lights speeds by, throwing up dust. She pulls the scarf more securely around her face and stays well back out of sight. The fence shocks her to the core. Rolls of razor wire backed by a barrier of metal grids secured by steel posts. The structure is topped by barbed wire, and she judges it is maybe four times her height. She can see an area of bare earth separates the edge of the field from the fence, dead land.

The whole thing reminds Daisy of Mum's detailed description of the Berlin Wall, and her phone photos of the portraits on the memorial to those shot attempting to escape. All ages, from teenagers to older women. It reminds Daisy too of the border fence built by the US president, and of migrant children forcibly separated from their parents after their long, death-defying journeys. A horrible picture of Lola having to flee somewhere with Elijah pushes itself into her mind, and of Lola having Elijah pulled from her arms by a faceless border guard. She imagines Lola's hoarse cries, snot and tears on her face. The mental images come thicker and faster as her breath rasps in time with their flow. An unexpected sob wrenches itself from her throat. She doubles over, the backpack straining her shoulders, and wretches at the base of a tree.

When she's finished, she straightens and wipes her mouth on the back of her hand, determined to banish the images. She's tired to her bones. She places her feet carefully one in front of the other, her canvas pumps rubbing her heels. You're such a fool, Daisy, she thinks for the hundredth time. Totally unprepared for this walk. Did you think you were simply going to arrive at the border and find Umid waiting there for you? She must keep reminding herself he's not waiting for her at all. More likely, he'll be horrified to see her if she ever finds him. This is his journey, not hers. She knows all this yet none of it makes any difference to her determination. *Remember those nights we spent together, Umid? Surely, they can't all have been for nothing!*

She can't walk another step right now, where can she stop? She scans her surroundings. A hundred metres or so further on there's a small brick shed, on the edge of a corn field. Concentrating on the terrain ahead, she thinks she catches sight of movement from the corner of her eye, in the long grass of a low bank above the cornfield. Several fleeting shapes, she thinks. But when she stops and shields her eyes, she can't see anything. Deer, perhaps? The sun's glare has retreated now, and the sky has dulled. Daisy lowers the scarf from her head and rests it on her shoulders. She promises herself she will stop at the shed for another sip of water and the remaining half of the first sandwich, maybe squat and pee again behind the shed, then haul herself back onto her feet and press on for a while. But where the fuck she's going she has no idea.

Umid might not even have gone in this direction. *You're a nutter*, Lola would be saying. *What the hell are you playing at?*

———————

Daisy continued walking after her stop at the shed. She must have fallen asleep on her feet. All the breath has been knocked out of her and she lies face down on pebbly ground. Stay calm, she tells herself, struggling to control a rising wave of panic. Finally, a huge whoosh of air forces its way into her lungs. She pushes herself up onto her hands and knees. Her right elbow and the side of her hand are stinging. Her right knee hurts, too, and the side of her forehead. Her water bottle has been flung free of her bag and leaks slightly on the ground in front of her. *Shit.* She reaches out for it with her good hand and places it upright. Slowly, she manoeuvres herself back into a sitting position, glad no-one has seen her. She feels dizzy and horribly nauseous. Lights flash at the corners of her eyes. *Not a migraine, not now.* She tries to steady her breathing but she bursts into tears instead from the shock and pain. *I want to go home.*

Pull yourself together, Daisy. There's no-one but herself to rely on, and whose fault is that? She whimpers as she tentatively swivels her right arm, flexes her fingers and examines the cuts in the fading light. Pulls up her skirt and inspects the grazed knee too. She places a finger on the side of her forehead, and it comes back with a smear of blood. What an idiot, is all she can think of herself. Out here in the middle of nowhere. Everything seems to be in working order though, if stiff and sore. She'll need to use some of her water to avoid infections in the cuts. Then she remembers the bottle of sanitiser that's been in the bottom of her bag since she first packed it back at The Cottages in Navengore. Mum said she'd used wet wipes a lot on her travels, but bottles of sanitiser produced less waste. *This is going to hurt just a little*

134

bit. She uses the edge of her facecloth to dab at the wounds and lets out a cry of pain with each application. *Owww.*

A chill has descended on the land. Daisy pulls the scarf up over her head again and arranges the bulk of it around her shoulders, throwing one end around behind her neck. She delves into the backpack for her long cardigan and slips her left arm into it, pulls the sleeve gingerly over her right arm. She buttons it all the way down the front. She screws the water bottle lid securely closed and tucks it back into her bag along with the folded cloth and the bottle of sanitiser. Carefully, she stands and shrugs the backpack back on. The lights in the corners of her eyes are fading, thankfully, and the headache she feels coming on is only faint. She has paracetamol in her toiletry bag if she needs it. *I can make it.* She has a destination in mind. Before she fell, (before she drifted off?) she'd spotted the shape of a building in the distance. A barn, a warehouse? She hopes she'll be able to sneak inside and find a safe nook to try and sleep in for the night. Then she'll have to decide what to do with herself tomorrow.

We had no rights in Kuwait,
no opportunity
to take control of our own lives.

22

Daisy

Border of Serbia and Hungary, August 2017

Her heels have been rubbed raw from the slip-on canvas shoes. If only she'd thought to bring her trainers or walking boots. She limps painfully towards the looming building, glancing nervously from side to side, squinting against the encroaching darkness. If only she'd stopped to think for one moment and make an actual plan instead of allowing an idea to rush wildly into her head and stampede all over her common sense. *Act in haste, repent at leisure*, her grannie used to say. Daisy's knee is sore, sticking to the folds of her long skirt, and the grazes on her arm and hand sting where they catch on the rough wool of her cardigan. The cut on her temple throbs.

She shivers as she approaches the closed metal doorway of this unknown building in the middle of a deserted field. In the dark. She must be mad. She's exhausted, faint and dizzy, probably dehydrated. And yet, with her pulse pounding in her throat and struggling to control her breathing, she feels suddenly acutely aware of her own visceral existence. Like it could end at any moment. Anything could be about to happen within that dark cavern. What does she have that she could possibly defend herself with? She can't think of anything.

Well, here goes, then. There are no windows on this side of the building. What if there are no windows on the building at all and it's utterly pitch dark inside? She doesn't think she could stand it. She and Lola have always needed to keep the curtains open a crack so they can see a sliver of sky. *What if there are rats inside? Bats flying around in the dark?*

She's tempted to dig her phone out of her bag to use as a torch but she's afraid that any hesitation means she will end up sleeping (or not sleeping) out here on the ground, too afraid to move any further. The door could be locked anyway, she tells herself, limping one step, two steps, three steps closer. I might end up having to sleep outside because there's nowhere else. It would only be for a few hours, then I'd move on at first light. Try not to think about what happens next, or tomorrow. She reaches the rusted metal door and places her good hand on it. Does she feel a faint vibration in the metal? Is it possible that she can hear the murmur of human voices beyond it, or could that be the material humming as it cools down from the heat of the day? She leans closer, feeling for a handle, a keyhole. There, the stout bar of a handle. Running her hand over it she explores the area beneath it with her fingertips. A keyhole. A sharp pain in her knee as she lowers herself towards it, straining to hear, to see or smell anything. Low sounds. A dim glow. The faintest scent of smoke, perhaps? Who would be in a building such as this at night if not for the very people she seeks? *What if Umid is in there? Oh. My. God. I must do this. I daren't. I must.*

Her heart pounds, the pulse resounding in her head, making the headache expand and threaten to explode. She pictures Lola with Elijah in her arms. If she had to choose a last vision that would be it. Lola with Elijah when he was first born.

With a sensation of ice in her chest she pushes the door, and when nothing happens, she tries pulling it sharply towards her. It opens. The headache is too bad, the dizziness too intent. Daisy tries to steady herself by hanging onto the door handle, but she loses her balance. She collapses on the stone floor at the entrance to a large, open area, aware that she's landed on her sore knee, and it hurts like hell. But overriding the pain is shock and fear. People moving in the dim space. A woman's cry of surprise, faces turned towards hers. From her foetal viewpoint she registers a fire in one corner, a head scarfed figure bent over a pot. The figure rises. Closer to, a pair of feet in black and white trainers striding towards where she lies, followed by two more sets of feet, the swish of long skirts.

Daisy can't seem to move. It doesn't feel like her, but she can hear a soft buzzing sound coming from her throat.

"Sister," a man's voice says. A hand with dark skin reaches out to hers, and after a moment's hesitation she grips it. *Save me*! The man helps her into a sitting position, then squats next to her, a frown deepening on his forehead. Two identical-seeming women, wearers of the long skirts, sink to their knees on either side of him. The three of them study Daisy with quiet eyes.

"Sister," the man repeats in his deep, rumbling voice. "You are safe. Dry your tears. Allow my sisters to help you. Food is almost ready, come eat with us."

She reaches into the bowl for a handful of rice, at their insistence.

"I have half a sandwich in my bag," she protests. "I don't want to take your food."

"Please. Eat. Take." The man who's name she's learned is Abdul, says. He touches the young woman's arm and indicates for her to pass Daisy the bowl of bread. Seeing that Daisy's good hand is occupied with rice the woman, Nadira –

or is she Aarifa? They are sisters, possibly twins, their features almost identical – Nadira, she decides, who wears her silver bangle on the right wrist. Nadira breaks a generous piece of bread off for her. It's pointless, and Daisy suspects insulting, to protest. She accepts the bread gratefully in her sore hand and forces herself to take slow bites. Her appetite has burgeoned into ravenous hunger.

When they had first raised her to her feet the two women had led Daisy across the room to a makeshift compartment partially secluded by a suspended cloth. Encouraging her to sit down on a folded blanket, they told her their names, patting their chests. She noticed that they both wore silver bracelets, on opposite wrists. One of them gestured to Daisy's brow, leaning forward to gently move the edge of her scarf away from the graze, while the other reached behind herself for a 2-litre plastic bottle of water. Daisy removed the scarf from her head, settling it around her shoulders, and tilted her face to the ministering hand. Together her new friends examined Daisy's wounds one at a time and cleaned them with water poured carefully onto a small piece of cloth Aarifa had taken from her bag. When they had finished, they used precious water to rinse the cloth out in a plastic bowl which they emptied out of one of the windows on that side of the building. Daisy felt guilty, thinking of the small amount of water left in her own bottle. She gestured to the milk carton.

"Where did you find water?"

Aarifa immediately proffered the plastic container at her, lifting it towards Daisy's lips.

"No, no. Thank you. I have water of my own. *Shkran*," She pulled out her own bottle of water and took a minimal sip, noticing Nadira's eyes registering the dwindling volume of liquid in it. "Do you speak Arabic?" she knows how to say thanks in Farsi, too, *mersi* – like French – but has forgotten any other language versions of the word she wrote diligently in her notebook back at the camp.

Nadira patted her chest again and tapped Aarifa on the shoulder. "Somali," she explained. She made a pinching gesture with her fingers, "Arabic, yes, but Somali my own language."

"And some English, too," Daisy said admiringly.

Cold air entered the cavernous room through the glassless window. Daisy shivered, then drew the scarf up over her head again, hesitant, not wanting to seem to be mimicking her new friends.

"I help," Aarifa took the headscarf and refolded it, neatening it either side of Daisy's face, taking care not to nudge the graze stinging anew on her temple. Aarifa spoke in Somali to her sister, who pulled out a pin from her own headscarf, and slotted it neatly somewhere alongside Daisy's jawline. Daisy hardly dared move her head, for fear of injury. The sisters laughed at her, bobbing their own heads up and down and from side to side, pointing gleefully at Daisy.

The hours are blurring into each other. It seems as if she has been part of this group for a long time. Not one of the ten migrants in the building has asked Daisy's purpose in being here. She's ashamed and guilty, thinking she needs to find the right moment to tell them the truth, but for now she basks in an overwhelming sense of relief and comfort. To be safe. To be in kind and caring company after her long, confused day. Umid is not here, of course. She checked the faces as soon as she was led out of the women's compartment. She can't believe now that she ever thought she might find him. *He doesn't want to be found by you.* Tomorrow she'll need to decide what to do: continue searching or take her passport and her privilege and return to the campsite: make amends with her mother. She hasn't felt able to take out her phone and make a call or even compose the email she promised herself she would write. It would feel rude.

The company eats together around the meagre fire made in a rusted metal oil can. Abdul is in his mid-thirties, Daisy thinks. He gives the impression of being the group's leader. His brother Mohammed closely resembles him but could be ten years younger. They tell Daisy they're from Sudan. There's another Sudanese man too, Daisy can't catch his name. Three young Eritrean men: boys really, Daisy thinks, they're called Hassan, Tesfay and Robel. Sitting slightly away from the fire are two Iraqi men, Shakib and Birwa. They introduced themselves when Daisy was first brought over to the fire but now seem intent on their own private conversation. All the migrants nodded politely when she told them she was from England. The awkward pause was barely perceptible. She is here, like them. For the moment she is one of them.

After the meal the men gather up the cooking implements and wash them with water poured from a slightly battered 5-litre container. Abdul notices Daisy looking.

"You need water?" he asks. She wonders if Nadira or Aarifa said something to him about her almost-empty bottle. "The relief truck came by today. They bring us water, a generator for charging our phones, and for shaving," he rubs the smoothness of his neck below his neat beard, touches the shaved sides of his head. "Even a portable shower. Please, let me refill your bottle."

She's learnt not to protest and to accept help gracefully. She hands over her bottle and feels relief at its new weightiness.

The two women gesture to Daisy to follow them outside. Leading her around the corner of the building, one hand each on the wall in the dark, they both dip out of sight behind the thin shelter of a bush. Daisy pees for longer than the two of them, embarrassed at how long it goes on. She doesn't want to have to go outside on her own again in the night.

Back inside the building, the fire has been left to die down. In the thick darkness Daisy sees that men are settling themselves around the walls of the building, here and there the light from a phone screen illuminating one or another of their faces. Aarifa (bangle on her left wrist) pulls Daisy by the arm towards their curtained off compartment.

"We sleep now."

Nadira uses light from her phone to find extra sweaters for herself and her sister. The sisters arrange their rucksacks as pillows. Aarifa opens the folded blanket on the floor and gestures for Daisy to crowd under it with them. At last, something Daisy can do to help. She feels inside her backpack for her own blanket and spreads it on top of the sisters' blanket. She rummages out her thin towel too and arranges it over the three bags to form a pillowcase. Finally, she struggles into her leggings under her skirt and pulls socks onto her feet. Thank goodness for the socks. She's pleased the sisters are wearing thick socks (and boots, more sensible than her) so she doesn't have to feel guilty. She stuffs her socked feet back into the canvas shoes. They pinch, but it's preferable to freezing.

She realises that Nadira and Aarifa are removing their headscarves. Nadira shines a light on the small tin they decant their pins into. Daisy removes her headscarf too, handing over the pin. They each wrap their scarves around themselves. The sisters lie down on their sides, one behind the other. The phone light goes off.

Aarifa says something in her language. Daisy feels her nudging arm. She only hesitates a moment before carefully angling herself into a c-position on the thin slab of cardboard, her back pressed against Aarifa's warm body, the blankets tucked tightly around all three of them.

My uncle helped me leave
so I could try
to become free.

23

Daisy

Border of Serbia and Hungary, August 2017

Daisy can't believe she's slept at all, separated from the hard concrete floor by only a sheet of cardboard, but she wakes up to the warmth of Aarifa sliding away from her back and to the sound of hushed, urgent voices. It's still dark, Daisy can barely see anything. The blankets slither off her, and as her eyes become accustomed to the darkness, she sees that Nadira and Aarifa are packing their bags, draping their scarves over their heads and around their necks.   Daisy scrambles into a sitting position, wincing as the fabric of her leggings is torn away from the wound on her knee.   She clutches her blanket on her lap.   Her heart pounds erratically.

"What's happening?'

"We go now," Nadira stands up and pulls down the curtain sheltering them, quickly folding it and stuffing it into her bag. Movement is going on all around the edges of the building, flashes from torches and phone screens dancing patterns on the walls and floor. A huddle of men in the centre of the room, an electric sense of anticipation. Panic beats in Daisy's veins.

"I don't understand." What happened to the seemingly secure, calm place to spend the night, where she would have time to decide what to do in the morning?

"Smuggler here," Aarifa leans down to whisper. She gestures with her arms and hands. "Time, go." She pulls the blanket out of Daisy's hands and stuffs it in Daisy's bag, along with the towel discarded on the floor. "*Degdeg ah*!" Impatiently, she gathers up Daisy's crumpled scarf and fixes it over her head and neck.

Nadira joins her and together they jostle Daisy up from the floor. "Must go," Nadira whispers.

The sisters shrug on their backpacks and one of them loads Daisy's onto her back for her. The two of them pull Daisy into a torch beam spotlight in the centre of the room, where the members of their group are gathering. No-one looks at anyone else. Daisy's head spins and she's afraid she'll throw up. *The smuggler. Oh god, this is really happening. What am I going to do now? Where is the smuggler?* She wonders what her new sisters will think of her if she makes a run for it. How has she got herself into this mess? She stands with Nadira's and Aarifa's arms linked into hers, feeling like a prisoner, yet knowing she will fall to the ground if they let go. And oh god, she suddenly needs to pee so badly she's afraid she'll wet herself. She wants Mum, she wants Lola. She wants to go back to yesterday morning and make the decision not to set out on this mad trail. But she's here, now, on a cold dark early morning in a random building on the border between Serbia and Hungary. And it seems she's about to be people trafficked.

There's a clank from the fire corner, someone collecting their pots from the night before. Abdul appears in the circle of torchlight, strapping the pan and spoons to the side of his rucksack. A shout rings out, in a language Daisy doesn't understand. A man she doesn't recognise pushes his way through the group, a cigarette glowing in the corner of his mouth. He stomps towards Abdul, wrenches the cookware from Abdul's hands and flings it away onto the concrete floor. Cymbals crash in Daisy's head. She feels a dribble of urine escape, clenches harder. *I'm in the middle of a nightmare.* Aarifa squeezes her arm. Nadira breathes in sharply.

The stranger shouts again and cuffs the side of Abdul's head with his fist. The sound of knuckles on Abdul's skull is sickening. Abdul's brother steps forward but Abdul stays him with an outspread hand. The Smuggler makes a noise like a snarling wolf. Daisy feels lightheaded. She trembles so hard she's sure she's making the building rattle. She can hear Nadira's breath coming fast and hard beside her ear.

The Smuggler surveys the group, shoving each member roughly as he counts them off on his fingers. *Oh god. Oh my god.* If she breaks free, he's bound to grab her. She doesn't think she would be able to stand up without the sisters' support, let alone run.

Nadira, Aarifa and Daisy are at the back of the group. The Smuggler reaches them after a drawn-out nightmare of counting. Nadira, *shove.* Daisy, *shove* (they're still holding onto each other) Aarifa . . . His hand stays in mid-air.

He shakes his head and shoulders, like a huge, shuddering beast. He turns and lunges back to the beginning of the line, where he starts counting again. Daisy's aware of a rustling amongst the group but nobody looks at her with the accusation she deserves. She turns her stiff neck and meets first Aarifa's eyes and then Nadira's in the dimness. She licks her dry lips, takes a shaking breath and withdraws her arms from theirs, though they try to hold on tightly. She steps back from the group, knowing it's pointless to run. At the doorway she's made out the shape of another hulking figure. It's he who holds the torch that has them all caught in the glare of its spotlight.

There's no escape.

The Smuggler counts Aarifa and Nadira. He pauses. Turns

to Daisy and lurches forward to grab her arm. She lets out a small scream. He shouts something in her face, she can smell garlic on his breath and see the cold glare in his eyes. He holds her there for a moment, then fumbles in his pocket for a phone. Taking his eyes off hers he snaps on the torch and shines it directly at her. As he moves his face half into the beam, she sees puzzlement rippling over it.

"Where from?" he barks.

She clears her throat, testing her voice. "UK," she whispers. "England."

"What the fuck?" he sneers and spits on the ground. "Where money? You owe me. Give." He shakes her arm roughly. His fingers dig into her skin.

Convulsing with fear, she reaches for her backpack straps but he's too impatient for her lumbering movements and snatches it off her shoulders. He throws her bag to the ground. To her horror, and she doesn't know why this is anymore horrible than the whole situation, he starts rifling through her things, tossing out the blanket and towel, her diary, reaching for her phone which he rams into one of the pockets on his jacket.

"Wait," Daisy cries. "My phone, I need that!"

With a lightening movement he's on his feet, his face thrust into hers. Before she can think he draws his hand back and lands it hard on her cheek. She reels backwards, pinpoints of light whirling at the corners of her vision. Her face stings and her jaw feels loose. *He hit me, he really hit me.* A swirling image of a handprint on skin hurtles through her mind. She doubles over, wrapping herself tightly with her arms. She forgets to keep control of her bladder. A hot release of urine soaks through her leggings and pools on the floor at her feet.

The Smuggler takes no notice. He turns her backpack upside down and shakes out the rest of its contents, ignoring the few remaining clothes and her toiletry bag. The curled-edged half of sandwich and her water bottle. He picks up her purse. She watches mutely as he withdraws the few notes of cash and slips her bank and credit cards out of their slots, flicking through the various store cards and her library card. He throws the purse onto the floor along with the rest of her possessions.

"Pick up," he orders, kicking the spare clothes and the bag towards her. She doesn't understand why he hasn't looked for her passport, then realises he must have assumed she doesn't have one, hence her presence in this building. Surely credit cards are a giveaway? Or maybe he just doesn't care. She pictures her driver's licence in the glove compartment of the van. With shaking hands, she stuffs the rest of her things into the bag and reloads it on her shoulders. My phone, she thinks. What am I going to do without my phone?

To her surprise, when she straightens up, he's holding out his own phone, displaying the 'notes' function. "Pin numbers," he orders. When she hesitates, he jabs the phone into her ribcage. She cries out again. "Pin numbers," he shouts. "Now."

She looks at the bank and credit cards in his other hand, her mind frozen. He jabs her with the phone again, making that awful snarling sound. He holds the phone while she types in the number for her bank card, but she can't remember the credit card one. Her mind spins sickeningly. Then she thinks, I could just type anything, he wouldn't know. And she wishes she'd thought of that immediately. *Unless he's going to march me to an ATM.* But she still can't remember it. She gives a shaky impression of considering hard, then quickly types in a random number.

The Smuggler seems satisfied. With a leer at her he backs away, holding his nose and laughing at the puddle she's left on the ground. She wants to curl up on the floor in shame, especially once Aarifa and Nadira hurry forward to bring her back into their midst, patting and comforting her, while all she can think about is the stink of her urine.

I flew to Turkey,
Crossed the Aegean Sea
in a crowded boat.
I walked through Europe,
took some buses and trains,
ending up in Denmark.

24

Daisy

Border of Serbia and Hungary, August 2017

Daisy's head is full of fog. The past night and day have felt like a lifetime, and when she tries to recall Lola or Mum it's hard to believe they're even real. Umid. She tests the name in her mind, but it feels paper-thin, a leaf on the wind. The only people real to her right now are Aarifa and Nadira, holding her closely on either side despite the narrowness of the path, and Abdul immediately in front of them, keeping his back straight and his chin tilted up even though from his profile when he half-turns Daisy can see his right eye and cheekbone are misshapen from the beating. He's her inspiration not to give up and collapse into a howling mess on the ground. Once they had all been pushed out the door of their overnight sanctuary and set on their trail through a channel of vegetation towards the border fence, Abdul had murmured to her that everything would be all right and that she must trust the young women to look after her.

"Soon we will all be safe, my sisters. *Inshallah.*"

The Smuggler, gimlet-eyed in the darkness, hisses at them to keep moving, and to stay quiet. Daisy's leggings are drying out in the night breeze blowing through her thin skirt. She wishes she'd taken the long-sleeved dress from her bag, put it on under her cardigan before she'd gone to sleep. However long ago that was. Nothing is real. None of this is real. A nightmare gone on too long.

"Stop!" the whisper echoes back along the line. Daisy bumps up against Abdul, who has come to a sudden halt. Daisy had been moving robotically, only half in her mind. She feels drugged, separated from herself.

"What's happening?"

Nadira wipes a hand over the back of her mouth. In the dark the whites of her eyes show. Daisy realises Nadira's terrified. There's a hot scent coming off her. She wonders why she herself feels so numb. Perhaps she isn't here, she thinks. *I'm back in the van with Mum, maybe spending another night at that campsite near Belgrade. Yes, that was the last real thing that happened.*

"We have reached the fence," Abdul explains. "We must be very quiet."

I can't go through the border fence! But neither must she do anything to jeopardise the chances of her friends. You've got yourself into this mess, Daisy, she reminds herself.

There's a feeling of many more people surrounding them than the ten that left the building they spent the night in. Bodies crowded together. *What's happening?*

She strains to see what's going on beyond the bulk of Abdul and his brother Mohammed. Aarifa's breathing is shallow, muffled by the scarf covering Daisy's right ear. Daisy takes her hand and squeezes it. Aarifa in turn reaches for her sister's hand. Am I seriously doing this? Daisy thinks. Her head is tight, an invisible band round her forehead. They stand still for interminable moments, until Daisy realises the line ahead of them is beginning to thin out. The Smuggler is placing his hand on the refugees' backs, one after the other, instructing them to make a run for the fence. Now it begins to hit hard, what's really happening. *Oh my god ohmygod.*

Clouds part to reveal a sliver of moon, casting the faintest light on the ground ahead of them. The Smuggler slithers back along the diminishing line of migrants, silent and sinuous. He has his finger to his lips. He stares at the three women. Reaches his arm out and slices their locked hands apart with his own, rigid as a chopper. He pulls Nadira and Aarifa away from Daisy and shoves them in front of him, keeping Daisy behind. *Why have we been separated?* Without the sisters, Panic floods Daisy all over again. Mohammed is running towards the fence. Abdul glances back at the women before it's his turn to go and then he too sets off, angling his body low against the ground.

In the space created by the absence of his bulk and in the thin light of the moon Daisy can make out the paler stretch of dirt road at the edge of the field and beyond it, severed coils of razor wire, cut and pulled apart to make a gap wide enough for a human to pass through. The dark shape of a figure wriggling through the clipped metal grid behind that is Abdul. He disappears from her line of sight, he's through!

The Smuggler presses his hand on Aarifa's back, sending her towards the fence. Daisy watches her running, hunched forward, and feels her own stomach drop. She gnaws at her fists. The smuggler by the fence is pushing Aarifa through, she's halfway there, but her skirt seems to have caught on the wire. Daisy's hands creep up her face, her teeth chatter. *Please, let her be safe.* She sees Aarifa tug at her skirt, ripping it. She's through, leaving behind a tangle of cloth like a bat flapping helplessly on the wire. The Smuggler grabs Nadira's arm and starts dragging her towards the fence, signalling Daisy to stay behind. *What, wait here on my own?*

At the exact moment she thinks this, there's an explosion of sound and light. Out of nowhere, two vehicles burst into view from opposite directions on either side of the fence.

Dark-clothed, helmeted figures spring out of the trucks screaming instructions, waving around what Daisy thinks are batons, or possibly guns. Wolf-like shapes pirouette at the ends of leads, their teeth bared, spittle flying from their jowls. Strings of saliva lit up in the headlights. Everything is bright, she's caught in the headlights. A shot is fired. Daisy can't help herself, she screams, drops to the ground. She can see Nadira ahead, also prone on the ground. Neither of the smugglers are anywhere to be seen but somewhere far behind her she hears another vehicle start up and drive off.

I was still only seventeen
when a family took me in.
For seven years
I went to school, got a job,
paid tax, did citizen things.

25

Daisy

Border of Serbia and Hungary, August 2017

Daisy shudders violently in the grass. She's on her knees and elbows, shielding her head with her arms and hands. Her scarf has fallen back off her hair. The ground reverberates with thudding feet, the air resounds with shouts. There is the hollow sound of something hard hitting someone's skull and closer by, the more deadened impact as of a blunt instrument on flesh. A man screams.

Daisy doesn't want to see or hear anything. She forces an image of baby Elijah into her mind, conjures the feel of him into her arms. Something pure, understandable. *Lullaby and goodnight*, she hums. *In the sky stars are bright.* In Navengore, right now Lola could be walking the floor with him, singing this exact song. She holds onto the image as hard as she can. There, the baby's asleep now.

Boots approach with a decisive rhythm. Rough hands grab hold of Daisy's backpack and wrench her to her feet. Shouting voices jar in her brain. She feels a hard shove in her lower back, causing her to stumble forward and dangle off the biting fingers gripping her arms. She retches. She shrivels, trying to make herself smaller. *Don't hit me.*

Daisy is crammed into the back of a Serbian police truck with Nadira squashed onto the seat next to her and *four-five-six-seven* other captees crowded into the breath-filled space around them. The men – she and Nadira are the only women in the car – hold themselves with dignity, their hands clasped on their laps or at their elbows. The smell in the car is bad, she doesn't think she's the only one who's peed herself, or worse. And there's a metallic scent too. Daisy only recognises one of the others, the smallest Eritrean boy who huddles into himself, biting his lower lip. He has a bleeding wound on his cheek. She thinks of Joe, the time he was knocked off his bicycle and walked all the way home from the next village with a bleeding head. He had the same expression as this boy, glazed eyes and a rigid jaw. Daisy feels a wash of sorrow for all the hurt boys. Who are these lost men in the van with her? Why does life have to be so cruel?

She doesn't think she can bear the pain, but she has no choice.

There must have been other refugees trying to cross at the same time as them. That would explain the sensation of being amongst many while they waited for their instruction to run to the fence. She supposes it makes sense from the smugglers' point of view to deal with as many people as possible at one go. She thinks she spotted Abdul's brother Mohammed being led to one of several other vehicles that had turned up after the first two. He walked in a line with others, nudged by two officers with guns. Mohammed's hands were up on the back of his head. She wonders what has happened to Abdul, and to Aarifa.

She's certain now that The Smuggler had intended to leave her behind.

Bastard. Having taken her phone and her credit cards.

She keeps having flashbacks to the shock of his hard slap

on the side of her face, the way her head snapped back.

She's so immersed in this nightmare experience she keeps forgetting she wasn't attempting to cross the border herself. She doesn't feel like Daisy anymore and she has no idea what's going to happen to her next. Her backpack was removed from her and thrown into the boot of one of the other vans, along with everyone else's. Her passport is in there, in the secret pocket. She trembles, hunching forward on the seat as the van careers over rough ground. Beside her Nadira is crying, but quietly, keening Aarifa's name under her breath. Daisy tries to comfort her by reaching for her hand, but Nadira has her fists clenched. It's the first time Daisy has seen her losing her cool. Imagine if it was herself and Lola who'd been separated so violently. It's going to be all right, Daisy tells herself. It's going to be all right. But she feels her face go hot with shame. However long things take to sort out she knows *she'll* be reunited with Mum before long, be back on the road. See her twin again. But for Nadira, Aarifa, Abdul and all the others she's briefly connected with, the future is uncertain, terrifying.

As it is for Umid, wherever he is. She allows one memory of him to flood her mind for a moment, a brief light in the current darkness. The night they stayed at the B&B on the island. The way he'd been smiling when he came out of the bathroom, freshly shaved, and wrapped his arms around her. God, she'd truly believed they were in love. It hurts so much. Bile rises into her throat when she pictures the border crossing. The cruelty of both the smugglers and the border guards. Has Umid attempted it yet? Her mind wanders. She glances at the wound on the Eritrean boy's face, then recalls the sharp crack of gun on skull. Maybe it happened to that man sitting opposite, his head bowed and the dark sticky gash fully visible. His body slumps forward. *He needs medical treatment!* Nothing could have prepared her for the viciousness of the past night. She doesn't think she'll ever forget the sounds and images.

The crunching bumpiness of the ride gives way to the whine of a smoother road surface. Lights start to flash by at the sides of the road. The man with the bashed head grunts and slumps forward further. The two men either side of him grasp his arms and pull him back upright, hold him in place. His head lolls to one side. Ice spreads in Daisy's chest. *How can this be happening*? Beside her Nadira draws in a long, miserable breath. She loosens her clenched fingers and uses them to straighten her headscarf around her face, lifts one corner of it and dabs at her eyes. She straightens her back, looking directly ahead, her nostrils flaring. But Daisy notices the tremble of her lower lip. Will Nadira allow her to take her hand now? It might help thaw the ice of panic spreading inside Daisy, too. The shuddering starts again in her bones. She reaches across and slides her fingers over Nadira's. Nadira squeezes back weakly. They glance briefly at each other, then down at their laps. Daisy thinks the man on her other side must be bothered by the shudders rolling through her, causing her leg to knock against his, but he's lost in his own resignation.

The vehicle makes a sharp turn, seemingly following the curve of a road. A feeling of anticipation grows within the cramped space. Soon they are surrounded by artificial lights, flickering through the windows as they slow down. There is the clank of high metal gates, Daisy can just make them out being dragged open. The van speeds up again along a short length of track and then comes to an abrupt stop. A moment later someone bangs on the roof. Daisy nearly flies out of her seat. The refugees and Daisy jerk their heads, glance around fearfully. The door is wrenched open by a police officer and yellow light floods into the car from outside. She can see her travelling companions' faces clearly for the first time. Take in the shock of full-colour congealed blood on skin and hair.

Their captor issues a command that presumably means 'out'. They start to pile out the car, flexing stiff limbs. If the passengers move too slowly, the armed officer violently 'assists' them. The man with the bashed head is dragged out of the vehicle and immediately collapses onto the ground. The black-clad, helmeted policeman kicks him, then calls over to his colleagues to remove him so the other passengers can alight from the vehicle. Daisy watches through the window as the broken man is carried towards a low, flat-roofed building, one of his arms dangling, fingers trailing the ground.

Daisy, Nadira and the rest of their able-enough carload are herded into line behind those emerging from other vans. Officers bark at them to *keep moving.* Police dogs lunge hungrily at the refugees, straining on overlong leads. One beast is almost at Daisy's skirt, trying to thrust its long narrow muzzle between her legs from behind. She lets out a cry, at the same time shrivelling inside at the realisation of what has attracted the dog. *I need a shower. I need clean clothes.*

But I wasn't recognised as a resident,
never would be.
I wasn't allowed to travel,
or be free.
Statelessness would never be enough for me.

26

Daisy

Detention Centre, Serbia, August 2017

Daisy and Nadira are in a room with four other women. The floor is bare apart from the bunk beds lining the walls. They've been given a sheet and a scratchy grey blanket each. Artificial light enters the room through a curtainless window from the spotlights outside, but the sky is lightening now too and soon it will be morning.

One of the strangers sits on her bed rocking back and forth. Two are curled up on their sides, their backs to the room. The other lies on her back, staring at the ceiling. Daisy descends her ladder, thinking of the wooden bunk beds she and Lola shared when they were little. They'd swap around once a month to both get to sleep on the top bunk. These beds are higher. Daisy's socked foot slips on the hard floor when she reaches the bottom, and her other knee bumps against the metal of the step above.

She must be covered in bruises.

She moves to sit next to Nadira on the lower bunk. Nadira hasn't spoken. She sits cross-legged, fiddling with the bangle on her wrist.

Daisy feels numb all over. Her vision is blurred with exhaustion. She has a hollow feeling inside her. She can't believe she's being held in detention; the whole night and the day before feels like a dream. Impossible to comprehend it was only the morning before that she stepped from Mum's van after a sleepless night, walked through a woodland path on the campsite, on her way to the shower block. She recalls turning around and around under the hot water as it rained like small pebbles on her head. She remembers the cymbal sound of the droplets echoing off the shower walls. *I'm English*, she'd explained to the female officer in reception. This is a mistake; I can prove it. You'll find my passport in my bag, but they took my bag. I need it back, please. Even as she pled her case, she'd felt hot shame at the thought that Nadira, patiently waiting her turn, might understand what she was saying. *Daisy the sneak. You'll do anything to get out of trouble.* Something Lola once said to her when they'd both done something wrong, and Daisy had tried to excuse her way out of it. It feels like she's letting Nadira down by attempting to leave. She supposes the empathy she feels with Nadira is because they're both twins. Daisy will eventually be reunited with her twin, but will Nadira?

"I don't understand you," the receptionist replied in perfectly adequate English. "You must follow procedure. You will be interviewed properly in the afternoon. Now you may use the toilet and we can give you water to drink. Breakfast is at 8 am. Here is your number. Next." The receptionist had fastened the paper bracelet too tightly on her wrist. In the bathroom, Daisy took off her leggings and rinsed them out. Pressed damp toilet tissue against the crotch of her knickers to freshen them but was too afraid to go without them. She swabbed her thighs and crotch with paper towels.

Nadira suddenly stops messing about with her bangle. She

163

half-glances at Daisy, before uttering an emphatic sigh. Then she lets her upper body drop to the mattress, lying on her side and curling her legs into a c-shape. She tugs at the blanket to try and cover herself, but Daisy's sitting on it. Daisy sighs too. Standing, she leaves Nadira to it, returns to the ladder and climbs back up to her own bunk.

Try to sleep, Daisy. It's Mum's voice she hears in her head. *Everything will be better in the morning.* She lies on the bunk, looking up at the spiderweb pattern of cracks on the ceiling, like roads on the map. Follows the imaginary roads in her mind. Where would she go? There's a buzzing in her veins, a sensation like she's still travelling in that packed van. When she closes her eyes, lights kaleidoscope behind the lids. Faces loom in, then zoom away. The faces of all the people she's met in the past twenty-four hours. The kindness of Abdul when she collapsed in the doorway of that abandoned building; the mirror-images of Nadira and Aarifa, so gently tending to her wounds. The Eritrean boy who somehow reminds her of Joe. The snarling wolfishness of The Smuggler's bared teeth.

There's a cacophony of noise in her head. A sharp crack rings out, and Daisy's head jerks up off the pillow. Trying to let go of the tension, she starts to drift off again, but soon afterwards The Smuggler slaps her on the face. Her body jolts back awake. From the bunk below she hears the soft sound of Nadira crying. A woman across the room snores loudly. Daisy hugs herself tightly, tucking the blanket around her like a tight sleeve. *I want to go home.* But she's no longer sure where that is.

Breakfast consists of bread and weak coffee. Daisy forces herself to eat, ravenous but with a swimming feeling inside her threatening to override the hunger. She presses a hand to her stomach, *please don't let me disgrace myself further by throwing up at the table.* She holds the food in her mouth for a moment, pauses, and when she's sure it's safe, swallows it down.   Opposite her at the table, Nadira posts bread mechanically into her mouth. Her skin has a greyish tinge. Daisy's afraid her friend is shutting down. Desperate to help her, Daisy scans the refectory for a glimpse of Aarifa, but she isn't among the countless others eating at the long tables. Over in the far corner, she catches sight of Mohammed, but there's no sign of his brother either. *How many days is it since I left the campsite, since I last saw Mum?* Daisy thinks it was only two mornings ago that she turned her back on the van, so glibly. Mum must be going frantic. If only she'd sent her another message before she went to sleep in the barn that night. Even though, rationally, Daisy understands that her situation will be sorted out and she'll be allowed to return to Mum, it doesn't feel that way now. She imagines long years ahead, in these same circumstances.   And wonders how the people around her will stand it.

After the meal the detainees are encouraged to go outside in the fresh air while cleaners work in the rooms. But as she and Nadira file out along with the others, Daisy notices a blonde woman with broad shoulders and pouches under her eyes calling numbers from a doorway. A few people are being ushered into a room off the foyer.

Daisy hesitates, then makes up her mind. "Sorry," she says to Nadira. "I just need to ... " She turns back and approaches the blue-shirted woman. "Please, can you help me? I'm here mistakenly. They took my bag and my passport. I'm actually English." She can hear the 'don't cha know' tone of her voice and feels ashamed. But she must do something about this. It's wrong to be living an experience that's not her own. She lays her hand on the woman's arm and tries to make eye contact.

The supervisor is wearing blue latex gloves. She shrugs Daisy's hand off and looks at her with horror. "No touch," she says shrilly. She points to the paper bracelet on Daisy's wrist. "Must wait turn."

Daisy is left hot with embarrassment and shame. Nausea

gets the better of her. She runs outside, her stomach heaving. Makes it as far as the fence and throws up in the grass at the base of a tree. As a child, she had always vomited when under stress. The habit seems to have returned with a vengeance. She shuts off her growing suspicion of another cause for her almost-constant nausea, and finishes, straightening up. She wipes her mouth with the hem of her skirt, which she's probably already peed on, she thinks bitterly.

She joins Nadira on a bench. Children play on a swing set nearby. A small girl with black curly hair and round dark eyes toddles up to them. Standing between Nadira's knees, the child opens her palm. In its centre is a speckled black and white pebble.

"*Ladayk*," she offers the pebble to Nadira.

Nadira seems to come awake. She leans towards the child, cradles the small hand in hers. "*Ana?*" she says softly.

"*Naeam lak.*" The little girl drops the pebble into Nadira's hand. Nadira strokes it with her forefinger. The child stares up into Nadira's face, watching her reaction. "*Bï*" she says then and turns and trots back to her friends.

The exchange has felt profound to Daisy.

"Do you know her?" she asks. "That little girl?" She indicates Nadira for *you*, and then the child, sitting cross-legged in the grass now, cradling a chunky piece of wood in her arms.

Tears squeeze out of Nadira's eyes. Folding her fingers around the pebble she turns to Daisy.

"I had," she says, gesturing towards the small girl. "I had *ilmaha dumar ah.*" She brushes her other hand over her eyes. "But no more."

Nadira had a child, Daisy guesses. She once had a child, but she doesn't have one anymore.

After a lunch of lukewarm soup and more bread, Daisy's number is finally called. She sits at a small desk opposite a thin-faced woman with brown hair scraped tightly back in a ponytail. The woman wears spectacles that have only one arm, but nevertheless stay perfectly balanced on her nose. She finishes writing something on a form, before peering over the top of the spectacles at Daisy.

"Daisy Galen?" Her English is heavily accented.

"That's right," says Daisy, thankful the woman speaks her language. She clears her throat. She's got that funny buzzing in her head again, and hopes she isn't going to pass out. She laces her fingers together on the desk in front of her.

"Why are you here?" the interviewing officer's brown eyes look Daisy up and down. "English woman, you say. What were you doing at the border?"

"It was a mistake," Daisy tries to explain. "I was, err, looking for someone." She coughs again, her throat inexplicably gravelly. "I was walking, and it got dark, so I slept in a barn. Excuse me, could I have some water, please?"

"This is not café," snaps the officer. But she reaches behind her for a bottle from a shrink-wrapped multipack and passes it to Daisy anyway. She scribbles something on the form. "Continue, please. This is not good explanation."

Daisy unlaces her fingers and unscrews the bottle. She takes a long drink, thinking how to explain her situation. "I'd had a fall," she says haltingly. "And the people in the barn helped me. The women ... " unexpected tears prick her eyes at the memory of Nadira's and Aarifa's gentle ministrations, how it had felt they'd become friends so quickly. She sniffs and continues. "They helped me and gave me some food. I thought I would sleep there for the night with them, and then I'd find my way back to the bus stop and return to the campsite in the morning. But a bad man came in the night." Her explanation sounds like a child's elaborately constructed excuse for a misdemeanour. The woman glances witheringly at her, then fills in another part of the form.

Daisy breathes in and tries again. "I didn't realise he was a smuggler. He hit me in the face and stole my phone and my money." She leaves out the part where she wet herself. "Then he forced me to march to the border with the other people in the barn." She takes in another shuddering breath. "He didn't give me a chance to explain. I was horrified when I realised what was happening. I had no intention of crossing the border." *Sneaky Daisy. Sanctimonious Daisy.* Lola's voice in her head. Then Moussa's *This is not about you Daisy.* Everything that's happened has been her own fault. She should never have been in that barn with the refugees anyway.

The interview continues with what seems to Daisy pointless questions: height, weight, defining marks etc. Each answer is being recorded on the form. Before long Daisy's attempt at humility dissolves and she's taking umbrage again: it's obvious she's English, she's not an asylum seeker, this is a complete waste of time. Meanwhile a tiny voice in her head is saying *you deserve this. They're taking all your details so they can easily identify you if they catch you again. You're not the victim, Daisy; this is not a game.* She imagines Nadira undergoing the same interview and she expects Nadira won't be walking out the gate at the end of it as she thinks she will be.

The officer turns over the last page of the form, then she reaches into a drawer and takes something out. As she turns back Daisy notices her glasses slipping slightly down her nose. The woman lays Daisy's passport on the desk and makes a show of copying the number into a box on the form. So, they had it all along.

Daisy wants to reach out and grab it. Wants to shout *give me my bag and let me go.* But what would she do then? She has no money and no phone. She must stay calm; she'll need to rely on the centre's help in reuniting her with Mum. She twists her hands around each other under the desk, bites her lip.

The officer pushes her one-armed spectacles back up the bridge of her nose and glances up at Daisy. She folds her hands over Daisy's papers on the desk, it looks like she's not getting her passport back any time soon.

"You can return to the refectory now. We'll call you later."

"What?" Daisy pushes her chair back and stands up. "Why won't you let me go?" The buzzing in her head grows stronger. "May I please make a phone call?"

"Later," the woman indicates the door with a flick of her hand. "We will call out your number when we're ready.

Nothing for it, then
than to set off travelling again
in search of somewhere I could be accepted
As a someone,
a person,
a citizen.

27

Daisy

Berlin, August 2017

Email from: Daisy_halfcrazy@dmail.com
To: Lola Galen

Subject: My mad adventure

God, Lola,
I mean, hey Lo ... Prepare for a long email!

It's a good job Mum made us memorise numbers when she gave us our first mobile phones. That was our eleventh birthday, remember? *It's no good telling me you don't need to bother because your phone will do it for you*, she said. *What if you lose your phone? What if it gets stolen*? Not in her wildest dreams would Mum ever have imagined it would be a people smuggler who stole my phone. Never in her wildest dreams would she have imagined I'd almost end up illegally crossing a border.

I can hear you asking, would I have done it? Crossed that border I mean. I keep asking myself the same thing. And the truth is, if The Smuggler (that's how I think of him, in capital letters) had pushed me between the shoulder blades and sent me running towards the fence after Aarifa and Nadira – they're the twins I was telling you about on the phone – then err, yes, I think I bloody would have done. If the border police hadn't turned up, etc. Yeah, I think I would have followed them. Anything not to have been left alone on that deserted field in the middle of the night. I never told you this on the phone (and I hope you've written down my new number!) but when The Smuggler hit me in the face, I wet myself. It must have been the shock; I was already desperate for a pee, and I forgot to hold it in. So that was one more humiliation. I had to march with the others in wet leggings and stinking like that poor girl who was in our class at school, remember?

It's hard to explain, but I was kind of imprinted on those twin girls, you know like baby geese are supposed to imprint on the first thing they see and think it's their mother? It's just that they picked me up off the floor and tended to my wounds and let me sleep with them. I know, I'm pathetic. But it still hurts to think of Nadira's blank-eyed stare when I said goodbye to her in the detention centre. She must have felt so alone.

Stop it, Lola, I know you're laughing at me for being in a detention centre. Yeah, I know it's mad. I can hardly believe any of it myself now. The truth is, though, I go hot and cold when I think of everything that happened. I keep having flashbacks: The Smuggler's slap, the border guards screaming at people and beating them up. There was a boy in the van with me who somehow reminded me of Joe when he was younger (not now, I can't believe how grown-up Joe's become, with a beard, lol). There was blood dripping down that boy's face, and he looked so lost. I keep wondering where they all are now, and what'll happen to them.

Anyway, it's a good job I knew Mum's mobile number off by heart so when I was finally allowed to make a phone call at the detention centre, I was able to ring her and ask her to pick me up. I'm not even going into her reaction when she found out where I was. You can probably guess, you know, that cold front she puts on. Suffice it to say she only spoke to me through Alicia – yeah, the dog – for the next couple of days. *Alicia, I'm making a cup of tea. Daisy can have one if she wants one. Alicia, Daisy might be exhausted after her adventures, but we still need her bed putting away, don't we, so we can move in this fucking van.* It was full-on cold war, I tell you. We were driving most of the time though, so I could pretend to be asleep.

Still, she's cheered up now. In her element with Electra and Rudi, grandmotherhood suits her. I love our niece so much! I never came across a more intelligent four-year-old in all the time I was teaching, and she's so quick-witted and funny too. I absolutely adore her. It's great that Rudi and our Elijah are almost the same age, isn't it? I can't wait for future family gatherings when the little cousins get together, those boys will be like brothers.

Speaking of – it was emotional to be reunited with ours. Jamie is just really, really, nice. It breaks my heart that he was out of the family so long, and we were deprived of him. Do you think we could have done something about finding him by ourselves, Lo? Instead of following Mum and Dad's lead and accepting he was gone. I worry that we've been complacent. Letting the same thing happen to our younger brother, too. What the hell was the matter with our family? Just imagine if something had happened to either of them during those missing years, and we never got to see them again. I've missed having brothers.

Right. So, there are two things I've put off writing about so far. The first: I know you're dying to ask, Lo. About Umid. I think last time I emailed you – and I'm sorry it's been so long – we'd just had that weekend at the B&B. God, that was one of the best nights of my life. I thought I really loved him; I still think that. Well. He left the island without telling me. I was humiliated (it's becoming a bit of a pattern, to be honest). I thought we really had something. Then a friend of ours, Moussa, made me see it wasn't about me. I keep forgetting Umid's a refugee, you see. I think he needs to make his own path and try and find a way of putting his life back together again, and there's nothing I can do for him. But it hurt that he left without saying goodbye. I suppose he must've known I'd make it hard for him. He doesn't need a madwoman like me complicating things.

Mum and I were already in Serbia when I got a message from Moussa telling me Umid was there too. It seemed to make sense at the time to try and find him and say goodbye. How simple that sounds, and how stupid.

So yeah, I've finally admitted it, I'm stupid.

Really stupid.

Because – and this is the second thing – I'm pregnant, Lo.

Okay, I can't write anything else right now, I'm going to be sick again.

Call you later.

Love, me.

I said goodbye to the family
that felt like mine,
the woman I called 'Mum'
and to my girlfriend.
I took a bus to Hamburg,
then another one to Paris
and from there to Calais.

28

Daisy

Berlin, August 2017

Email from: Daisy_halfcrazy@dmail.com
To: Lola Galen

Subject: The thing I just told you

Hi again, Lola.
Sorry I ended the previous email so abruptly. At least I sent it, so you'll have had time to digest my news. Sorry I didn't answer your call, either. I just couldn't face it after being sick. Not with so many listening ears around. Our Electra doesn't miss a trick, you know. She's extremely well-informed about babies and childbirth and explained the complete process to me from conception to afterbirth when I was holding Rudi on my knee earlier. To be honest it was a shock hearing those words come out the mouth of a four-year-old.

Leilja cornered me on the landing outside the toilet and made me admit I'm pregnant. See, she noticed even though

Mum didn't. Mum's going to feel so let down by this. I was always 'the sensible one'. Not anymore. God, Lola. What have I done?

Yeah, it is my fault. Before you ask, 'coz I know you're about to, I wanted it to happen.

So now you and Leilja know. Oh my god, Lola. I'm going to have a baby. Another cousin for the clan! It didn't feel right, with you having a baby and not me. Does that sound terrible? Probably. But I am happy, I can't help it. Even though I know I'm stupid.

What do you think of our sister-in-law? I can't make her out. I don't think she's very keen on Mum and Mum's made the odd snipey comment about her. I think Leilja feels Mum's a bit too possessive over Jamie and Joe – ironic, really, since that was probably why they both stayed out of touch so long in the first place – and Leilja's been the one looking after Jamie all these years. But Leilja was kind to me. She made me go back in the toilet and take a pregnancy test; she had some left over from last year when she found out she was pregnant with Rudi.

I knew already, I've missed two periods, Lo. Well, I kind of knew but I couldn't really believe it. Anyway, the test confirmed it.

Everything's been going around my head on repeat. I go numb for a while – in my body I mean. And when physical sensations start to come back, I get a pins and needles feeling all over. This morning when I had Rudi on my knee (he was asleep) I sort of drifted off for a while. When I came to I couldn't connect for a moment: like I thought what's this warm thing in my arms? Then I remembered I was holding baby Rudi. The past few days I've found it difficult to concentrate on anything. Nothing feels real. I keep expecting to wake up in the van with Mum and find out the past week or so has all been a dream.

Do you think I'm going mad, Lo?

I'm sitting on the blow-up bed in Electra's room writing this on my laptop. Mum's sleeping on Electra's bed – not now, I mean at night – and Electra and Rudi are staying in their

177

parents' room. But I can hear Electra downstairs asking where I am, so I'm going to sign off now.

I'm sorry I haven't asked anything about you and Elijah, and Dad. How is everything?

Tell me it all in an email and tell me everything you think about what I've written here. I'll call you in a couple of days – or wait, there's that big family Skype thing tomorrow, so I'll see your face again, and Elijah's.

Love you both,
Daisy xxxxxxxxxxxx

I went back to the beginning.
Sat round a fire
in a migrant camp,
and waited for the smuggler's command.

29

Maya

Berlin, August 2017

Daytime

Maya's oldest son was setting up a screen on the wall opposite the window in the living room. They were having a whole-family Skype session later. It would be odd to see Con again, especially now she knew about Susannah Metherington. Lola had let something slip on their last video call. When she came to think of it, the woman had been all over Con at The Cottages Christmas party. More fool him for falling for her snaky charms.

Maya remembered Susannah's shockingly flirtatious behaviour in a club on the village mums' bi-annual night out, back when the children were small. Pasting herself all over a young bricklayer at a twenty-first birthday do. The poor lad had seemed terrified. She reminded herself again that it wasn't her business what Con did anymore; he was her ex-husband now. *That was what you wanted, Maya.* She only hoped Susannah wasn't going to be included in this family call. Daisy must've known about her father's new 'relationship' too, she thought; she and Lola told each other everything. All trying to hide it from her, protect Mum's delicate feelings.

She shuddered. The six-month-old asleep with his head on her shoulder clenched his body, lifted his head and turned his face into her neck, mouthing her skin with his petal soft lips. She rubbed his back until he settled again, his body going limp against her arm. She'd get a disapproving glare from Leilja if Rudi woke before the end of his expected nap time. Maya hadn't realised how difficult dealing with a daughter-in-law would be. Leilja was highly-strung, she liked everything doing just-so. Maya got the impression Leilja felt she, Maya, was what her mother would have called lackadaisical, letting sons slip through her fingers and running away to 'find herself' while her family was in crisis.

"I'll be back in a minute Mum, just got to fetch another cable. You okay with Rudi?" Jamie stepped down from the stool he'd been standing on, a coil of wires in his hand. "You looked like you were drifting off yourself there."

"I'm fine, son, just relaxed. He's a very restful baby." Maya brushed her lips against the top of her grandson's head. That familiar ache in her chest when she thought about Jamie as a baby, as a little boy. "You have a wonderful family, Jamie. I can't tell you how proud I am of you," she surprised herself, blurting that out loud. But she wanted to add *And I'm sorry. I'm sorry, so sorry, about everything that happened in our past.*

Jamie's eyebrows knitted as he stood hesitantly in the doorway, looking back at her. His hair had grown longer since she saw him in January, it was now caught up on the back of his head in a man-bun. He'd shaved his beard – trimmed it much shorter anyway, he looked more like the boy she remembered, despite now being a father of two.

Back then – in January that is, not when he was a boy –

he'd kept her at a distance, couldn't quite seem to believe the dreadlocked woman who'd written that crazy blog pretending to be Joe was his mother. The mother he remembered as being timid and mousey, always on her husband's side. She'd turned up after more than ten years, sat down with a guitar and sung him back to his childhood. He'd talked to her about this the previous evening. He'd said it was Electra's easy acceptance of her that helped thaw his resistance to letting her back in. It wasn't about him anymore. And now there was Rudi, too, the children needed her in their lives, Jamie said. It was the first time he'd spoken so openly, maybe she was finally on the road to his forgiveness. She cupped her palm over the back of the baby's head and his small hand tightened on the neckline of her t-shirt. She hoped she could make amends with grandmotherhood.

Jamie shifted his weight from one foot to the other. "Okay, cool. Look, Mum, you don't have to . . . ah, never mind. Be back in a tick. Want a drink or anything?"

On the screen Con appeared healthy and tanned. Perhaps he'd started making time for walks and fresh air, something Maya had often suggested they do together, but his work had kept him busy. Or perhaps it was a spray tan. Lola had told her he'd started going to the gym. He sat on a black leather sofa she'd never seen before, in the living room of his new apartment on the ground floor of their old family home. There was a fluffy white rug atop the grey carpet. What happened to her exquisite, embroidered sofa and red velvet armchair? The Persian rug they'd had so long? Maya, you must let go of the past, she told herself yet again, pasting a smile on her face as she greeted him. The property was Con's, now. She had the financial equivalent of his half in the bank. At least Susannah Metherington wasn't present at the get-together.

Lola sat next to Con on the leather sofa. Elijah was on her lap, reaching out towards the laptop screen, his pudgy hands seeming enormous against the foreshortening of his body. He'd grown so much since she last saw him at three months old, a different child now. His eyes had darkened to the colour of treacle and his head was covered in a cap of tight curls.

"Hello, baby," she called out to him. "Elijah, it's Gramma. Look, here's your cousin Rudi," she lifted the baby on her own lap, turning him to face his cousin on the screen. "You two are going to be such good friends."

"That baby is *my* cousin too, Gramma," Electra pointed to the screen. "I did meet him before, when him and Rudi were even smaller. And I met that lady," she ran over to the screen on the wall and pointed up at Lola, and then Con, "and that man. He's called my grandpop. Is that right, Papa?"

"That's right, Lecky. And the lady is *my* baby sister. Her name's Lola." He waved at his sister up on the wall. "She's your aunty."

Maya watched Jamie's face closely. His baby sister. She pictured him as a five-year-old, 'helping' her change the twins' nappies. *Oh Jamie.*

"But I thought *Daisy* was my aunty," Electra ran back over to Daisy, sitting in the only armchair, and climbed into her lap. Maya saw Daisy's arms tightening around her, noticed the way she sniffed Electra's head. A bell rang, as if from far away, in the back of her own head.

"Daisy is your aunty too, Lecky. You can have more than one. Daisy and Lola are twins, can you see how their faces look the same?" Jamie had moved to perch on the arm of Daisy's chair. "Can't believe you two are the same pesky little sisters I remember." He ruffled Daisy's hair. She jerked her head away, but she was smiling. Jamie leant down and whispered something in her ear. Daisy reddened.

"No," she spoke quietly but the general chatter in the room had stopped at that moment. "Not now."

From the corner of her eye Maya noticed Leilja nodding at Daisy. Daisy's expression twisted. She kicked the base of the armchair with her heel, making Electra laugh as she was bounced up and down on Daisy's knee.

"What is it?" Maya said sharply.

Lola leaned forward in the screen on the wall. "Go on, Dais," she said. "The rest of us know. You can't keep Mum and Dad in the dark for ever.

"Know what?" Con's voice, and at the same time Joe's, coming into the room late. "Hi Mum." He squeezed into a space on the sofa next to Maya.

"Sorry Amar couldn't come," he said to everyone. His voice contained less than its usual ebullience. "Err, he had to wait in for someone at the apartment." They were in the process of moving in together. Maya suspected they'd had a row. She patted Joe on the arm, and he leaned in close, tugging the ends of her hair. "I liked it when you had dreadlocks, Ma. Anyway, Daisy. What is it you've got to tell us?"

"Oh fuck," Daisy said. She wrangled the hem of her peasant blouse into a rope with her free hand. She tapped Electra's leg with the fingers of her other. "Sorry, Lec." Electra playfully slapped her fingers down, like a game of whack-a-mole. "You said a rude word!"

"Okay, you might as well know Mum and Dad. And Joe," Daisy said, "while the whole family's here. I'm pregnant, and I don't want to talk about it right now."

Night-time

Christ, she was still furious at Daisy, horrified by the recklessness of what she did in Serbia. Her spiralling thoughts refused to allow her to sleep. Maya lay restlessly in Electra's too-small bed while Daisy snored on the blow-up mattress on the other side of the room. Maya missed her dog; Alicia had been relegated to the little room Jamie called his studio, off the kitchen. She'd barked the previous night and Maya had to keep getting up to quiet her down. The second time she went down she found Electra already there. She was lying next to the dog on the pile of blankets Joe had brought back from the flea market where his boyfriend had a

184

stall. Faintly lit by a distant streetlight casting a meagre glow through the studio's small window, the dark-haired child lay on her side with her head on Alicia's white back. She was murmuring to the dog in German. Alicia barely stirred when Maya walked in, fumbling in the dark of the corridor.

"Sweet pea," Maya crouched beside her, stroking the child's hair and the dog's fur at the same time. "You should be asleep upstairs."

"I can't sleep, Gramma," her granddaughter climbed into Maya's lap and curled up, her thumb in her mouth. "Papa snores too loud."

"So does your aunty Daisy," Maya leaned close to Electra's ear to whisper. "But don't tell her I told you."

Electra twisted around and patted Maya on the chest. "Aunty Daisy said you snore, too, Gramma."

The dog had just begun a faint rattle from her nose, pressed into the blanket. "So does Alicia. I bet you do too, little pea, when you actually do sleep."

This night there had been no sound from Alicia. Either she was getting used to the new situation, or the little girl had gone down and curled up in the blankets with her, at least they would both be getting a good night's sleep.

Maya wasn't planning to go down and check. Despite her restlessness, her body felt exhausted. Her mind continued to spin with thoughts of Daisy, disguised in a group of refugees trying to cross a border. Maya had heard about the dangers of that border crossing – the violent pushbacks, the shootings. Imagine if Daisy had been beaten up or shot, how would she, Maya, ever have borne it? It would have been her fault, somehow. She hadn't paid enough attention to Daisy, too immersed in her own role at the camp. Daisy had been unhappy, needing something Maya hadn't given. Pregnant, of course! The lethargy she'd suffered, the occasional sickness, how could Maya not have realised?

She felt she'd lost her way somehow, as a mother and a person. She'd only really known who she was when she was travelling alone, with a backpack. She hugged herself in the cramped bed. Daisy had been so hard to talk to lately. She went cold at the thought of her running off after that refugee boy, she'd had no idea of her daughter's strong feelings for him. Maya could barely picture him – this Umid. Despite her fury with her daughter's actions, at the heart of her concern was the fear Daisy had fallen prey to the same kind of obsession as before. After her breakup with Dan, in Newark. She'd been accused of stalking, dear god. Maya hadn't been there for her then, either.

She probably should have been kinder to Daisy when she picked her up from the detention centre. *A detention centre*, for god's sake. Her mind jolted fully awake again. Those days of worry when she didn't know where Daisy was. She'd been on the point of calling Con. He would have blamed her. Said she should have taken the time to listen to her daughter rather than coming up with a constant string of diagnosis from food poisoning to mononucleosis. When all the time her daughter was pregnant. It was a miracle Daisy hadn't suffered a miscarriage. She'd been hit by a people smuggler! Shoved about by a border guard! Maya turned over onto her other side, images a vortex on her mind's screen, juxtaposed on the wall in the dimness.

She lay awake, listening to the sound of her girl's breathing. Pictured the embryo inside Daisy's stomach, cells dividing at the rate of the spinning images in Maya's mind. To think that Daisy's eventual child was once inside Maya, an egg in the uterus of the foetus that became Maya's own daughter.

Sleep, she begged herself. Sometimes the magnitude of everything was too much for her consciousness to handle. *I can't think about any of this anymore. Let me sleep.*

My life
Was under threat.
I had to come to this unknown country
with a different language.
But many people here
have big hearts.

Part III

Nobody can feel it
unless they've experienced it —
you have to be ready
to die.

30

Umid

**A makeshift camp on the outskirts of Calais –
March 2018.**

Interview with Libby L. a filmmaker.

L: Okay, we'll start recording. For the camera, could you
tell me your name please?

U: My name is Umid Habibi.

L: I won't use your surname, for obvious reasons. Can we
do that again with only your first name?

U: Hi, my name is Umid.

L: It's nice to meet you, Umid. How are you?

U: Is nice to meet you too, Libby. I'm doing okay. Mostly
okay anyway – no, don't put that in, I just say I'm okay, right?

L: I'll cut it if you want, but it's fine to show people how you
really are. Can you relax a bit more? Tell me something about
yourself. What would you like people to know about you?

U: I . . . well, like I say, I'm Umid. I'm twenty-four years
old. I'm happy person, normally, ha.

L: You seem like a happy person. You have a cheeky glint in your eyes.

U: Ha.

L: What do you enjoy most?

U: I like dancing and music. I like cooking, I'm good chef.

L: You're a good chef, have you done that as a job?

U: Yes. I worked as chef in Iran. And I volunteer in kitchen on Samos. I cook for many, many people.

L: And what about the dancing, have you ever danced professionally?

U: No. Is just for fun. Ha. That was joke, right?

L: I don't know, I saw you dancing earlier when those musicians visited, you had some moves! Anyway, Umid. You mentioned you were on Samos, the Greek island. How long did you spend there?

U: I was on island for more than two years. Long, long time.

L: And what was it like for you there?

U: It was very hard. I never realised I would have to stay there so long. I used to watch ferry leave every day and wish it was me.

L: It must have been difficult. Why did you have to leave Iran?

U: Because I was protesting, against government, you know? I had warning that police were coming for me. They took my friend.

L: How old were you when you left, Umid?

U: Twenty-one.

L: Can you describe the journey that has brought you here to Calais?

U: I walk from Iran to Turkey and got boat to Samos. I found charity there and they give me mat and blanket. Then they just ... send me out onto hillside. I thought, what? I have no family and no-one to help me. I was so lonely at first.

L: I can imagine you would have been. How did you leave the island?

U: In the end I bribe asylum services to give me travel card.

L: You had to bribe them?

U: Yes, everybody does that if they can, it how system works. I stand in line, watching money passing over counter. They tuck it away under folder. When it was my turn, I hand over money. Like magic, travel card appears. Ha.

L: If you don't mind me asking, where did the money come from?

U: From my biggest brother, in Iran. I sell him my car when I have to leave. I ask him to keep money for me.

L: And where did you go then, was it Athens?

U: Yes. But I couldn't stay there, it was terrible situation in Athens. Refugees homeless and hungry, crowded on streets. I decide to leave.

L: What did you do then?

U: I walked. I take buses and trains. I sleep everywhere. Sometimes deserted buildings, sometimes in one-stop camps. I stay two months at detention centre in Serbia, in the grounds.

L: Why in the grounds?

U: There was no room inside.

L: Why were you in a detention centre?

U: I was caught at border, the first time. Here, do you see? Scar on my arm. My arm feel broken, but it heal by itself. Only took few weeks.

L: Yes, I see. That must have been painful.

U: Beatings, prison. It's same for everyone.

L: There was no other way to get to France safely?

U: You're right, Libby. No safe route.

L: What happened then?

U: I found different agent and they got me across border. Then I walk more, at night, you know? You have to hide in jungle during day. I stay four weeks in camp in Belgium. It was nice place, but waiting list for interviews too long. I wanted to go to UK.

L: Do you have any family in the UK?

U: Yes, aunt of my mother's, who I was . . . when she left, I am six. She pinch my cheeks and leave red lipstick on my face. She lives in city called Peterborough with my cousin. Not far from Cambridge. Is famous university, yes? Her son got job there at technology firm.

L: Did you consider staying in France?

U: No, I do not want to stay here, they do not want us. Have you seen what they do to us here?

L: Sorry, I didn't mean to upset you. Can you give me an example of the treatment you've had?

U: Okay. When I arrive in Paris, I get off train in Gare du Nord. Amazing station. I ask Sudanese guys with backpacks where can I go. They take me to small settlement near sports stadium, but the gendarmes raided camp the next morning and we have to move on. They do this many times, Libby.

L: I'm sorry. Not such a romantic city for refugees. Tell me more.

U: We find another place to sleep under railway bridge. Buzzing sound wakes me. I open my eyes and see drones hovering at entrance of tunnel. Police again.

L: Drones?

U: Yes. They use drones to find us. At first, I thought shouting voices were in dream. I was back at protest march in Tehran. In the dream I watch my friend Amin being dragged away. Then I feel someone pulling my sleeping bag, the zipper press against my throat. There is blow on my shoulder, at first numb and then pain. The gendarme beat me again with solid object, he's shouting, "Sortez, sortez!" They treat us like animals. The police grab our things and throw them in car. Then they spit at us before they drive away.

L: I'm sorry. You came to Calais next?

U: Yes. We decide to walk here. It took four days. Raining most of time. We only have black bin bags to try and keep dry. I was hungry, Libby.

L: Speaking of which, I think we'll leave it here for today. I'm going to take you for a coffee now and maybe for some of

193

those crepes from the stall by the beach, if you have time? I'd appreciate the company.

U: Yes of course I have time, Libby, and thank you. I'd love to go for coffee with you.

The smugglers are like Mafia,
I saw a man shot, a woman screaming
and when I intervened,
my arm was broken.
I went to the hospital, had my arm set,
then returned to camp.

31

Maya

Calais, May 2018

Email from: Maya Joy Galen
To: Daisy_halfcrazy@dmail.com

Subject: Your beautiful baby and you

Oh, Daisy my darling.

Please don't be too sad about your baby's father. I'm sure it will work out in the end. I'll ask at the various camps around here, to see if anyone knows of him. Trouble is the refugees are always being moved on so there's not as much cohesion as I imagine there was in the days of the 'Jungle'.

If you ever feel things are really getting on top of you, please let me know. I'll come back if you want my help, I promise, and I'll stay for as long as you need.

You seemed so cosy and settled in the flat with Lola fussing over you. Avalie was feeding well, and your sore nipples were better. I thought it was okay for me to leave. To be honest I felt a bit in the way there, but that's just me being sensitive. I should have paid more attention to how you seemed to be feeling. Just let me know, sweetheart. I'll try and call you this evening. Not too late, as you need your sleep. I'm sure Lola will help by walking the baby around if she cries at night, as you helped her with Elijah.

Thank you for those pictures of my precious granddaughter. I just wanted to put down in words how privileged I felt to be present at her birth. You were so brave, you reminded me of a lioness, my love. Roaring your baby into the world. Especially with all those cats howling at each other outside and the full moon shining directly in the birthing centre window. Wasn't it amazing? If you can, do try and keep the feeling you had then in mind to see you through these difficult days of new motherhood. You are strong, you are amazing for what you did. One day Avalie's father will be as proud of you as I am, don't forget that.

You were asking me how I'm getting on back in Calais. The weather's been beautiful the last few days. It's a pleasure to wake up on the campsite and see the early morning mist steaming off the trees. There's a lady staying in a caravan, who loves Alicia. She's started looking after her while I'm out. It gives Alicia a break from our van.

There's a new team of volunteers since I first came here last autumn. Apart from Bill, of course. You know, the friendly widower from Newcastle who invited me for Christmas dinner. Yes, he's nice but I'm not looking for a man in my life, you know that! Bill doesn't think he'll ever leave. Some of the new volunteers stay for a week or so, others come for months. Like me! Well, what else can I do until I come up with a better plan? You're correct in that I could buy a property close to you and Lola, help look after the children, possibly get another receptionist job or something similar. But what happens if you and Lola decide to move on in the future, Daisy? I know you can't imagine it, but you might meet someone new and want to settle down somewhere else. Okay, I can feel you getting upset at the thought of that. Perhaps you will eventually be reunited with Umid, then. Somehow. But you'll have a life of your own one day with your own family and it's important that I build a life of my own too. So that I don't become a burden to you and Lola one day. Your father certainly seems to be moving on with his life. Albeit in the same place.

Anyway, sorry for going off at a tangent.

Have you been getting out for walks? Fresh air will help keep your spirits up. I remember you and Lola taking Elijah out to meet some of your old schoolfriends in the village a week or so after he was born. Now that Avalie's a few weeks old, she might enjoy the carrier more if she doesn't like the pram. There are some lovely walks along the clifftop, looking down at the fields. Remember how we used to go for picnics there when you were little?

I'm having a cup of tea in my van before crossing the road to the warehouse for morning duty. I'm going to help unpack a new delivery of t-shirts and joggers from the UK and bag them up for this afternoon's distribution. They had a film crew in the warehouse yesterday, interviewing some of the newer volunteers about why they're here. Bill and I didn't fancy it. Apparently, they – well, it seems to be a young woman mainly – are interviewing refugees as well. It's for a TV documentary I believe.

Take care, Daisy,

Lots of love to you and Avalie (I'm writing separately to Lola)

Mum xxxxxxx

At five A.M the water was quiet.
We set off in a fragile boat,
Fifty-five of us, too many by far.
Women and children crying made us nervous,
so many people in that small boat.
Dolphins arced through the sea on either side,
it felt like they were guiding us.

32

Umid

Calais, May 2018

Second interview with Libby L. a filmmaker.

L: Hello, Umid. It's good to see you again.

U: Hi, Libby. Welcome. Yes. Is good to see you too. Is that new camera?

L: Yes, I'm surprised you noticed.

U: Ah, I thought so. I don't know if I tell you this, but I wanted to make career in media.

L: Is that so? Have you had any experience in that kind of thing?

U: Yes. I show you, later. My videos on Internet. I had many followers.

L: I'm intrigued. What kind of videos?

U: I film protests. Interviews, things like that.

L: Is that another reason you had to leave Iran?

U: Yes, of course.

L: Okay. You can send me the links and I'll look later. Did you have any training or were you self-taught?

U: I have degree in media studies. I want work for BBC, you know, Libby. That's why I go to England, ha.

L: I admire your ambition and I hope you're able to achieve your dreams, Umid. Following on from where we left off last time, did you ever think you would end up in the sort of situation you're in now?

U: Are you kidding? No, I never imagine it will take so long.

L: Would you have stayed in your own country if you could?

U: Yes, of course. You think I don't miss my mother? It's more than three years since I see her! Sorry. Of course. Nobody puts themselves through this for fun. Everyone here had no choice. I had no choice.

L: I understand. I'm sorry to ask difficult questions. Are you okay, Umid? If you don't mind me saying you seem a bit down.

U: Yes Libby, I struggle since you last came. I am too sad. I thought I would have left by now. But I need to have hope. Like my name, ha.

L: I'm sorry. Apart from safety, of course, what do you hope for?

U: I want to study, improve my English. I want work hard and make something of myself, I have to start again, Libby but it's hard to do that here.

L: I can see that. How about cooking, had you thought of making that a career? I loved the meal you cooked for me over the campfire, so clever.

U: Thank you, I know I'm good cook. I'm glad you like my lentil soup. I would make you even more delicious meal if I have proper cooker. In kitchen with shining tiles on walls and stainless-steel things. Yes, I work as chef in my home country, but like I say, I want work in media.

L: You could combine the two with your own cooking show. No? Perhaps not, then. Moving on, can you tell me how your parents felt about you having to leave your country, Umid?

U: When my parents discover I'm missing they call police. I don't tell my parents for two weeks – it was safest for all of us.

I was out of country by then. My mom say officers come to house, asking questions. She scream at me on phone. What have you done? Have you killed someone? I say of course not; how can she ask that of her own son?

L: It must have been a terrible shock for her to learn you had gone.

U: I tell her I going to make my fortune in Europe. She still thinks I'll be coming back one day.

L: Do you get to talk to her often?

U: Yes, on WhatsApp once or twice a week. She thinks I should be married by now; she keeps choosing brides for me, ha,

L: Is it usual for a mother to do that?

U: Yes, in my country mother chooses wife for son. I don't want to get married for a while. I want my freedom first.

L: That makes sense. What are you thinking, Umid? You've gone quiet. Tell me . . .

Look, I'll turn the camera off. You were blushing, that's all.

U: What, Libby? Why you looking at me like that?

L: Do you have someone you're especially fond of, a girlfriend, maybe?

U: Girlfriend, what, here? Of course not.

L: Okay.

U: What do you mean? I'm not blushing. Stop it. Okay, okay. Not anymore, but I had girlfriend on Samos. She was volunteer, an English girl. Little bit older than me.

L: Ah. I'm switching the camera back on. Umid, I understand you were seeing an English girl when you were on Samos. Have you kept in touch with her?

U: She was nice girl but no, I haven't been in touch with her, is too difficult. She would back to comfortable life, and what about me? She must forget me, Libby. Look around you, only waste ground and police tearing down tent. No olive groves or golden beaches to make feel romantic here.

L: Can you tell me about the English girl?

U: All right. Her name Daisy. She was teacher in UK. She will forget me, for sure.

L: If your circumstances had been different, might you have continued the relationship?

U: Maybe. In different life, maybe. Turn camera off, Libby.

L: Let's take a break, we'll go and eat.

L: Are you okay to go on?

U: Yes. Thank you. Burger was delicious, and it was nice to feel normal for while.

L: I understand you've been volunteering with a charity here?

U: Yes. I try be useful. I help with distributions. Try and deflect trouble when start to kick off. All these people, cultures that don't normally mix. They cut a lot of trees down you know. Tore up undergrowth. So we have nowhere to hide.

L: I imagine there's a high turnover of people here, some leaving, some arriving.

U: Yes. One of my friends go out last night and not return. I hope he get to UK. Before, he try hide himself in fishing boat. But they have searchlights out there you know. He nearly die of hypothermia.

L: Where do you think he went last night?

U: I think he try lorry.

L: What about you, Umid, are you planning to try leaving soon?

U: Yes, I have no choice, Libby. I need find courage for ask my father for pay agent, I have no money left.

L: You've tried before, haven't you?

U: Yes. Last smuggler never showed up with boat. Ones before brought boat but shoved back in van when police came. And first boat sank as soon as we pushed it out in sea. You have to wade in up to your chest then pull each other into boat when it float. I was last one in, and boat already sinking.

Smugglers don't care. They point gun at you if you try argue with them.

L: You must be scared of trying all over again.

U: Of course. Come on, who wouldn't be? But what else can I do? We know when we set out, we might die. Everyone here accept that already. That's how it is here.

Every day I went to school
I had to pass through
the dangerous neighbourhood.
Life felt precarious:
violence, gang recruitment, drugs.
Even with all the problems,
you can try to live a good life.
go to school, do your job,
but never feel secure
that you will come back alive.

Part IV

The journey was long,
eight or nine hours.
I nursed my broken arm,
if I had fallen in,
I couldn't have swum.

33

Maya

Kintyre, Scotland, July 2019

Electra had grown into a rangy six-year-old. Maya's first grandchild had lost the baby plumpness her limbs had still had when Maya first met her, aged three. The girl had long legs (from her father) and a narrow face but with the rounded cheekbones of her mother. She ran towards Maya, who was on her way back from walking Alicia along the beach below the campsite. Maya's pockets were full of rose quartz, that she thought perhaps she might be able to chip into little jewellery pieces when she ever gave herself the time.

On the beach she had breathed the salt air deeply, rested among some seal-like rocks for a while, and watched gannets plunging head-first into the surf. Tried to clear her head. The sea sounded like voices, clamouring, hungry. She closed her eyes. When she opened them again, she felt cleansed somehow, refreshed. The voices had died down.

Alicia panted, slumped onto the grass at her feet. Electra tugged her little brother Rudi along behind her, attached by a tie-dyed scarf. Maya called out that it might be too tight around his wrist; the dear, pudgy wrist of a toddler transitioning from toddlerhood to childhood. A child she had last seen in the new year at his home in Germany.

"It's okay Gramma," Electra insisted, cantering to a stop. "Good dog," she said to Rudi, behind her. She spoke in perfect English, spacing her words slowly and evenly as if she believed Maya's hearing to be defective, or had forgotten what language her paternal grandmother spoke. Electra was multilingual — German, Bosnian and English — and you could almost see her brain computing before she started talking to anyone. "My mama tied it for me. Rudi likes it, don't you, Rudi? He likes being my dog."

"Dod!" Rudi stamped his feet delightedly.

"What do dogs say, Rudi?" Maya asked him. Her knees creaked as she lowered herself onto the grass next to her actual dog, pressing down on her weak wrist. She half-fell into a sitting position with her legs crossed. Why was she so stiff? In her early fifties she'd felt invincible, carrying her life on her back. She was now in the final year of that decade. Electra and Rudi watched her solemnly, while she wondered where her supple body of only a couple of years previously had gone. She made an effort to smile, fought an urge to grab the two-and-a-half-year-old boy and squeeze him. But he narrowed his eyes, pre-empting her leaning body's intent.

Alienation from her grandchildren was the price of her life choices. *Look what I've given up, and for what?* Not for the first time she wondered if she was making any difference at all. *I could have been a hands-on grandma.* Her feeling of loneliness refused to abate, despite being surrounded by her family. She shivered in a gust of breeze off the sea, feeling it go through her. The people surrounding her, this vivid and visceral family, had lived their lives largely without her the past few years: the visitor. Grandmothers were supposed to be needed. But she hadn't been there often enough.

"What do dogs say, Rudi?" Electra repeated Maya's

question, still in English. The little boy's face lit up and he bounced forward, play bowing, for all the world like a real puppy. At Maya's side, Alicia sat up straight and tilted her head.

"Row, row," barked Rudi. Maya's yearning fingers involuntarily reached out to him, but his bark turned into a growl, and he backed away. He strained at the far end of his tether. Maya's sinuses burned. She ran a finger under her eyes.

Electra didn't seem to notice. "Good boy, Rudi," she said. "He's clever, isn't he, Gramma? That's because I taught him. Me and Uncle Joe did anyway.

"He is clever," Maya swallowed. "And so are you, darling. Perhaps you should untie him now though, can you see his skin is becoming red?"

Maya watched Electra struggle with the bow around Rudi's wrist, her tongue poking out between her lips. The little boy thrashed his arm and started to whine. As his face darkened, Maya had a sudden memory of Jamie at his age, having a tantrum at his day nursery when she tried to hand him over to the staff. *Oh, Jamie.* Here were his children. A beautiful pain seared her ribs.

"I can't do it, Gramma," Electra's lower lip wobbled. "Please will you help me?"

Finally, a chance to feel useful. "Of course, sweet pea." Was it Daisy or Lola she used to call that when they were little? The other one's pet name had been 'Poppy' for some reason. Maybe that was Lola, then. She'd always wanted a name like Daisy's. *Her flower girls.* "Try and hold his arm still for me, will you darling?"

Maya could see Leilja leaning forward in her camping chair, ready to spring up at any moment and come to the rescue. Maya's face burned. Useless Gramma. She breathed deeply and forced her fingers to work. As she finally released the bow, Rudi's arm flew up and hit the side of her jaw and she let out a *whoosh*. The scarf fluttered onto the grass. Maya pressed her hand to her face while Rudi ran wailing into his mother's arms. Electra stood in front of her, watching Maya take another deep breath and compose herself.

"Are you all right, Gramma?"

"I am, little one.   Now, have you got a hug for your gramma?"

Dutifully, Electra leaned forward and allowed Maya to hold her. Her black ponytailed hair swung against Maya's cheek. She breathed the child in.

———————

Maya couldn't put her finger on it, but she felt Con was behaving shiftily. He couldn't seem to look her in the eye. Almost as if he was feeling guilty about something. But they were divorced, weren't they, so whatever he was trying to hide was no concern of hers. Still, it rankled. She cut him off on his way back from the shower block, deliberately walking diagonally across his path.   He overreacted, stepping back comically.

"Oops," he said. "Trying to trip me up, are you?"

"Don't be daft," Maya folded her arms. "Haven't lost your dancing skills though, I see. Some quick moves there."

"Yes. Well, I've been practicing lately, as a matter of fact."

"Have you?"

He paused. "Yeah, they were running classes in the village hall. You know, ballroom, Latin and all that."

She looked at him properly. He seemed healthy, his hair thick and longer than the last time she'd seen him — longer than she'd seen it since they'd been students, in fact — his shoulders straighter. An air of confidence about him. The blue bath towel hanging over his arm was not as fluffy as it had once been. It had once hung, corners rigorously aligned by their cleaner, beneath its partnering hand towel in their en-suite bathroom at The Cottages. Hers, hanging next to his, had been a dusky pink. She wondered if he still used the pink ones or if they were now upstairs in Lola's flat. For a moment

211

it was difficult to catch her breath. *I haven't lost anything, I made choices.* She didn't know what the matter with her had been since she'd arrived here in her battered van. Everybody else already set up in their hired vans, her daughters and Electra running out to greet her — why the constant ache in her throat? She swallowed. They stopped at the side of his fancy hired camper van, three times the size of hers. Alicia pressed herself against Maya's leg, as ever, suspicious of Con. Maya cleared her throat.

"How are you, Con? You've hardly spoken a word to me since we arrived. You're looking well."

"Thanks. You ... look well too Maya." His hesitation told her it was a lie. She didn't feel that well to be honest, tired. *So tired.* "I like your hair now you've cut it; I always said it suited you short." He smiled, but not with his whole face. Surely, they were both remembering how he had begged her to have it cut short when he visited her in Paris, the last year they were together. Her hand went up to her neck, fingertips still surprised at finding soft loose waves to nestle into, even these years later. The dreadlocks had served their time when she was on the road, on foot. *Don't think about that now*, the halcyon years of her self-discovery.

"And we only arrived yesterday," said Con. "There hasn't been much chance to catch up yet, has there?"

"I suppose not. Just checking you weren't avoiding me."

He shook his head. "Why on earth would I?" But there was a definite tensing up of his face beneath her searching gaze. She knew him too well. Or she had done.

"No reason." She forced a smile. No sense in getting off on the wrong foot before their family holiday had even properly begun. "Well, it's good to see you anyway. Perhaps we could have a proper chat later, I'd love to know how it's been going with you and the girls all living together again, with our two grandchildren! Hard to believe, isn't it?"

Con nodded. "It *is* hard to believe, Lola and Daisy being mothers together. And *Daisy's Day Nursery* seems to be running successfully. But we're not exactly living together, Maya. I do have a life of my own you know." He shook out the towel from his arm and draped it over the wing mirror of his van to dry off. "So do the girls, and it's handy that they've got each other to babysit, because I'm not always available any longer." He gave her a 'so there' look.

She felt herself blushing. "Of course you're not, I didn't think you would be. Anyway, we'd better get back to our van," she bent to fondle Alicia's ears, turning her reddening cheeks away from him. "The kids'll be back from their walk soon and I want to get freshened up, too."

I looked straight ahead,
to whatever would happen next.
If it was my day to die,
I accepted it,
but I was spared.
A grey boat appeared on the waves
and took us aboard.

34

Maya

Kintyre, Summer 2019

Maya woke from a doze on her bed with Alicia, a pleasantly edible smell filling her nostrils. She remembered: Jamie and Con were setting up a barbecue for the evening meal, using a fancy appliance that'd come with Con's hired vehicle. Tubes connected it to his gas supply, and there were two decent-sized grills to cook on. She bet Con was in his element, master of the burgers.

One time when Jamie was a teenager, he'd enraged his father by pouring too much fuel on the barbecue Con had meticulously set up in their immaculate garden at The Cottages, one of his prescribed 'happy family' times. All the sausages on the barbecue had been ruined. Con sent Jamie to his room, only to discover later that his son had climbed out of his bedroom window onto the garage roof below and jumped down from there to the ground. Coming in drunk later, Jamie taunted his father with the information that he had written 'loser' on the garage window. It was only with his finger dipped in the rainwater barrel by the back gate. All while Con had been inside the garage putting away the barbecue. "It was so fucking dirty," Jamie said. "Not so Mr Perfect after all, are you, Pa?" Later, when she was already in bed, Con left the room, and the outside light came on. Maya knew he couldn't stop himself going out there to wipe the garage window clean of Jamie's contempt.

Her heart contracted now in empathy for the difficulty of the father and son relationship. But it was all better now, wasn't it? Back when she and Con had been reunited with Jamie after their long estrangement, Con confided in Maya that Jamie had told him he could understand his father better now he had a child of his own. That was when Electra was smaller. Now Jamie had a son of his own, too.

She relaxed and breathed through the open window of her van. For a moment she was transported into the less distant past than her years as a wife and mother, back to the community in Catalonia where she had lived for a while with a group of mostly young people and their 'leader', Wild Eric. Observing and listening to the disparate young travellers at the evening meals around the fire there, had brought her to many realisations about her own children, the understanding that she needed to let them go in order to regain their trust. Now here she was, amid her whole family and she felt alone, cut adrift. Con was the one they relied on these days. The patriarch. Maybe they had deliberately cut *her* adrift. She wasn't like them anymore.

Oh, stop feeling sorry for yourself, Maya. Alicia's inquiring nose sniffed at the saltwater on Maya's cheeks. She gave a tentative lick.

"Oi, get your slobbery chops out of my face!" Maya pushed her away, laughing now. A slight bump on the side of her van. She sat up. Beneath her window, against the background sloshing and sighing of the sea and the distant banter between her ex-husband and son, she heard children's voices. She wiped her sleeve across her face and peeped out of the window gap, down towards the ground. It was her two little grandsons, Rudi and Elijah, both two-and-a-half. *Jamie's boy and Lola's boy.* Maya pressed a hand to her chest.

The toddlers were passing a stone back and forth between their two sets of dimpled hands, chattering to each other, but she couldn't make out what they were saying. Slowly it dawned on her that Rudi must be speaking his mother's language — Bosnian — and Elijah was responding in a made-up babble of his own. Somehow, they were communicating with each other in vernaculars that neither of them could understand. *Oh, my heart.* Like the children she'd been involved with at the camps on Samos and in Calais. How they would play and sing together in a multitude of languages when the visiting artists came, or when one of the aide workers found time to try and organise them into a game or a music session.

Language consisted of more than words.

She leaned away from the window and scooted off the side of the bed, placing her feet firmly on the floor before attempting to stand up. She ought to take advantage of the shower block, but she felt shy of meeting any of her family on the way there or back. *Where've you been, Mum?* They might ask. *We were just talking about you, wondering what you were doing. Why haven't you been out here with us, we see you so rarely as it is?*

No, she was unprepared. It felt too complicated to explain her exhaustion. Coming away from France, where you couldn't afford to indulge your own vulnerabilities, where you only had to look at the situations of those so much worse off than yourself to feel ashamed of thinking you were tired — she felt hit by a sledgehammer now. Back in the 'real' world. Where her family were safe and happy and thriving.

She moved to the front seat area and locked the door with the central locking, *just in case anyone remembers I'm here* — it seemed her brain refused to put a stop to the self-pity

— and pulled down the blinds in the centre of the van before stripping off. Squeezing herself into the tiny bathroom cubicle she used the cassette toilet, flushed it and then ran a sink of cool water. Taking a flannel, she washed herself, starting by running the flannel over her short hair, allowing the water to run down the sides of her face and onto her shoulders. Face, neck, underarms, arms and torso. Fleshier again now she wasn't constantly walking. Thighs and lower legs. Dipping the flannel in water again she washed front and back between her legs. Feeling refreshed and clean, she sat on a towel on the closed toilet lid and carefully washed her feet: tops, soles and between her toes. She'd seen too many foot infections in Calais from lack of access to washing facilities.

The cool water on her body calmed her racing mind. Wrapping herself in the towel she slipped back into her bedroom area and dressed in fresh clothes: bra, vest top, a pale soft cotton shirt she'd bought three years ago from a market stall in Lleida, Spain. *Where I met you, Alicia.* The dog wagged her tale as if she could read Maya's thoughts.

She left the shirt unbuttoned. A bit creased but never mind. She pulled on underwear and loose linen trousers (from a charity shop in Inveraray on her way up to Kintyre) and slipped her feet into her old sandals.

"Right, I'm ready to face them all, Alicia. How about you? Good dog." Maya encouraged her off the bed. Alicia stretched and yawned, then shook herself in the narrow space between the kitchen sink and the bathroom.

"Thanks for all those hairs," Maya said, shaking her head. "That's another sweep-out session for me, then. But not yet, dog. It's time to go out there and drink up every moment with my lovely children and grandchildren, don't you think?"

Sometimes I think it is only me
who has problems like these,
but during my travels
I've met many people
with problems worse than mine.

35

Maya

Kintyre, Summer 2019

Someone had arranged camping chairs in a semicircle around
the barbecue. The smell of slowly-cooking food mingled with
the scent of the sea, and the sounds of her family's voices were
accompanied by its background symphony. The sun was still
high in the sky.

Alicia left Maya's side and half-crawled beneath the big van
to lie on her side on the cool grass. Maya stood for a moment,
shading her eyes with her hand. Con and Jamie were intent
on the barbecue, Jamie wearing a tie-dyed apron, Con with
a tea towel tucked into his shorts' waistband. He glanced
up and gave her a friendly nod. She half-smiled back from
beneath her shielding hand. Jamie spotted her.

"Oh, hi Mum, I wondered where you'd got to." *His eyes.* In
his bearded face she could still see her tousle-haired toddler.
Her firstborn. A tug of love in her chest.

He looked so like his father.

"Looks like you're doing a good job, son," she gave him an open smile.

"I'm helping Papa and Grandpop," announced Electra, descending the steps of the van with a bag of bread rolls under one arm.

"You're doing a good job too, sweet pea," Maya said.

She stood a moment longer. There were her family ranged on camp chairs and stools. Two — no three — camping tables were wedged together in front of them, covered in cloths. Bowls of salad, crisps, and dips had been placed there, awaiting the arrival of the main food.

Maya smacked a hand to her mouth. "Oh, sorry. I haven't brought anything out. Let me see what I've got in the van!" *A few eggs, half a wilted lettuce, some oats. Not much more.* "Oh dear."

"Seriously Maya," Con said. "Not to worry, we've got more food than we know what to do with out here. Even with these gannets." He tapped his granddaughter on the head as she laid out the bread rolls, and she crinkled her face at him. How familiar they were with each other. It can't only have been that the rest of the family had arrived slightly before Maya. Since the family reunion at the beginning of 2017, Con had maintained regular contact with his sons and grandchildren in Germany. *A pity it took the breaking of our marriage to achieve that,* Maya thought.

"Hey Mumma," Lola came up behind her and planted a kiss on her mother's neck. "Did you have a nice rest? You look refreshed. Me, on the other hand ... " She mimed tearing her hair out. "Now I understand why you used to lose your temper with us so often when we were kids. Come back here, little man!" She ran off after her son, who was tugging at a tablecloth, edging a glass bowl of salad closer and closer to his head. Lola disengaged his fingers in the nick of time, pushing the salad bowl into the centre of the table and simultaneously sweeping the little boy onto her hip. She chided him, kissing his tight curls repeatedly.

221

Maya watched her settling into a chair next to Daisy, who was nursing Avalie. Daisy had a faraway expression on her face that Maya had noticed more than once since she arrived. She studied the twins faces, now turned towards each other. As girls they had drawn together and apart in cycles, sometimes wanting to be the same and sometimes fiercely different.

Did I really lose my temper with them often? Funny how her children — especially Lola — pictured their childhoods differently from how she did.

"Mum, Mum. Here you are, come and sit next to me!" Joe dragged a chair closer to his and patted it. Her dear boy. Her renegade — her vagabond inspiration. He'd left her when he still had the rounded cheeks of a boy, and when she found him again his face had lengthened, untamed russet beard covered his jaw.

She moved around the semicircle and seated herself next to him. He snuggled in closer, tactile as ever. Maya put her hand up and stroked Joe's now expertly trimmed and groomed facial hair. Joe laid his hand on her arm.

"It's so good to see you again, Mum. I keep missing your visits because of one thing or another." He leaned over and gave his mother a kiss on the cheek. "You'll have to come and stay with us in Germany. Any time. We've got the apartment perfect now, Amar, haven't we?"

He threaded his fingers between his boyfriend's on the arm of Amar's chair.

Amar leaned forward, smiling at Maya. "We'd love to have you, Maya-mum. I think you'd love the 'Blue Room', that would be your bedroom. And we can't wait for you to meet our little Chi-Chi, she's this big, now." He made a measuring gesture with his spare hand above the chair arm, indicating the size of the Chihuahua puppy they'd recently adopted. "She's been asking when her other *oma* is coming to see her."

All the tension in Maya's stomach relaxed. A warm laugh bubbled out of her. "I'd love to come and stay with you two,

222

and I can't wait to meet Chi-Chi." *I'm not so sure what Alicia will think of her, but I won't mention that now.*

"Then it's settled. We'll check our diaries and get the Blue Room ready for you." Joe squeezed her arm, resting his cheek on her shoulder.

A comfortable pause followed. Maya found herself gazing at Daisy again, across the barbecue, sitting next to her twin.

"So perfect she looks, nursing her baby at her breast. Like a real-life 'Madonna and Child', no?" Amar followed the direction of her gaze. He was right, Daisy looked comfortable as a mother, back in tune with Lola again too, who cuddled a now sleepy Elijah on her lap. *My girls all grown up with children of their own.*

"I'll fetch you a drink, Maya-mum," Amar untangled his fingers from Joe's and pushed himself up out of his chair. "What would you like? White or red?"

"Hmm, I think I'll just have a soda water if there is one. Thank you, Amar. I don't tend to drink much alcohol these days, tends to give me a headache."

"I will see what I can find for you." Amar squeezed between his chair and Lejla's, sitting on his other side, and set off for the makeshift bar Jamie had put up behind the barbecue.

Joe tightened his grip on his mother's arm. "I'm glad you liked my book, Mum. It was thanks to you bringing my journal back to me that I was able to finally get it finished. And I even sneaked some of your blog posts in, tee-hee, so thanks for them as well."

Maya pressed her hand to her forehead. "Oh don't, Joe. I feel so embarrassed about that now. Still, my trickery helped me find you again, didn't it?" *To think I would never have known Jamie's beautiful children if I hadn't posted a blog pretending to be Joe.*

"I was so mad when I first discovered that fake blog," Jamie grinned at her. "But you were clever to think of it, Mum. I just didn't know how to get in touch with you again. It never occurred to me you were following my footsteps around the world, backpacking and eating food out of bins! It was such a surprise to find you had my journal." A short pause and then her son's face crumpled. "Poor Nick."

"I know darling." Maya took his other hand and squeezed it. She swallowed the threat of tears. "That poor boy." She sucked in a breath of salt air, her eyes stinging. Being called to identify a body the Australian authorities had mistakenly believed was Joe had been the most horrific experience of her life "At least he was able to be identified, because of your journal. That is something, you know. In however a tragic way he was at least reunited with his parents."

Joe and she both wiped tears out of their eyes.

"I know," Joe said. "I contacted them, you know, his parents. Just to let them know what a good friend he'd been to me. I told them about our walking adventures. They were grateful."

"That was kind of you— oops!" Electra had come bouncing over, carrying a plastic cup of liquid. Drops spilled onto Maya's linen trousers as her granddaughter handed it to her over-enthusiastically.

"Sorry Gramma," Electra said, not sounding it at all. "Uncle Amar said to give you this. 'Cause he's gone to the bog, he said. It's erm, soda water he said."

"Thank you, sweet pea." Maya took a long sip, before placing the cup carefully on the ground beneath her seat. "Would you like to sit here on my lap for a while?"

"Nein, Gramma. I'm far too busy for that. Let go of me please, Uncle Joe!"

"But I'm trying to capture you for your gramma," Joe said, wrapping his arms playfully around the child."

"*Das ist genug*, stop it now," Electra said sharply, and Joe's arms dropped away.

"You have to respect my personal space, Uncle Joe," Electra said, brushing herself down. Two chairs away from Joe, Lejla laughed out loud. "That's my girl!"

Electra planted her feet firmly in front of Joe. "Now, are you sorry?"

"I'm sorry," Joe hung his head, peeping up at Electra from under his eyebrows.

"Fine, then," said Electra. "I've got to get on. See you later Gramma."

"See you later sweet pea."

Maya gave Joe a similarly reprimanding look. "That's told you." She gestured across the chairs at Daisy, disengaging a sleeping seventeen-month-old Avalie from her breast and settling her into a more comfortable position on her lap. "Bear it in mind in future, because you've another niece over there who's likely to know herself just as well as Electra does, and good on them. I wish I'd been more like Electra when I was young." I wish I was now, she thought.

My story is sad.
But I can make up
a happy story for you
if you want.

Part V

I am only one in a long line.
In prison the window is small,
we see only a small amount of ourselves
And a small amount of the sky.

36

Maya

Calais, late September 2019

Alicia mainly stayed in the van while Maya worked in the warehouse, though on the days that were still hot Maya tethered her outside in the shade of the row of containers. A truck of donated goods had arrived the evening before. Maya helped unload a builder's bag stuffed with sleeping bags, followed by several black sacks packed with small men's winter coats, then some laundry bags full of boots with their laces tied together, and finally several large cardboard cartons packed with individual boxes of new trainers from a shop that had gone out of business in the UK. All the items had to be thoroughly checked by different teams before being stored in relevantly labelled cubby holes. Maya had volunteered to help sort the sleeping bags, shaking them out and checking for cleanliness and state of repair before labelling them 'winter' or 'summer'. The row of shelves she worked at was at a right angle to the ones where shoes were stored. She glanced up when Annie, a twenty-two-year-old care assistant from Newport in Wales, let out an exclamation.

"These are amazing!", Annie had opened and gazed wonderingly into one of the new boxes. She tipped the box to show Maya. A bright pair of yellow and black trainers glinted under the overhead light. "Absolutely brand new. It was so kind of the shop owners to donate these. They could have offloaded them to some discount store and made a profit, couldn't they?"

"Yeah, most businesses would," agreed Laurie, a new volunteer from Brixton. "That's how Capitalism works. These guys must be a one-off."

"Not necessarily," said Bill, Maya's friend. "It's amazing the kindnesses you see when you've been doing this long enough. It shows you that there are good people in the world, despite what we see out and about round here, and all the bad stuff they show you on the news."

The older man paused in his unloading to stretch his back. Then he leaned in front of Annie and lifted a shiny yellow trainer from the box.

"Good quality these are," he said admiringly. My Peter would've proper fancied a pair o' these when he were a nipper. Linda would never buy the kids branded trainers though. Said there was nothing special about 'em for the money you had to pay. If it was down to me, I might've given in. But she was solid, my Linda. Knew what was important." He held onto the trainer sadly for a moment, most likely thinking of his late wife, before replacing the shoe in the box. Bill was a veteran volunteer. Three years earlier he'd taken early retirement from his job as a train driver after his wife died, and he hadn't known what to do next. Nothing motivated him, he could only think about all the plans he and Linda had made for their old age. One of those plans had been emigrating to France or Spain. Bill thought he might like to do some travelling, but it was hard deciding where to go and he suspected he'd feel lonely without a real purpose. "All the gumption was knocked out of me," he'd said another time in the warehouse (young Annie had just been talking about her depression after her dad died — grief was the motivation for her first trip to Calais too).

Then Bill had watched a thing on the news. A film about refugees drowning in the sea. He'd never really thought about the people in the life jackets before, their faces blurring into each other. Never wondered who they might have been in their former lives.

Losing Linda had brought home how fragile everything was though — how you could so easily lose the lifestyle you'd taken for granted. He said realisation'd bubbled up in him like a volcano. Those faceless people had once felt their worlds to be as normal, as stable as his had been before Linda died. Then something blew their safety apart — could have been war, drought or disease. Or some other threat of violence he couldn't comprehend, he'd lived an unthreatened life after all — always had a steady job, enough to eat, a summer holiday every year and some savings in the bank. Never really into politics, though he'd voted Labour all his life just because.

That night he listened to a right-wing politician speaking about the 'hostile society' they wanted to create to stop people seeking sanctuary in the UK and he was livid. To hear those sneering words set against the film of such desperate people stoked a rage he hadn't realised was there. Bill personally was aware of a young family local to him (the parents were the same age as his kids) who'd fallen into debt because of job loss, got kicked out of the home they'd saved hard to buy and were forced to live in some grotty hostel, relying on handouts.

The young dad fucking hanged himself, said Bill, talking to the other volunteers in the warehouse. *They found him in the park the next morning.* It still made his heart want to burst out of his chest. Found by a dog walker, the lad was. It was all over the local papers. Same age as Bill's son. How fucking more hostile could society get? Annie'd put down the box she

231

was lifting from a pallet that day and thrown her arms around Bill's neck, sobbing noisily.

When it had all calmed down, Bill told them how he'd made the decision there and then to rent his home out and travel to Calais to help in the 'Jungle'. This was before it had been destroyed, cleared out by the authorities. He'd told the others that what he saw during the days of violence and confusion when the camp was burned down shocked him so much, he decided to rent himself an apartment on a more permanent basis (just as he and Linda had once planned) and stay in France. His children were grown up and had moved away — one to Devonshire and one to Australia, and there was nothing to keep him in Newcastle.

Now living on the outskirts of Calais, Bill had set up a charging station in the small garage which came with his apartment, open whenever he was at home, and where he daily left out jugs of water to drink and snacks to eat. Maya frequently directed migrants to Bill's garage to charge their phone and connect to the internet long enough to contact a worried relative somewhere in the world. Bill also provided buckets of water for migrants in the mornings and evenings, along with wash kits he'd persuaded local businesses to donate.

Once he'd even allowed a family with a newborn baby to sleep in his garage overnight, but a neighbour reported him and the police had come by the next morning, hammering on the garage door and insisting the family move on. Then Bill had paid for a B&B for the family until he'd managed to advocate for them, and temporary housing was (reluctantly) provided by the authorities. He was a veteran volunteer now. He always said it was because of that young father who'd hanged himself, he was that desperate. No more and no less desperate than the migrants clutching their babies in those flimsy boats on the sea, really.

"You're one of the best, Bill," Annie replaced the lid on the box of vivid trainers. The box rattled as she slid it up onto

232

a shelf labelled with the correct shoe size.One of the brand tags must have worked its way loose. "They should do a news article about you, they should. That'd cheer everybody up."

"Ah get away with you now," Bill mock-cuffed her with the side of his hand. She shrieked and dodged. Maya had to smile, thinking of how jokey Con's and Lola's relationship had become since she'd been out of the picture. She blinked and turned her face away, concentrating on her own job, tightly stuffing layers of checked sleeping bags onto the warehouse shelves. They all worked quietly for a while longer, and then Bill let out a low gasp, followed by the words, "Oh, my god."

"Didn't think you were religious," quipped Laurie, lifting another stack of shoe boxes onto a shelf high above his head.

"What's the matter, Bill?" Something about his tone had sent a quiver of worry through Maya. "Are you all right?"

"Aye, yeah. It's not me. And it's nothing to joke about, young man!"

"Sorry," Laurie let down his arms, then folded them, probably as startled by Bill's sharpness as she and Annie were. It wasn't like him. They all stared at Bill: hunched, tense.

"What is it?" Annie said at last.

Bill breathed out. His voice was hoarse. "My wedding ring's gone off my finger. I don't know where it can be!" The fingers of his other hand worried at the etched whiteness where the ring must have sat for so long.

"Oh my god," Annie began crawling around on the floor. "What can've happened to it?" Maya moved across and felt along the edge of the shelf where most of the boxes had been stacked. Laurie activated the torch on his phone and aimed it into the now empty cardboard carton the boxes had been lifted out of. Bill's brows knitted together, his brain obviously teeming with possibilities.

"I knew I must've lost weight," Bill muttered, as they continued to search. "And my hands are cold, I could feel the ring loose. I kept meaning to have it altered. What am I going to do? Oh no. Linda would never forgive me!"

Annie pushed herself up from the floor and patted Bill's back. Laurie shone his torchlight to the back of a half-empty shelf.

"I bet it's in one of the boxes," Maya moved along the shelves. "The one Annie had. When you took out the shoe, Bill, and talked about your son. I heard something sliding about when Annie lifted it up there." Her eyes roved the stacks of identical boxes ranged along the shelves. "I've just got this feeling."

Laurie groaned. "D'you mean to say we have to get every one of those boxes down and empty them out? What if you're wrong?"

Bill and Annie turned and stared at her, Bill's eyes brimming with hope. Annie gestured with her palms outstretched at her sides. What?

Maya tipped her head back and gazed at the rows of white boxes with bright yellow stickers on. Now where had Annie been standing when she put it away? Her feet took her forward. Around there. Lucky guess, she hoped. She raised her hand, pointed. Her finger came to rest on a box just above and to the left of her head.

"I reckon this is about where you were standing when you put it away, Annie. Size 42, weren't they? Can you slide that one out, Laurie, without the whole pile coming down？" *Please let it be in there, or at least one of the boxes close to it.* She felt so bad for Bill.

"Good grief," Bill said when he opened the box to find his ring exactly where Maya had predicted it would be. "You're just like my Linda, you are. She could always find anything I'd lost. Just seemed to have a sixth sense about where I might have left things, even when I hadn't got a clue. I'll never be able to thank you enough for what you did there, Maya." He dabbed at his eyes with a handkerchief while Annie rubbed her hand up and down his back.

Maya felt overcome by a sudden rush of emotion, fondness for Bill. She turned and busied herself with the sleeping bags before anyone noticed that she had tears in her eyes as well.

Sometimes I dream
about my mother, my father,
and my three sisters.
I dream about water,
Which is in short supply
in my homeland.

37

Maya

Calais, early October 2019

Maya had spent two hours standing at the back of the hot drinks van handing out plastic cups of coffee, tea and hot chocolate, along with the permitted two biscuits per cup. It had been a busy session at the most crowded site of the five or six the charity visited once or twice a week. There was a chill breeze. She rubbed her hands to soothe the ache in her joints, pausing to admire the plaited bracelet on her wrist, gifted to her by a young Egyptian man who'd spent the afternoon at the sewing table. He'd made at least one gift for each of the volunteers, bedecking Annie from head to toe with a necklace, a bracelet, and an anklet, along with a headband, which she wore across her forehead. Its colours were vivid against her dark hair. He said he wanted to marry Annie when he made it over to the UK. He said Maya could be his mother at the ceremony, since his own mother would be unable to attend. As was happening to Maya often lately, her eyes filled with tears and she had to turn away.

"Are you all right there, Maya?" Marguerite, a youth councillor who spent two weeks out of every three months volunteering in Calais, took her arm and guided her to one side. "I'll finish up here. You take a walk around if you want to, it gets cold standing still." Maya must have been staring into space again. People were starting to notice.

She nodded and blotted the corners of her eyes with a folded tissue, blaming the moisture on the wind in her eyes. She wandered over to the games table where there were several intense games of Connect 4 underway between volunteers and refugees. There were still several men sitting in canvas chairs at the hairdressing station, some standing over others with razor blades held against the teeth of combs, meticulously styling the edges of hair and beards. She could see Laurie mentally counting the number of blades in circulation – each used one would have to be counted back into the plastic box in the pouch at his waist. At her introductory talk in the warehouse, she'd learned that refugees would sometimes ask for blades so they could cut into the top of a lorry and been warned to be meticulous with them when working at the station.

She cowered as a football soared over the top of her head, narrowly missing hitting her. Enthusiastic games wound in and out of the various services the charity provided, and it was a wonder no-one had been injured with a razor blade or a pair of scissors.

"Okay, folks, time to get packed up now." Neil, their team leader, called out. "No more hairdressing clients, please. Finish up."

Maya set to packing canvas chairs back into plastic bins and helping gather boxes of books, games and sewing materials to load into the van.

Stretching her back, she gazed out over the bleak site, watching young individuals and families heading across the scrubland towards a line of trees where their tarps and tents were hidden. Earlier that week there'd been another eviction by the police, and the charity had distributed 300 emergency sleeping bags to the site's residents. Her throat ached. She'd struggled to settle back into the whole routine since returning from Scotland. Her spot on the Calais campsite had been taken by a large, noisy family celebrating an older member's 'big' birthday and she'd retreated to the corner nearest the woods, further away from the shower block.

Later that evening Bill called by and invited her to his apartment for supper. They sat out on his balcony. The sun was setting behind the church opposite.

"You seem down," He regarded her steadily. His eyes were deep, an unusual dark grey. "Are you having second thoughts about coming back here?"

Maya answered too quickly. "No, of course not. I miss my family, that's all." She cast her eyes down at her plate. Picked up her knife and pushed some salad to one side, before selecting a single cherry tomato and popping it into her mouth.

Bill scooped up a forkful of pasta, chewed thoughtfully. "Why didn't you stay in the UK with them then?"

"What?" Maya looked up and met his gaze but couldn't hold it. She glanced to one side and fixed on the curl of steel-grey hair that hung over his forehead instead. "Because there's so much that needs doing here, of course."

"Seriously, Maya." Bill finally stopped staring at her. He speared another forkful of penne and savoured it in his mouth before swallowing and looking at her again. "New volunteers arrive every day. Most only stay from a few days to a couple of weeks. But there are always enough. We don't *need* you here." He tutted at the sound of her shocked gasp. "You know what I mean, you don't have to look at me like that."

Tears stung her eyes, but she blinked them away. Her voice came out smaller than she meant it to. "I know. You're right, of course. I'm not sure what I'm doing here anymore. I just want to feel useful; I suppose."

Bill leaned forward and patted her hand.

"You are useful, of course you are. I didn't mean that you weren't, only that we could manage without you if needs be. And without making you big headed — compliment alert," he waggled his two forefingers in the air in front of his face, "—you have such compassion in you, anyone can see that." He smiled at her. "Marguerite mentioned that you're particularly good with the younger chaps, that they look up to you as a mother figure." He leaned back in his chair again, regarding her from under his bushy eyebrows. After a moment he resumed eating.

"I have sons older than some of them," Maya said. She hesitated. "It's perceptive of you to ask me that question, Bill. Why I don't go home to the UK, I mean. You want the full story?"

Bill cleared the last of the salad from his plate, laid down his fork and nodded, folding his arms.

"As you know, I first came here after I'd been back in England a while when my daughter and I returned home from Greece," Maya laid down her own fork. She wiped her mouth on a corner of the linen napkin Bill had placed by her plate. "I say home, but it didn't feel like that anymore. I couldn't find my place there — at least not in the house my children had grown up in. I was already divorced from their dad. You know I left him to go travelling? Backpacking, I mean. It seems crazy now, a woman of my age ..."

"Stop that," said Bill, jutting his chin at her. "There isn't one person in our situation who hasn't been called crazy by their family or friends at home for the unorthodox choices they've made. Rest assured; I speak from experience."

She could see it in his eyes, hurt, pride as well. She was aware from a previous conversation that his daughter didn't speak to him anymore and his son thought of him as a 'silly old man'. That pull or push of family — it was always there, for everyone it seemed. They were both silent for a while.

"You mentioned the full story," said Bill. He picked up his glass and drank his beer down. Reached for another bottle from the cool box at his side and used a bottle opener in the shape of a black cat. He poured beer into his empty glass, glancing over at Maya's half-full one. "You want another one? No? Very well, I shall drink alone." He took a sip. "What's the full story then, Maya?"

She fiddled with her bunched-up napkin. "I say I left my husband to go backpacking, but it wasn't that simple. My son had gone missing — my youngest son that is. My older son had been out of contact for several years, it was all such a mess." She looked up into Bill's intense gaze. "That's an even longer story, I won't go that far back ..."

"Families," said Bill. "There's always a long story. I won't judge you, Maya."

"I left Con after we were called to identify a body in Australia, which turned out not to be him, but instead our son's friend. It was such a shock." she paused to draw a trembling breath. "The experience threw everything in my life into context. The boy was carrying my son's journal. My Joe's special book, that he'd shown me so many times on our video calls. Until he cut me off."

Thirsty suddenly, she reached for her glass and swallowed the remaining beer in one go. She placed the empty glass on the table. Without saying anything, Bill opened another bottle and refilled it.

"Joe had drawn maps and written entries describing all the places he'd travelled to, from Australia to Iceland, to Denmark and Germany. Then it just stopped. He must have given his journal to the dead boy. Somewhere, my Joe was still alive, and I wanted to find him, Bill. I wanted to find out what made him tick, so I decided to trace his footsteps. I chose to become a vagabond like him. It was the only thing I could think of to do."

She breathed out slowly, not even realising she'd been holding her breath until then. She glanced up at the dying sunset, a blaze of orange outlining the old stone church across the street. After warming up later in the afternoon, a slight chill had crept into the air again.

"The thing is, I found myself, Bill. Probably for the first time in my life I seemed to know who I was. Travelling, mainly on foot, carrying everything I would need on my back. I met so many young people — and some older travellers like myself — who taught me to understand what was of real importance, and I started to 'get' why Joe had severed all contact, and why Jamie had left home so many years before. Con and I had cut off their air supply, you see, tried to force them to be what *we* wanted them to be. I needed to discover that before I could make peace with them again."

She paused for another drink of beer. Bill's face had taken on shadows in the dimming light. But his eyes shone out under his eyebrows, his gaze steady. He was a good listener, she felt compelled to go on.

"More that that though, as the years went on and Con continuously tried to persuade me to return home, I realised that I didn't want to. I was enjoying my freedom too much and I would have felt stifled back in our generous — but oppressive — home in a village where everybody knew everybody else's business. I didn't want to go home."

Bill raised his glass to his lips, drank. Lowered it again. "You were reunited with your sons?"

"Yes, with both. They were living near each other in Berlin. Joe had found Jamie, which made Con and me feel even more guilty for not making more of an effort to find him ourselves, all those years. But I needed to go home before that because my daughter was having a baby, my other daughter that is. Daisy's twin, Lola. She'd been through the whole pregnancy without me, and she resented me for that." Maya rubbed her hands together and drew her cardigan more closely around her, trying to hide the fact she was shaking slightly. "Now my Daisy's had a baby as well," she said. "And I realise I'm missing out on being a grandmother. But I don't feel they need me anymore, Bill. They've got used to being without me."

"Hmm." Bill twisted his wedding ring, a habit she'd

noticed often, especially since its near loss. "So that leaves you where?"

Maya shifted in her seat. A question she'd been asking herself a lot lately. Heat rose into her cheeks. She'd been moaning on to Bill for ages, and this was supposed to be a 'welcome back to France' meal.

"I'm not sure," she unfolded her arms to stack the empty plates. Bill moved her hand away with his own, glancing at her questioningly.

"Go on . . . " he pulled the plates on the table towards him.

"I think I want to go travelling again," she finally confessed. "But in my van this time. It's felt important to do the work I've been doing here, but in the end, it's still staying in one place. I'm becoming stuck again. This isn't what I set out to do. Maybe by travelling some more I'll find the place I'm meant to end up?" Her voice rose at the end of the sentence, like one of those people who spoke as if everything was a question, she thought. As if she needed validation.

Bill half-smiled and nodded to himself. "I hope you don't think I'm speaking out of turn," he said, pushing himself to a standing position. "But I think you'd be doing the right thing in leaving. Seems to me you've got a bit more finding yourself to do yet, Maya. Whereas me, this is where I'm at. Even without the work we're doing, I mean. I've made an offer on this flat, I'm planning to stay here." He carried the stacked plates and dishes to the door into his apartment. "I was never the travelling type, if you know what I mean. But it suits me here, easy to get back to the UK and far enough away from my past life to make a new start."

The orange sky had diffused into semi-darkness. A moth battered itself against the wall light by the open back door. Bill carried the pots into his apartment.

Maya nodded at his shadow as it disappeared inside, feeling an inexplicable sense of loss in her gut.

Chad is in the centre of Africa.
It has five states, and seventeen million people.
From my village, you had to walk one hundred
     kilometres
before you could find a telephone.
I lived with my wife and unborn child,
he's three months now.
He has never seen my face,
nor I his.

38

Maya

Calais, 31ˢᵗ October 2019

Maya returned to bed with her mug of tea. Drawing aside the curtain by her head, she peered out at the grey mizzle and at the quiet campsite. Her van was parked close to the woods, pressing in on this dull and misty morning. It felt like mist inside the van too as her hot tea spread steam on the window. Wiping the glass with a corner of her bedspread, she watched, mesmerised as a broad wraith of flowing white wound its way along the ground from the open field beyond the campsite, creeping towards the forest. There it divided, wrapping itself around the nearest tree trunks, swirling into the darkness under the trees. She shivered, thought of all the small animals that must be in there, feeling the mist's cold fingers punctuating their fur, dragging over their skin.

In other copses and scrabbles of woodland nearby, mist might be creeping under the flaps of tents, settling on babies' eyelashes as they twitched and moaned in fitful sleep. *Oh, their mothers.* Her stomach clenched, a sudden visceral memory of baby Joe in her arms as she watched rain trammelling down the windows in her conservatory at The Cottages, one autumn morning so long ago. Lucid recollections had hit her more and more often recently — her children as babies again — she could feel the heavy warmth of them, their weight in her arms.

She pulled her woolly cardigan more closely around her, sipped the hot tea.

It was the last day of October. Still early, time enough to try and relax, attempt to clear her head of the previous night's tangled dreams — the visceral memories of her own children, her grandchildren too, and of the children and the families and the young men she worked alongside daily. If circumstances had been reversed . . . Sometimes the years of not knowing where Joe was, the constant ache of wondering what had happened to Jamie — it all hit Maya in flashbacks. She might wake up sweating, temporarily forgetting they were both safe, living happy and fulfilled lives in Germany. And the wash of subsequent relief would threaten to drown her. It was all so fragile, she knew that now — all too aware of other mothers across the world, possibly living in situations of terror themselves, hoping and praying their sons were safe.

In the way she had of reading Maya's mood, Alicia stretched at the end of the bed, yawned and nudged up closer to her human companion. She placed her nose on Maya's lap, her eyes, dark-shadowed in the white of her face, holding Maya's.

"I'm fine. Good dog." Maya laced the fingers of her spare hand into Alicia's warm fur, sipping the last of her tea. "Better get up I suppose. Give you a little walk before we set off for the day."

Maya's rubber boots and Alicia's long-toed paws made the only footprints on the grass verges of the campsite that morning. The last few remaining caravan owners had departed as the English half-term had ended a week earlier. The landscape felt eerie, the woods somehow threatening. Silly, but it might have been something to do with the date.

246

Hallowe'en. Her girls had loved dressing up, trick or treating in the village. The route pre-planned and timed so that other mothers with their small children could take their turn visiting the same circle of homes. Joe had hated it, never one for 'surprises', however carefully constructed. Jamie and his teenage friends had caused trouble later in the evening when the little ones had gone to bed. Post-Halloween mornings, toilet roll hanging from hedges and trees of the houses that had a 'No Halloween Callers Please' — everything in Navengore always polite — hung on their door handles or placed in the window. Jamie had never fitted in such an environment.

On the inside of the dunes outside the campsite the dawn mist had dissipated. Alicia ran off after a rabbit and returned, thankfully empty jawed. They tramped along the path and watched the sun fully rise above the swell of the hills. Maya rubbed her hands together as they made their way back down the track to the campsite. It would be time to get out her woolly gloves soon.

After a breakfast of two eggs, scrambled, and the slightly stale end of a baguette, Maya washed her plate, cutlery and tea mug in the van's tiny sink, sparing as ever with the water. She dried the pots and replaced them in the cupboard above the sink.

"Almost time to go, Alicia." It was cold enough (no danger of Alicia overheating) to leave the dog in the van while she worked in the warehouse, though she had occasionally taken her out on a distribution run.

"Why you have dog for pet?" A young Eritrean man named Kemal, having waited patiently in line for the small package of supplies she eventually handed him, once asked her. "What is point of that? Dogs for guarding, for hunting yes. But pet, what the point?" He edged back from Alicia's sniffing nose, brushing a speck of nothing from the hem of his coat with his right hand. Maya recognised the almost new blue thigh-length coat with a diagonal white stripe from the warehouse the week before. Astonishing that he'd managed to keep it so clean. He cradled the package in his right arm, high above reach of the dog's nose.

"She's my friend," Maya tried to explain. "My companion. She comforts me, keeps me warm."

"Dog keep you warm? Hah. You no have husband?" Maya noticed the twitch at the corner of Kemal's mouth. It was the second time she'd met him. He assessed her reaction with his flickering glance, meanwhile continuing to dodge the curious dog. He was light on his feet, the soles of his black trainers encrusted in mud. She pictured him kicking a ball with mates on the playing field at Navengore, judged him to be around eighteen — the age Jamie was when he left home for good. Catching his eye at last Maya read there a combination of watchfulness and a desire for fun. She laughed.

"You are being cheeky, Kemal. I don't need a husband, thanks. My dog keeps me quite warm enough. Now off you go and get yourself something to eat."

Before Samos, before Calais, she'd imagined only misery in the camps, thought there would be an 'every man for himself' attitude. Instead, she usually encountered warmth and generosity amongst the refugees. At the end of distribution, they would offer to share their rations. "Come eat with us, Madam. I make you my special soup."

Once, on a day she'd left Alicia in the van, she'd accepted an invitation from Amir, one of four Somalian youths who'd been in the queue together. She'd had to gain special permission from her team leader. Amir and his friends inevitably reminded her of her sons, also of the youngsters she'd lived with in the Catalonian community the summer before she found her own sons again. She squatted on an upturned drum at the entrance to a four-man tent that had seen better days, hidden in woodland. "You must sit there inside, Madam," Amir, who appeared to be the oldest, told her. When she protested, he insisted, dragging the stool inside the tent's flaps for her. He began cooking on a battered stove fed with damp sticks. She worried her extra portion would cause them to go hungry for longer before the next distribution. She saw how the boys each contributed a handful of lentils to the pot. One shook in some spices, another salt. They chatted with her in halting English about football (about which Maya knew precisely nothing — Jamie had never wanted her to watch him, at least had pretended he didn't, and neither Joe or the girls had been interested) and one of the youths picked out an impressive but limited arrangement of notes on a scratched-bodied guitar. The guitar had only three strings, she noticed.

Around her the late afternoon hummed with voices in different languages from other members of the temporary camp. Before long it would be raided by the French authorities, and the refugees would muster what items they could snatch up before dispersing into the woodland, only to gather again once the police had gone, after slashing their tents and confiscating clothes and possessions. Other faint music played in the background. Through the unzipped doorway of the tent, she caught an intermittent medley of movement through the undergrowth nearby. Smells, of cooking and of fouler things, drifted on the air. She felt lulled by the day's work and by the young men's animated conversation, relapsed into their own language now.

When she dipped a spoon into her portion of soup — from a wide-necked olive jar, how clean could the water have been in which they'd washed it? She dared not examine the receptacle too closely — the taste sang in her mouth. Cumin, she guessed. And perhaps cloves.

"Delicious. Thank you for a lovely evening," she smiled as she got up to leave, her behind numbed by the improvised stool. "I must cook for you boys some time." She would bring them something she'd prepare in her van, which they could reheat. But then again, she was aware that after she'd gone, Amir and the other young men were likely to pack up their possessions anyway and head off to a lorry park or a beach in hopes of making a crossing to England that night.

Maya was straining to swivel the stiff driver's seat back into position facing the wheel when Alicia let out a startled 'woof'. The dog turned suddenly on the passenger seat and pressed her nose to the window. She drew in a few deep breaths and proceeded to utter a high-pitched whistle, her ears shooting up.

"What is it, Alicia?" Maya straightened her back. "Have you seen a rabbit or something?" Then she, too, caught a flash of orange as a shape passed by the window; heard the weighted press of feet on grass, then crunching on the gravel outside the van. And something else, a child's voice, that of a toddler, with a note she recognised.

A pain, not quite a pain, more a sudden emptying and filling feeling in her chest. A decisive knock on the van's door.

"Daisy!" Maya's voice was hoarse as she pushed open the sliding door. Her heart beat out of rhythm. It really was Daisy, with Avelie strapped to her hip and a rucksack on her back. Her darling girl, though with shorn hair in place of Daisy's customary ponytail. Shorn hair at the sides and a pink blaze on the top that caused Maya to blink hard. Was this really happening — was it really her daughter standing there? Daisy-not-Daisy fumbled with a tied strap at her waist and released the toddler from her bindings, lifting the woollen-clad child up to her chest, then outwards towards Maya.

"Here you are, Mum," Daisy laughed, her voice sounding to Maya like bubbles breaking the surface of water. "Have an Avelie, while I get this thing off my back. Feels like it's filled with stones. Go to Gramma, baby. Remember your gramma? She took you paddling in the sea. Here you are, Mum," she had to repeat; the child held in midair.

Dazed, Maya reached out for the precious child. Silken black hair under her lips. Soft, warm body-filled wool in her arms. Avelie lifted her head and met Maya's besotted gaze, the child's pursed mouth falling open. A bubble appeared on her lower lip, reminding Maya of her first glimpses of her as a newborn. Of course, Avalie *was* still so new. *When I was one, I had just begun.*

"Gramma," she said, the baby. "Gramma, down." But Maya only squeezed her granddaughter tighter.

My country is at war,
our president was killed.
My job was terminated,
and I volunteered with the Red Cross.
We looked after the military
and we looked after the rebels.
Everybody, said the doctor I worked with,
is a human being.

39

Maya

Calais, 31st October 2019

Maya lowered Avelie onto the bench seat where she flapped her hands and patted Alicia with gusto. The dog blinked and lowered her head in submission. Maya turned back to the doorway and helped Daisy up into the van, wrenching the door closed behind her with her other hand. She drew Daisy into her arms. Daisy was taller than her, Maya's face at her daughter's neck, above the collar of her jumper and below the fuzz of her cropped hair. She breathed in Daisy's scent — faint sweat and the remaining smell of the soap she must have used the last time she had a chance to wash — and clung on hard.

Daisy flinched slightly. "Okay, Mum," extricating herself, she stepped back within the confines of the small space and slid the rucksack off her back, leaving it against the door. They were still only inches apart. "Let me look at you. How are you doing?"

"Daisy," Maya found it difficult to speak. "I'm fine. But you, you and Avelie. What are you doing here? I only spoke to you on WhatsApp two days ago, you never said a thing about coming."

She sat down heavily next to her granddaughter. Avelie laughed and knelt up beside her, patted her face. "Gramma?" She climbed into Maya's lap and lay her head on her chest.

Maya nuzzled her face into Avalie's hair. "Hey, sweetheart."

Daisy shuffled towards the passenger seat and fitted herself into it. Her boots stuck out into the dining space between them. Maya tucked hers in against the base of the bench seat. *Where will they both sleep?* Her thoughts swirled. *It was cramped enough when it was just me and Daisy (and the dog). Now there's Avalie as well. There's no room to move!*

"I just got this urge to come. I don't know what hit me really, I just felt so restless." Daisy busied herself unthreading the straps of the baby carrier and sliding them off her shoulders. She unwound the rest of it from her waist, folded the corduroy as small as she could on her lap, glancing up at Maya from under her eyelashes. "I needed to be here. In case, you know, he comes. Don't worry, I can help. I won't mess it up this time, I promise."

Maya felt the weight of Avalie sinking against her, the child was falling asleep. Another weight, emotional, descended on her too. *I'd made up my mind to leave.*

"Daisy," she said helplessly. "It's been two years, more than. What makes you think he'll arrive here now?"

"I don't know," Daisy sounded so miserable. Maya hadn't realised it had been eating into her all this time. "Why not? There could be any reason it's taken so long. There could have been trouble along the way — he could have stopped off to work somewhere for a while, earn some money before deciding to come here . . . " she trailed off, met Maya's eyes.

He could have got hurt, beaten up so badly at a border that he couldn't go on. He could have been sent back to Greece. He could be in prison. Maya didn't say it. Instead, she tightened her arms around Avalie. Would she ever know her father?

"Well, you never know," she said, aiming to lighten the mood. "Perhaps he will turn up here. Meanwhile, what am I going to do with the two of you?" She reached over and stroked her daughter's leg.

"Mum," Daisy said. "Stop that, I'm not a dog." A ghost of a smile at the corners of her mouth. A mouth that used to be so close to smiling all the time and now tended to turn down slightly.

"Sorry love. I'm so used to Alicia I think everyone needs a good stroke sometimes." She leaned forward and launched herself into a standing position, the sleeping Avalie in her arms. "Let me at least put this one down for a nap on the bed, she must be exhausted. Then we can have a cup of tea and a proper chat, work out what we're going to do. Oh, and I need to make a phone call." *Bill will be wondering where I've got to, I was supposed to be on distribution this afternoon.* She edged into the gap between the bathroom and the kitchen sink, angling Avalie carefully so as not to bump her head or knock her small, booted feet on the units.

"Here you go, darling." Avalie meowed softly like a kitten as she set her down and nestled herself into the quilt. Maya left her uncovered because she was wearing so many layers, but she unzipped and gently slid those tiny boots off her feet. She stayed there gazing down at her for a moment, brushing sweat-stuck hair from the baby's flushed cheeks.

"Do you think I should take her coat off?" She turned to glance back at Daisy. "I don't want her to overheat."

"Not much chance of that, Mum," Daisy was pulling the edges of her own knitted jacket together, then folding them across herself. "It's cold in here. I suppose Avalie and I need to get used to it, hey?"

"You're both planning to stay in the van with me then?" She couldn't help the note of anxiety — petulance, Daisy might read it as — that crept into her voice. Damn, she thought. Daisy was already bristling, if she was a dog her hackles would be rising. Alicia sensed it, getting up from the floor and pushing her nose into Daisy's hands. Daisy stroked her absently.

"Oh, we won't trouble you if you don't want us," she glanced up at Maya, tears brimming in her eyes, which were dark-shadowed. "I thought you'd be pleased to see us. You said in the summer you were sad at missing out on your grandchildren's lives." She bit her lip, lowered her gaze to the dog's and held it there. The dog stared steadily back at her.

Maya assessed her. The girl must be exhausted. She put the kettle on, then slotted herself back into the bench seat in front of Daisy.

"I do want you, love. I've missed you terribly since I came back to France, you know I have. I'm just worried about you that's all. This seems so sudden. And what about your nursery? I thought you were happy running it."

"I was, sort of anyway," Daisy sniffed, fished up her sleeve for a hanky. Maya felt a buzz of warmth, it was one of a set she'd sewn for Daisy last Christmas on her old sewing machine. She'd managed to embroider daisies in the corner — on the machine. Lola's set was decorated with three teardrops. As a teenager Lola had adopted these as her symbol, having pointed out the meaning of her name was 'sorrow'. Maya had been shocked when she found out — she and Con had chosen the name after the song by The Kinks and never investigated its actual meaning. She was glad Daisy had chosen a meaningful name for her Avelie: it was Persian for 'strong', 'a visionary'.

"But Lola can manage it fine on her own," Daisy continued. "She's better at the business side of it than me. And she doesn't want to leave Navengore, she's happy there. I'd never really intended to go back and live at home again Mum, you know that."

"Yes, but then you had Avalie. Babies change your plans, darling girl." The kettle whistled, and Maya rose to hush it

256

before it disturbed her sleeping granddaughter. "I had all sorts of ideas about what I would do with my life, but in the end, I put them aside because of you children ..." She stopped and cleared her throat. Pouring water over the teabags in two mugs she turned to face Daisy's accusing eyes, her arms crossed tightly.

"Bloody hell, I can't believe I just said that. Sorry, darling girl. It was an absolute choice I made, Daisy. I always wanted to have children; you know that. There's nothing I would have rather done." She finished making the tea and handed a mug to Daisy, who reluctantly unfolded her arms. Maya held her own mug over to one side as she slid back onto the bench seat. "Here, I'll pull the table back out." She'd pressed it into its folded position against the wall in preparation for driving, immediately before Daisy arrived.

With the two mugs on the table between them she leaned forward and examined Daisy's face more thoroughly. "You haven't been sleeping, have you?" Daisy shook her head.

"Is it Avalie, does she wake you up at night?"

"No, she sleeps like a log, you'll be pleased to know." Daisy took a noisy sip of tea, then replaced the mug on the table. "I've been having dreams if you want to know. Dreams about her father drowning in the sea. I wake up in a sweat, struggling to breathe. I thought it might help if I started doing this kind of work again, help to focus my mind, think about others for a change. Everything's so *nice* in Navengore, if you know what I mean? I have to be so polite all the time and no one talks about anything that really means anything. You do know what I mean, don't you Mum?"

Maya felt a laugh like a volcano in her chest. The tea in her mug started sloshing from side to side as the laugh broke out. She replaced the mug on the table before it spilt all over, then let go of the laughter completely. Soon Daisy was laughing too.

"Oh yes," said Maya when she'd calmed down. "I do know what you mean. Everything is so *nice* in Navengore."

One day a general came to the Red Cross.
He asked why we were treating the rebels
and the doctor said
'Everyone is a human being.'
The general shot the doctor dead
in front of us, and we volunteers were arrested
for protesting.

40

Maya

Calais, 1st November 2019

She could hear Avalie snuffling in the early hours of the morning, while she, Maya, lay awake worrying. What if the child got a cold, pneumonia even? It would be impossible to cope in the confines of the small van. She hadn't realised until the moment of waking but she was angry at Daisy for bringing her one-year-old-daughter into this unforgiving environment.

Maya and Daisy had argued about it the previous night, quietly. They were making up Daisy's bed with Maya's one spare set of bedding, and the memory foam topper she'd had under her own sheet. Now she'd have to put up with the uncomfortable ridge in the middle where her mattress folded back for lifting the bed-base.

Daisy disagreed with Maya that it was wrong to bring Avalie. She said she wanted the child to one day understand the things her father had gone through, and she didn't think

Avalie ever would without seeing the conditions refugees were forced to live in.

"I don't want to bring her up on a diet of princesses and unicorns, Mum," Daisy shook out a pillowcase before stuffing the corners of Maya's spare pillow into it. The heating in the van rumbled. "It's hard enough for her being a girl in this life as it is—" *what the hell had this apparent copy of her daughter with a completely different outlook from before done with the real Daisy?* Maya struggled to contain a splutter of nervous laughter. Daisy gave her a hard stare. "—Avalie needs to be prepared, to understand real life. If I never ..." Daisy laid the pillow down at the head of the narrow bed and smoothed the pillowcase repeatedly. She paused, biting her lip. "Avalie might one day have to take up the search for her father. I'm determined she's going to know him, Mum."

"I can understand how you feel, love," Maya ran her hand along the side of the duvet cover to make sure the edge of the quilt met up with the seam. "It just seems an odd time of year to come out and start the search." She stopped herself just in time from adding *but don't mind me, you must know what you're doing,* in the way her own mother would have done. And finishing off with a particular sniff that meant *you obviously don't.* She pressed her lips together, folded a red blanket she usually kept in the cupboard with the towels, and laid it over the end of the bed. In the continuing silence — apart from Avalie's noisy breathing at the front of the van — Maya turned to fill the kettle at the sink. They'd need hot water bottles tonight, and a soothing drink of camomile tea before bed.

"I felt as if I was going to burst," Daisy said, breaking the moment of quiet. She sat down on the grey quilt, pulling Maya's neatly folded blanket towards her, and reached for her daughter on the passenger seat. Avalie had been chewing absently on the foot of a small floppy rag doll Maya had made for her the previous Christmas. Dressed in a warm pair of footed pyjamas and a woollen cardigan, she now fussed and pulled at Daisy's jumper, asking for 'mulk'. Daisy lifted her jumper and tucked the toddler's body in against her stomach, drawing her knees up into a cross-legged position. "Every day was the same. And I couldn't stop thinking about Umid. I need to find him, Mum, and even if I don't find him here at least there'll be some chance I might meet someone who knows him. There's a tiny chance isn't there? I need to believe that, at least."

Maya poured hot water over camomile tea in a glass pot. *It still doesn't seem right to bring your innocent daughter along on your mission, even if it is Avalie's father you're seeking.* But she didn't feel the same confidence in her motherly opinion as she had once. Look where it had got her, two lost sons and a rejection from Lola at Elijah's birth. She chose her words carefully.

"There's always a chance, love. But it won't do to set your heart on it. It's tough here now winter's coming, and you need to be here because you believe in what we're doing, not only because you're desperate to find someone."

"Mum! God. How selfish do you think I am?" The sharpness of Daisy's tone made Avalie jerk her head back from her mother's breast and stare at her, milk dribbling from the corner of her mouth. The toddler's lower lip trembled. Despite her brown eyes and almost-black hair, the child reminded Maya so much of Daisy at the same age a pain of nostalgia shot through her.

An evening not long after her young family had moved into their new home in Navengore, leaving London and a recent upset behind. Con had finally got Jamie settled in bed and had come down and handed Maya a glass of wine where she was stranded with the twins on the L-shaped brown cord sofa they'd bought for their enormous new living room. The twins still had a feed before bed, though not long after the move they stopped breastfeeding altogether. Maya remembered Daisy jerking away from the breast at her father's entrance, the way Avalie had just done. Remembered gazing down at the curve of her daughter's cheek, her sleepy, surprised eyes, her rose-coloured, half-open mouth; feeling the exact same love and an emotional sense of her own power: to be the grower and nurturer of this exquisite being, that Daisy's gaze on Avalie's face expressed now.

Maya touched her eyes with the corner of the towel hung on the outside of the bathroom door before lifting the teapot and mugs to the outer edge of the small worktop, where she'd be able to reach for them from the van's passenger seat. She was an onlooker now, Daisy and Avalie's world an exclusive entity. Maya couldn't go inside; she could only attempt to be a haven at its outskirts.

"I didn't come just for that," Daisy shuffled her now-sleeping daughter on one arm while she pulled down her jumper, completely unaware of her mother's whirling mental adjustments to her sense of place in her family. "You know I wouldn't do that. I enjoyed the NGO work in Greece, and I never completed the timescale I set myself. I want to do it better this time. I promise I will."

But you still have Avalie to think of. Maya didn't say anything though, as she squeezed herself between Daisy's makeshift bed and the fridge. Instead, she nodded with apparent understanding.

Alicia shuffled up the bed on her belly and licked Maya's chin. Maya hadn't realised a leftover tear from a dream about her children being young again had trickled slowly down her face. She wiped the rest of it away with the edge of her duvet. The dog panted hot breath on her face.

"Shhh," she put a finger to her lips, then wafted her hand under her nose. *Dog breath*! Alicia seemed to wink at her. Maya's hand, stroking the dog's ruff, was cold. She pushed back the quilt and knelt upright to reach the heating dial. She wouldn't have bothered for herself but with Avalie here … she pulled the quilt back over her legs and body. The heating kicked in with a huff of warm air, and set up a steady rhythm, a continuous out-blown note. Maya heard Daisy's breathing falter for half a second, then resume with a rumbling, not quite snore. Avalie coughed in her sleep, and another wave of concern swept over Maya. *Please don't let her become ill.* Maya wondered if the child was up to date with her vaccinations. Daisy had hesitated over the one she'd been due at a year old, (something she'd read from a group that purported to have alternative information than the mainstream) then 'given in' as she put it, under pressure from Lola. Daisy wouldn't have brought the child into her current environment without every possible protection, would she? Avalie coughed again, then seemed to settle with a contented *mmm-mmm* noise. Though Maya couldn't see her daughter and granddaughter from her bed, the awareness of their presence was overwhelming.

She pushed aside the curtain. It was just getting light. "Do you think it would wake them if I put the kettle on?" Alicia cocked her head and shrugged, or so Maya read it. I've been alone with this dog too long, she thought, unfolding her creaking knees from the quilt and stiffly lowering her feet to the floor where she slid them into her slippers. With the kettle on, she took some time to study her daughter and granddaughter tucked up tightly together in the put-down bed. Avalie's arm was flung over Daisy's neck. Maya wondered how her daughter could sleep like that, she'd always found it difficult to sleep with her own babies, too aware of their every move. Con would never allow their little ones to stay in the bed with them anyway.

"Hey, you're awake," she whispered to Avalie, who stared unblinkingly at her. Maya moved forward a step or two, her finger on her lip again. Daisy appeared so vulnerable asleep, her cropped hair exposing her neck. They'd have to rig up a curtain to give her a sense of privacy.

Avalie shuffled onto her bottom and sat back, holding up her arms to Maya. "Gramma," she coughed again, but only slightly. "Carry'oo."

"I'll carry you, darling." Suddenly it meant everything that her daughter and granddaughter were here, they'd manage somehow. What a privilege to wake up to this precious face every morning. She reached over so that Avalie could climb into her arms, moulding her warm, pyjama-clad body against Maya's as if it were they two who belonged together.

The kettle panted towards its warning shriek. With the child nestled on her hip, Maya turned off the gas and poured water over her morning teabag.

"You can come into the big bed with your gramma and Alicia," Maya told the toddler. "How about that. Let your mum sleep on a bit, eh?"

I spent months in prison
then I fell ill and was taken to hospital.
I saw a chance and fled.
I left at three am, walked fifteen hours until I
    reached a telephone.
I managed to get a message to my wife,
she sent me the money
that saved my life.

41

Maya

Calais, late November 2019

Maya surreptitiously rubbed her aching hands in the guise of folding and refolding a tea towel, not wanting Daisy to see she was struggling. Nevertheless, a shock of pain took her by surprise, and she had to suppress a yelp. Recovering, she threaded the folded gingham cloth through the bar fastened narrowly beneath the cupboard over the sink and tugged the ends even. She remained there a moment, practising calm breathing. Feeling something bump against her, she glanced down into the wide dark eyes of twenty-month-old Avelie, tugging her jeans' leg.

"Gramma, *me* dwess."

"Oh, you dressed yourself, sweetheart," Maya said. "Aren't you clever? And you look so pretty."

"Tell her she looks strong and ready for anything, Mum." Daisy's voice came from behind the half-open curtain now erected next to hers and Avalie's bed. "Or say something like, 'those red dungarees suit your shiny dark hair'. Don't just tell her she's pretty, that's fatuous."

"Oops," said Maya. "Sorry." She reached down to pull Avalie up into her arms and settled the child on her hip. Grimaced into the tiny mirror next to the sink. Avalie's face against hers, she felt the bubble of Avalie's laugh vibrate before it burst out of her perfect bow lips. "I keep forgetting. It's just that she is — so pretty I mean. Aren't you, pet?"

Hearing Daisy's exasperated groan and feeling the van rock as Daisy stood up and pulled the curtain fully back to reveal herself in the narrow walk-through space, Maya had to hide a smile. Daisy had changed so much in the past years, not least in a visual sense. Gone were the plump cheeks and long hair, the floaty hippy dresses on a girl who'd done her best not to offend anyone. Anything for a quiet life, had been Daisy's motto in the past. Now, at twenty-nine, the shaved sides of her head set off the bright pink of her remaining tousled hair. Maya couldn't get used to her new lean appearance, her skin tanned and weatherbeaten. In place of her former floaty dresses and crotchet cardigans, Daisy's customary uniform here in Calais was jeans or dungarees, and a thick flannel shirt over a thermal vest and a long sleeve cotton tunic, topped off with an oversized jumper. She wore thick wool fingerless gloves, and thick woollen socks inside her Doc Martin boots. Sorrow and motherhood had worn her. She looked like she acted: tough, capable, no nonsense.

To be fair, Maya dressed in much the same way, and little Avalie's wardrobe consisted of similar clothing. Living in a van on a campsite in Northern France, in winter, it was all about keeping warm. Nights were the coldest, but Daisy and Avalie had each other to keep warm against in their snug bed, and Maya of course had her beloved dog.

"You've gone soft in your old age," Daisy grumbled as she sat on the edge of her bed again and pulled on her socks. "Pretty this and pretty that." She glanced up at her mother and Maya felt a tug in her stomach at the shadows that lingered constantly in the backs of Daisy's eyes, even when she was laughing. Maya's protective instincts threatened to overwhelm her sometimes. Daisy may be a grown woman and a mother in her own right, but she would always be Maya's baby. She pulled herself together though, before Daisy noticed and gave her a stern lecture for dwelling on things. These days it sometimes felt like Maya was the daughter and Daisy the mother.

"And don't think I didn't see you rubbing at your hands. The arthritis is playing up again, isn't it?" Daisy said softly. "You can't do a good job with other people if you're in pain yourself, Mum. Have you taken your painkillers?"

"I was just about to," Maya lied. She'd been thinking about taking her latest prescription to work with her, in case anyone needed it more than her. But Daisy was right, it didn't do to act like a martyr, she'd be neither use nor ornament to anyone. For the zillionth time she cursed the arthritis gene she seemed, after all, to have inherited; recalled again the crippled hands and fingers of her own mother and grandmother, which she'd had reason to hope she'd avoided until the past couple of years. But no.

"Here you go poppet," wincing, she lowered Avalie onto the bed next to the snoozing dog. Alicia opened an eye and her tail thumped faintly on the bed as Avalie stroked her and threw herself down alongside the dog, making exaggerated kissing noises. "Wuv'oo!"

Maya pushed two pills from the blister packet and swallowed them with water. "There we go, that'll do the trick. Anyway love, we'd best get going." No answer from Daisy, who had her back to her and was rifling through a pile of divested nightwear, trying to bring some order to the tiny space. "Do you want me to walk Avalie over to day care for you, love?" When Daisy still didn't answer, Maya tried again. "Alicia could come too and have a final wee before we leave her locked up in the van for most of the day."

Daisy sniffed hard and cleared her throat. "If you don't

mind, Mum. I'll finish tidying up here while you're gone, turn the front seats around and all that." She sat back on her bed, part of which would soon become the driver's seat again. Despite Maya's protests Daisy refused to take the double bed at the back for herself and Avalie.

Daisy had a defeated demeanour. These sudden plunges in mood seemed to come out of the blue. "Come here Avie, give Mama a kiss and I'll see you later, okay? Love you so much, baby."

Maya swallowed hard, watching the little girl fold herself into her mother's body. She couldn't help thinking of her other grandchildren. Jamie and Leijla were expecting their third child any time soon —another boy. I must visit them in the new year, Maya thought. If I go and Daisy wants to stay here, she'll have to rent a van of her own.

"Come on then poppet." She shrugged her arms into her thick winter coat (it barely fastened over her bulky jumper) and lifted Avalie's down jacket from the pegs by the door, helping the little girl on with it. She tried to hide how much her fingers hurt as she struggled with the zip.

"B'bye, Mama," Avalie pushed her feet into her bright red wellington boots as Maya held them steady for her.

"See you later baby. Love you so much," Daisy blew her daughter a kiss.

Maya paused to watch Daisy roll the cushion loaded with quilts and blankets back on itself from the foot of her bed, fold back the hinged wooden base and struggle to wield the heavy front seat round into its driving position.

We can't go on like this. It was a repeated refrain in Maya's head, even though Daisy insisted they were managing fine. *Daisy should have her own van. Avalie needs more space to play.* Everything felt fragile now, and she was constantly torn between her desire to leave, resume travelling again, and the need to remain with her daughter and granddaughter.

The pain Maya was suffering due to the cold didn't help. She took a deep breath, glancing at Daisy a final time.

"Come on then, Chickadee." She reached for the child's hand.

"Yay!" Avalie loved daycare, which thankfully was being provided free by a local childminder who wanted to assist in whatever way she could. Maya helped her granddaughter down the step. The dog bounced joyfully out into the biting cold, and Avalie squealed, laughing at hers and the dog's breath fanning out onto the air in front of her. They crossed the camping field, Avalie stamping footprints in the dew. She slipped over once, her hand pulling out of Maya's. Maya cried out, her mind flashing back to a dream she'd had, in which Avalie had been taken from her. Shaking slightly, she resettled her granddaughter back on her feet, brushing her coat and dungarees down and making sure she was steady again.

"Sk-sk-, Gramma," Avalie's lower lip trembled. She was trying to say 'skid', a word Maya had taught her when she herself had skidded on frosty grass the day before. Avalie's eyes were bright with the threat of tears.

"You did, petal, but you're all right, aren't you?" Maya bent awkwardly and kissed the child's rosy cheek.

"Ya," replied Avalie, bravely. She set off again with a clumsy attempt at skipping, pulling Maya along with her. The dog barked, circling them.

"You are a brave girl!" Daisy would approve of that, Maya thought, as they progressed across the site towards a row of lodges along the road at the bottom. The first belonged to the campsite owner and the one separated from it by a wide strip of garden was the owner's daughter-in-law's, the childcare provider.

"Ya," Avalie blew breath out into the cold morning. She roared. "Disaur!"

"Yes, you are. The youngest, sweetest dinosaur around. And the toughest," Maya remembered to add.

She held her granddaughter's hand tighter. She remembered she'd had that dream — the one about losing

Avalie — after hearing a story from a refugee mother who'd been separated from her child. In a writhing mass of people at a border fence, someone took the child out of her arms, trying to help, and suddenly the baby had disappeared from her view. Thankfully she had eventually been reunited with her child, but there were plenty of others who hadn't.

Maya tried not to think about the worse things when she was with Avelie. In the first days after Daisy had arrived in Calais, she'd brought the toddler in to work with her, strapped to her back, wearing an oversize charity vest over both of them. On their first distribution, young refugee men crowded around, wanting to touch Avalie's cheek, offering her treats from the packages they'd received after their long wait in line. Their faces had lit up with smiles, those who could speak English mentioned their baby sisters and nieces. Or their daughters. Many of the men were married and had not seen their children for a long time. One or two took out their phones and showed Daisy photographs of their family members.

Daisy smiled and nodded at their photos, then with a look of determination took out her own phone. Scrolling through, she showed them photos in her turn, redownloaded from the cloud as soon as she'd bought her new phone in Serbia, she told Maya later. Once she'd confessed to the pregnancy, she hadn't been able to stop talking about her baby's father. Maya hadn't realised how many photos of Umid Daisy had. Her insides churned. The relationship had been much more serious than she'd realised.

"Have you seen him?"

Maya's heart felt close to breaking when she saw the disappointment on Daisy's face each time, as they shook their heads. Avalie picked up on her mother's sadness too, leaning to pat the side of Daisy's face and frowning at the damp on her fingers when she pulled them away.

271

Avelie trotted into the childminder's warm kitchen, already chatting to the other two children in there and laughing at the big, fluffy cat as it chased a cotton ball along the corridor. Maya blew Avalie a kiss and thanked the young woman, before turning back out into the cold morning. She felt a weight in her chest at the thought of the day's work ahead. It took her a moment to acknowledge the feeling as dread. What's wrong with me? She thought. I know the work I'm doing is meaningful, why is it that I only want to escape?

Bill had waylaid her in the warehouse the other day.

"Maya," he'd laid a hand on her arm. "Much as I love your company and will miss you if you leave, I really think it's time for you to take a break. I'm concerned about you. You were planning to leave more than a month ago, remember?"

Maya had shuffled her feet. "I know but, now Daisy's arrived . . . "

"Maya, it's your own health and wellbeing you need to take care of. What use will you be to your family or any of the service users here if it all becomes too much for you?"

"I know you're right," Maya said. "I just need to work out how to tell Daisy."

She stopped off at the toilet block on her way back to the van. *Just another few minutes to myself.* The strange weight she was experiencing now seemed to have settled on her shoulders and felt as if it was pressing her down into the ground. *What's wrong with me?*

She used the toilet; grateful she wouldn't have to manually sluice away the waste later. There was so much work to do now Daisy was using the van toilet at night as well as Maya, it required emptying more often. Straightening wearily, she pulled up her layers of clothes and flushed. When she moved over to the sinks to wash her hands her footsteps were slow, dragging. She soaped her hands liberally, anticipating the pleasure of hot water, a luxury of limited supply in the van. She raised her face to the mirror as she soaped her hands, noticing the deep, dark grooves below her eyes; no wonder Bill had seemed concerned about her. Those same eyes stung as she continued to stare at her reflection. I'm not doing well, she finally accepted. And again, *I can't carry on like this indefinitely.*

Unable to look at herself any longer, she lowered her gaze to the sink. Nudged the tap with her elbow and waited for the expected relief of the hot water. Nothing, no water at all. *Come on.* With her soapy hand, she wrenched the tap more fully into the open position. Still nothing. *Damn.* With tears of disappointment pricking her eyes, she turned on the cold, bracing herself for the shock on her painful knuckles. But no water came out of that tap, either. She tried the next sink. Nothing. Then, without warning, her breath caught in her throat, and she couldn't release it. Her hands tingled and her chest tightened to the point of pain. Still, she didn't breathe. *Am I having a heart attack?* She leaned on the sink with her soapy hands and fought panic. *Stop it, Maya, what if someone comes in?* and she realised it couldn't be too serious if she was thinking that.

Slowly, she regained her breath. Straightened her back and forced herself to meet her own eyes in the mirror again. *You're stronger than this, Maya.* But she wasn't. With the release of breath tears burst from her eyes at an alarming rate, soaking her cheeks and dripping into the neckline of her winter coat. And she couldn't wipe her eyes with her hands because they were all soapy! Breath tore out of her in rasps, she hunched over and sank to the floor beneath the sinks, no longer caring if anyone should come in and find her, it didn't matter.

"Mum, Mum. What's the matter?" Daisy's voice filtered through the fog surrounding Maya. "What are you doing on the floor? Come on, get up, you'll freeze down there."

Daisy was pulling on her arm. Maya became aware of the sound of gushing water. Allowing Daisy to pull her to her feet, she saw that two of the sinks were spluttering water from both taps.

"Why are all the taps on?" Daisy reached over to turn them off.

"No, don't." with her teeth chattering, Maya plunged her hands under a hot tap, so hot it burned, but she held her hands there. Steam obliterated most of her reflection in the mirror, and she saw herself as a ghost. That was how she felt.

"Mum, that's really hot, you'll scald yourself, stop it." Daisy tried to drag her hands away, but she resisted. "You're shivering, what's happened, tell me!"

Maya's body rattled with the shudders ripping through her. She tried to grit her teeth but couldn't seem to hold her jaw in place. She whipped her hands out from under the scalding water.

"I've had enough, Daisy," she managed to articulate between ragged breaths. "I'm tired, and I want to go home. I'm sorry, I know you want to stay, but I can't anymore."

Even as she spoke the words, she was wondering where home was. She'd have to do something about that.

Daisy stared at her mother, her face crumpling. "Mum, you should have said. I didn't realise you felt this way. We can go home, of course we can. We'll go home for Christmas. You can stay with Lola and me, and we'll look after you, I promise. You can spend a cosy time with Avalie and Elijah, think how nice that will be." Daisy rubbed her hands up and down Maya's arms as she spoke, and Maya began to feel warmth returning to her body while her hot hands dripped onto the floor. "I'm so sorry, Mum," Daisy said. "I was selfish, and I didn't realise how difficult things were for you. We'll go back to Navengore, where everything's 'nice', yeah?" She continued rubbing Maya's arms. "Come on, surely that deserves a little smile?"

Maya's shivers started to subside. For Daisy's sake, she forced the corners of her mouth to upturn so it looked as though she was smiling. But inside, she felt afraid. In all the years she'd been travelling, she hadn't lost control of herself like that. The last time she remembered feeling in any way similar was back in Navengore when she'd received a phone call from an Australian police officer, informing her that her son might be dead. In her imagination now, she'd been given a similar piece of information, only it was the loss of herself she was being asked to come to terms with. She felt numb, empty. Unsure who Maya was anymore.

I rented motorbikes
And made my way to Cameroon,
on the border with Chad,
to the home of a friend.
From there I travelled to my aunt's, in Yaoundé,
where a friend of a friend got me a visa to the UK.

42

Umid

Kingston Upon Hull, early February 2020

Final interview with filmmaker Libby L. before TV documentary is broadcast.

L: Hi, it's great to see you again, Umid, even if it is only on Zoom. But at least I'll see you at the screening of the documentary in a couple of weeks. You look good, I like your new hairstyle.

U: Thanks, Libby. It's good to see you again too. Yes, I get my hair cut in a barber shop now instead of around a campfire, Ha. How are you?

L: I'm very well, thanks. As a matter of fact, I'm getting married soon. Look, can you see this on screen? My fiancé and I have the same ring. It's a snake, to symbolise infinity.

U: Getting married? Wow, that's great news, Libby, congratulations. I love your ring.

L: Umid, massive congratulations to you too, on being granted your leave to remain, I was so happy when I heard. How are you, really?

U: I'm fine, thank you. Trying to start again. It's hard to believe I'm free, I waited so long for a decision. It was hard, Libby.

L: You've had to go through so much. And finally, you're here.

U: Yes, I'm here. Sometimes I can't believe I've made it, Libby.

L: But you have! Umid, the reason for this call is to summarise what's happened since we finished our interviews in Calais. There will be a short text passage about each refugee at the end of the film. Can you tell me how you made it to the UK?

U: Yes. I came in a small boat. We all thought we were going to drown. Nobody was speaking, even the children were silent.

L: Children?

U: Yes, there were two families in the boat. The engine had stopped working. The back of the boat was broken, and water was coming inside. We had been on the sea for eight hours already and we were only halfway across the channel. Libby?

L: Sorry, excuse me. And what happened then?

U: We saw the Border Force Boat with the British flags. Suddenly everyone started talking at once. Laughing and shouting. We were so happy.

L: How did the Border Force officers treat you?

U: They were lovely. There was a lady who was so kind to the children. They asked us if we needed anything, like water or to go to the toilet. I'll never forget them.

L: Where were you taken then?

U: To a detention centre in Kent, for two days. Then a hotel in Leeds. I was there for six months, and then I came to a shared house in Hull.

L: Is this the house you're currently living in?

U: No. You have to leave Home Office accommodation when you get refugee status, Libby. I had to move into a hostel, but

I have a nice room and I only share a bathroom with one other person. I'll stay here until I can afford a place of my own.

L: How easy do you think it will be to get your own place?

U: I'm not expecting it to be easy. I'm happy for now. I go to college to improve my English and I work evenings in a restaurant. I've applied for a university scholarship, to study for a master's degree in Film and Media.

L: That's great, Umid. I have to say I've noticed the improvement in your use of the English language. Now ... one more thing I want to ask you about. The girl, Daisy, that you met on Samos. Have you ever heard from her, or would you like to?

U: Libby, why do you ask me about her? This was two and a half years ago. Come on, what do you expect me to do?

L: I don't expect anything. Do you remember her email address?

U: Yes, I remember because it was funny. Daisy-half-crazy. I lost my phone soon after I left Greece and I didn't check my emails until I was in France, at an internet café. She had emailed me, but I deleted without reading it.

L: Why did you do that?

U: I told you; I wanted her to forget about me. I don't know, Libby. It was not a good time. I deleted my old email address and now I have a new one so she can't find me anymore.

L: Have you thought about—

U: Yes, I think about her sometimes. I don't want to intrude on whatever life she's living now. I need to focus on myself, Libby.

L: I understand. I'll change the subject: have you met up with the great aunt you told me about, in Peterborough, wasn't it?

U: Yes, I visited my aunt in Peterborough, but she hasn't been well. She's moving in with my cousin. She was pleased to see me, and she cried when she asked about my mother.

L: It's nice that you have family in this country. Umid, are you looking forward to seeing yourself on TV?

U: Yes, I'm excited about the documentary. It will be strange to see myself back then in Calais. And all my friends. I'm still in touch with some of them. I have one friend who is still there, Libby, he has never managed to leave.

L: I imagine it will be difficult to watch in some ways.

U: Maybe, but the bad memories will show me how far I've come.

L: That's true. Lastly, how do you feel about going up on stage at the preview and speaking to the audience about your experiences?

U: I'm nervous, of course, but I won't let you down, I promise. Thank you for choosing me to represent all the refugees you met in Calais, Libby.

I spent more than a day in Heathrow Airport,
Unable to find the exit, tired and ill with malaria.
When I found my way out, I took a bus
to a friend in Newcastle.
It was he who persuaded me
to hand myself in to the police.

43

Maya

Porto, Portugal, early February 2020

Maya still felt shaky at times, but the blood in her veins had slowed to a steady stream rather than hurtling around her like a rushing waterfall. She'd been for a check-up with her old GP, who pronounced her (reasonably) fit and well, although clearly suffering from stress. He recommended some herbal pills to help calm her, since she refused to take drugs unless completely unavoidable.

"Take some rest," he told her. "Enjoy your family for a while. I admire what you do out there in the refugee camps, Maya, honestly. But you won't be any good to anyone if you don't look after yourself." Just what Bill said. Since leaving Calais for good, she'd been thinking a lot about Bill. Wondering if he ever got lonely over there.

The girls treated her to a surprise trip to Berlin after Christmas. They'd wanted her to fly direct to Berlin with them, but she needed to drive because it would give her an opportunity to begin her longed-for road trip through France and Spain afterwards. Maya drove to Hull for the ferry to Rotterdam and the girls and their toddlers left Navengore a few days later. The whole family was reunited in the spacious living area of Joe and Amar's apartment, where Maya and Alicia would be sleeping in the Blue Room. After a few hours of adoring harassment from Chi-Chi, Joe and Amar's tiny dog, Alicia had given in and allowed her ears to be delved into by Chi-Chi's tongue, and her white fur buffed and polished to spa standard by her miniature canine friend.

Lola and Daisy were staying nights at Jamie and Leilja's with the children. Bedtime would be fun, Maya imagined. Lola would need to relax her strict expectations of timings.

After a few magical though exhausting days with them all, she kissed her children and grandchildren goodbye. She felt for the first time that every one of them had surpassed their need for her, though towards the end of the visit she'd caught Daisy having a cry in Joe's bathroom.

"Is it because I'm leaving again?" Maya had asked her. "If you need me, I'll be there, I promise. Do you want me to go back to the UK with you?"

"It's not about you Mum," Daisy had replied, slightly irritated. "I'm still upset that my daughter hasn't got a father. That's not going to go away until I find him. You don't seem to get that."

"I'm sorry, love." Maya tore off some toilet paper and passed it to Daisy to wipe her eyes. "I really hope the Red Cross or some of my contacts in Calais can help you."

She took off then, driving from Germany through France and Spain, without a plan; using a park for the night app to find safe places to sleep. The hairs on her arms stood up in Vigo, Spain, not far from the border with Portugal. At a camping spot near the estuary, she stood looking out to sea, her arms outstretched. She recalled a night she had slept on a beach in Catalonia with Alicia, just before learning about Lola's pregnancy. She toyed with the idea of bringing her quilt and pillows out of the van and spending the night outside now, then it started raining. It fell like a thick sheet, the kind of rain she'd only seen in movies before. Shivering and laughing, she called for the dog, running in hysterical circles, to come back to the van.

The following night she arrived in Porto. Maya didn't know what made her suddenly decide to book a small Airbnb apartment for three nights. Maybe the idea of space to move around; a bath, or simply the novelty of feeling that she had her own place. It felt like luxury, though the accommodation was basic. The bedroom with its deep windowsill reminded her of a medieval cottage. She immersed herself in a hot bath the first night, Alicia peering over the edge as if concerned Maya was going to drown.

"You could probably do with a bath yourself," Maya dangled a hand dripping warm water over the dog's nose, and Alicia drew herself up to her full height, avoiding eye contact, though seemingly determined to remain in place, guarding her mistress.

Maya slept solidly for the first time in a while. The apartment was one of five units in a stone building across the road from the beach. She struggled with the lock on the outside gate, despite detailed instructions from the owner, almost giving up until the correct combination of pulling and pushing finally enabled her to turn the key.

"Come on then," she said to Alicia. "At last. Let's go for a walk." Alicia seemed affronted at having to wear a lead, but Maya thought it was best, not knowing what the rules were. "Stop complaining," she told the dog.

They followed a boardwalk that ran beneath a high stone wall alongside the beach. Maya felt its spring under her feet and the vibration whenever a walker or runner passed by. Below the boardwalk smooth, giant pebbles hunched together like seals and further out toast-coloured rocks slanted towards the sea, sheltering distant rockpools that mirrored the cerulean blueness of the sky. Off the rolling sea's back, frothing waves hit the rocks, the spray blowing towards Maya. She tasted the salt on her tongue. Spread on amber sand between the rocks, sludges of dark green seaweed lightened in the sun.   everything seemed hyper-coloured, lucid.   She felt as though she was in a dream.

She pulled her wide-brimmed hat down against the glare of the sun and set off along the boardwalk again. Rounding a corner flanked by a wide green bank, she stopped to listen to perplexing sounds coming from the grass surrounding rockpools below: birds perhaps? Alicia's ears pricked up and she stared intently at the green-black water.   But Maya couldn't see anything.   She lowered herself to the planks, ungainly as ever, and sat with her legs dangling over. It took some intense scrutinising of her own before she was able to make out the small, jumping shapes of miniature frogs, camouflaged against the rocks.   Their high and urgent chirruping morphed into almost dog-like barks as she watched.

Struggling back to her feet, she moved on and came across a beachfront restaurant, where she sat outside on a glassed-in deck with Alicia, watching the sea, eating *tosta de quejo* and drinking a *café com leite*.

Later she found a quiet spot on the beach where she allowed Alicia a frenzied run and a swim in the sea. Back at the Airbnb she dried the dog off with an old towel out of the van, and they both had an afternoon sleep. In the evening they ate outside a restaurant in the town, a blanket over Maya's legs. She slept soundly again that night.

Another morning of leisurely walking on the beach and the boardwalk, and a return visit to her now-favourite beachfront café for the cheesy toast and coffee – a late breakfast. That afternoon she left Alicia in the flat and took a tram into the city centre. There she walked downhill, street after street leading eventually to the wide river. She browsed shops and market stalls along its edge and chose a riverside restaurant specialising in fish for her evening meal.

Later, back in the apartment, she answered an email from Ned in reply to one she'd sent him a few days before. He'd passed on the contact details of a friend who knew of a community she could go to for a while, in central Portugal.

She wanted to try community living one last time: she'd been so happy in Catalonia.

I was born in Saudi Arabia
but my father was from Yemen
so I am considered Yemeni,
a lesser thing to be
in the country where I lived and worked.
My wife is a pharmacist,
I was an actor and model,
and later a phone technician.
Then things turned difficult with the government.
An 80,000 riyal penalty, demanded of a company
employing those whose passports say
they are Yemeni.

44

Maya

Central Portugal, late February 2020

Email from: Maya Joy Galen
To: Daisy_halfcrazy@dmail.com

   Subject: A new community

Hi my darling girl,
How are you now? I was sad to see you feeling so down just
before I left.

   I hope you hear back from the Red Cross soon regarding
Umid's whereabouts, and that it will put your mind at rest once
and for all. Yes, I know what you mean about closure, and I
agree he should know about his daughter and Avalie should
know about him, too.

   It was so nice to see Avalie reunited with her cousin at
Christmas. Those two are so cute together. Elijah had grown
so much since I'd seen him in the summer. I was thrilled to be
able to celebrate his third birthday with you all, and then get

to celebrate Rudi's in Germany as well. He's so proud that he's now a big brother to Emil, isn't he? And Electra loved having her English cousins to stay – and boss around, sorry I know you don't like that word: direct them, I should say – how I love that girl! We had a good trip, didn't we? Me and my twin girls with their babies. And to see all five of my grandchildren in one place at the same time, and all my four children together, well it was heaven! An experience I'll never forget. I can't stop looking at the photos Joe had made into a book for me. It's wonderful to see him so happy with Amar, and I'm so excited that the two of them have started the adoption process at last. It's been a rocky road to acceptance of the whole process in Germany, hasn't it? They'll both make wonderful dads.

Thank you for organising the trip, Daisy, and to you and Lola for looking after me, I was such a mess when I first got back from Calais. I'm sorry, you shouldn't have had to see your mother breaking down like that.

I just want to say, don't think I ever take you beautiful people for granted, I don't, honestly. I think of my children all the time and if you ever need me, I'll come. That's a promise.

So now, let me tell you more about this place. It's a community like the one where I lived in Catalonia. Where Alicia found me, remember? The landscape is similar in some ways and different in others. Whereas in Catalonia we lived on a gentle slope, here the land is terraced. The owners are creating a permaculture forest, an ecosystem in which all the plants and animals contribute to the wellbeing of each other. Almost everything we eat has been produced on this land and one day it'll be fully sustainable. Most people here live in pods built onto the terraces, but Alicia and I sleep in our van on the flat area up by the road. There are twenty residents here. Some of them are families with young children. There's a large roundhouse where communal meals are served. I've been helping mostly with the cooking and in the laundry, and I sometimes help in the school. The manual work on the land is a bit much for my poor old joints, I'm afraid. My knee's started playing up again. And my hands!

You asked if I'm happy now Daisy, and that's a hard question to answer. I feel calmer than in Calais, but perhaps I only needed a break. A good, long break, to be sure. And I really wanted to travel again, in this van. But have I become stuck here now? Should I move on, just keep travelling through Europe, or settle in Portugal? It's tempting to stay here, I've seen a few properties I'd be interested in, though I could only remain here for three months at a time without putting myself through a tortuous administrative process. Or perhaps I should return to the UK and look for a property not too far from my daughters. But what would I do there, Daisy?

Thing is, I've got to admit that since volunteering in the refugee camps, I don't know if anything can ever make me feel quite as needed and fulfilled as that work. I just seem to 'get' people who are refugees, I don't know why. Whereas I'll admit to you that I'm struggling with my fellow volunteers here. Don't tell Lola, she already thinks I'm bonkers for coming here in the first place! What's the answer? Maybe your mother is simply too difficult to satisfy. Perhaps I've had too much freedom for too long.

I know I'm going to have to decide soon, because this Covid thing I keep hearing about on the news seems to be getting out of hand. What's happening in China sounds terrifying …

Sorry my love, I'm afraid I've got to sign off now. Someone's just hammered on the van door calling that the pigs have escaped again. That means all bodies are needed to round them up and help repair the electric fence once we've got them back in. Alicia has proved particularly useful herding both the pigs and the sheep, as a matter of fact, though she's distrustful of the chickens. She got pecked by a rather terrifying cockerel that was trying to attack me, just after we arrived here. Fortunately (sorry cockerel) that one had already been selected for the pot as there were too many cockerels and they were all fighting each other. It's good to see Alicia with a purpose, though. Now I just need to find one for myself.

I'll get this sent off now, Daisy, while the Wi-fi is still on (they switch it off at night to save the power from the solar panels, at this time of year). All being well I'll give you a call later.

Lots of love to you, Avalie, Lola and Elijah,

Speak soon,

Mum xxxxxx

By the time the six pigs had been rounded up and the pen made secure again, Maya felt exhausted. She'd joined the rest of the (reasonably, in her case) fit and able residents of the permaculture plantation in an organised charge along the road that ran across the top of the property, before being forced to scramble down one rock-edged terrace after another to head the animals off at the stream in the valley below. Alicia had streaked ahead, cutting in front of Betsy, the lead pig, and turning the herd back towards the residents with their sticks and the boards they used as ramps to guide the pigs back up the terraces to their pen in the olive grove.

Jenna, the plantation founder, had shut herself in her cabin, distraught that the youngest pig, Molly, had injured a hind leg. The vet had been called and the fear was that the pig might have to be put down.

It had been an emotional afternoon. Maya dropped a homeopathic remedy onto her tongue. She rubbed her aching knuckles and elbows in the warmth from the van heater. Later she smoothed in some 'miracle' cream Lola had bought her for Christmas and pushed her fingers into the special cotton gloves that had come with it. Despite various herbal supplements, her arthritis was no better than it had been in Calais, three months before. Nothing seemed to ease the pain. Cradling a mug of fresh ginger tea in her gloved hands she drew her knees up to her stomach and leaned back against her pillows, cocooned in bed for an early night.

It was too late to ring Daisy; she'd be putting Avalie to bed, and Maya didn't want to disturb the routine Lola had encouraged Daisy to follow.

Maya swallowed ginger tea, wondering why she felt such isolation in this community that had been recommended to her in an email from Ned's friend, a man who'd now moved on. The people here were nice enough. She just hadn't managed to gel with anyone. Perhaps I'm broken, she found herself thinking. I don't think this is the life for me anymore. But what is?

Sitting back, Maya allowed her mind to wander over memories of the weeks she'd spent in her daughters' flat, depleted of energy and feeling like a zombie.

In Navengore her feeling of disconnect had been strengthened by the knowledge of Con's separate existence from hers, in the rooms they had once watched TV in as a family, where she had cooked, and her children had played. The enormous kitchen in which she had waited for Con to return home from work, keeping his supper plate warm; her two sons missing and her two daughters living their own lives: was now reconfigured as Con's still larger than average kitchen and bathroom. Their old through lounge had become Con's living room and bedroom. He had his own hallway and utility room too. There was still space on the ground floor for the renamed 'Lola's Day Nursery', once Daisy's dream but where she now worked with Lola as an assistant. Like her mother, she felt unable to commit to permanence – in her case until she'd found out what had happened to Avalie's father. The day nursery was completely closed off from the downstairs flat, with its own entrance that had used to be The Cottages' side door. It consisted of two good-sized rooms: once the family's 'ironing room' and 'playroom', as well as a small kitchen partially adapted from their old 'mud room' and a children's bathroom utilised from the other half of the mud room along with the old downstairs cloakroom. Maya still shuddered to think their family had once felt the necessity of all those rooms to themselves, along with the former five bedrooms and four bathrooms upstairs – now converted into a sizeable flat for Daisy, Lola and their children.

Daisy had been quiet and pale after they drove home from Calais. Once Maya had gone to use the bathroom in the early evening and heard her daughter crying. She hesitated at the kitchen door, spotting Lola with her arms around her twin. Daisy was sobbing that she'd failed her child; failed herself by allowing the pregnancy in the first place. Now she was back in the UK she didn't think she stood a chance of ever finding Umid. She'd failed him too, by being unable to inform him he had a daughter. Maya watched her twins a moment, Lola with her thick dark hair and Daisy's growing out at the sides now, a lighter brown than Lola's and soft pink at the lower edges. She hoped Daisy would regain some of the roundness she once had.

Lola caught sight of Maya over her sister's shoulder. She shook her head gently at her – *I can deal with this*. They'd dealt with so much on their own without her. Maya backed off and returned to her room.

For the days leading up to Christmas she'd mainly lain in bed in her daughters' flat – unheard of for her. Alicia had been allowed to sleep in her room with her, though not on the bed, an edict from Lola. Instead, Lola had bought a faux fur dog bed that Alicia had quite taken to. It was Lola who took the dog out for a walk first thing in the morning, along with Elijah, her early rising dog enthusiast three-year-old. Daisy's old cat, Tink, had moved permanently into the downstairs apartment with Con, a former self-professed cat hater.

Tink wasn't the only one who had moved in with Con. Susannah Metherington (S.M. was Lola's name for her) had finally left the home she'd shared with her estranged husband for the past three years since she'd started, as Lola put it, sniffing around Con. She was now apparently living with Con full time. Lola reckoned Con was a bit put out by the amount of stuff the woman kept bringing in; the bachelor pad he'd created at the ending of his marriage to Maya now becoming distinctly feminised. Lola said S.M. kept dropping hints about herself and Con looking for a place of their own.

"Do you think he'll agree?" Maya asked tiredly. Do you think they'll get married?" She raised herself on her pillows to sip the lemon tea Lola had brought her. On the luxury dog bed Alicia stood up, stretched and sighed, before turning around in a circle and flopping down again in the same position as before. Maybe Alicia needed the rest as much as Maya did. Maya struggled to comprehend her feelings about Con and Susannah, a former 'best friend'. Though had they been really? They were fellow mothers at the primary school gates, they went to the same dinner parties in the village and shared a table at the extortionately priced summer balls. That had been considered friendship. It'd been enough then. Everything in her former society seemed small and pointless now, even her travelling years did, in comparison to the stories of enforced migration she'd become familiar with. She tried to analyse her reaction to the progression of events in her family and failed, too tired. Perhaps that meant she wasn't bothered about Con and Susannah, but she hoped she'd be able to find renewed enthusiasm for *something*.

"I dunno," Lola said cheerfully. "I think Dad usually just goes along with whatever she suggests. Maybe."

Lola was accustomed to S.M. being around now, Maya thought. Her father's relationship status was of no consequence to her. Maya studied her daughter's profile as she leaned to stroke Alicia. Her lovely curves, the fluttering of dark brown lashes on her rounded cheeks. Her hair, which she kept shoulder length and coloured a rich dark chestnut, swinging forward as she moved her head. A pain of love burned in her chest. Lola had always been the twin she worried about, before she took Daisy away to Greece. But since having Elijah, Lola had matured, blossomed into the capable young mother who managed her own business and co-parented with Elijah's father. She had a new partner now too, Jake: a teaching assistant at the school where she'd used to work. Though she said she had no intention of altering her living arrangements, not for a few years at least.

I'm proud of you, Lola," Maya said. She couldn't help reaching up to touch Lola's shining wall of hair. She also couldn't help noticing Lola's infinitesimal flinch when her fingers contacted Lola's shoulder. Things had never been the same between them since Lola, feeling abandoned, had gone through her pregnancy without informing her mother. Maya wondered if she could ever heal that wound.

"Give over, Mum," Lola said as if to cover her slight withdrawal. "Anyway, I can hear Elijah and Avalie having one of their set-tos in the playroom, I'd better go and rescue Daisy. You try and get some more rest before dinner, okay?"

Christmas Day. Maya was relieved that the family had booked dinner at one of the hotels in the village.

It had felt excruciating sitting at the expanding table in Con's living room the year before that, the first Christmas meal S.M. had cooked for them. Maya had only returned for a brief break from Calais that year, having promised the girls she would try to be around for the grandchildren on special occasions. The year previous to that one, 2017, Maya had only been in Calais a month or two, and she'd eaten Christmas dinner with Bill in his flat, before going out on a special distribution with a hot food van. She'd returned to the UK for Elijah's first birthday in January 2018, before visiting the boys and their families for Rudi's birthday in Germany; then back to the UK for the birth of Avalie in March. Between family visits, she had repeatedly returned to work with the beleaguered refugees in the moveable scraps of camps around Calais since then. It had felt too long of a drive all the way back to Greece after she'd dropped Daisy off in Navengore following their aborted expedition, and she didn't want to be so far away that she couldn't be available for her children and grandchildren, should they need her.

"I've been an itinerant too long," Maya told Alicia, stretched alongside her on the bed in her camper van on the Portuguese homestead. The ginger tea had cooled in her gloved hands, and she drank it down in a last gulp before leaning forward to place the cup on the draining board. She pulled the curtains over the back doors closed and shuffled down in her bed, pulling the covers up under her chin. "Another early night for me, I think. It's cold outside, and already dark."

If it had been sunshine and warmth she had wanted, she should have driven down to the Algarve. Bill had sent a text message recently: Lucky you, spending your winter in the sun. But so far, her weeks in the foothills of the Sierra da Estrela mountains had offered mainly thick clouds and often rain, with only a few bright days of sunshine between. It felt much like the endurance living of Calais in winter, but without the emotional satisfaction of the refugee relief work there.

On those brighter days, however, when she was able to take long walks in her time off from duties, Maya found the vistas of tree-studded slopes; the forested terraces of oak, olive and chestnut trees with shade-loving perennial vegetables growing beneath; the waterfalls and the rock-edged paths leading to sudden mystical clearings of damp, silvery grass; a balm for her troubled soul. The ground erupted with fungi – much of it gathered daily by Jenna and her partner, Adam, for drying or immediate consumption. Overhead a canopy of wild grapevines and brambles tangled together. Trodden-in, prickly chestnut shells crunched under her feet and fallen acorns rooted themselves in the thick mulch of the forest. Once when she rounded a corner on the twisting path, she came face to face with a deer. They stared at each other a moment before the deer backed into the foliage at the inner edge of the path and disappeared so quickly Maya wondered if she'd imagined it. Another time she was shocked by a sudden squeal off somewhere to her right. Scrambling for foothold as stones at

296

the edge of the path tumbled into the steep slope of the forest, she managed to jump backwards and cling, hidden, to the trunk of an oak just in time to avoid being trampled by a frighteningly bulky wild boar the size of a small cow, that charged across the path followed by a litter of shrieking piglets and careered into the undergrowth of the terrace below.

On those mornings when it wasn't pouring with rain, she chose to eschew the solar powered showers in favour of the spring at the bottom of the valley. A stool was kept there, and a simple 5-litre water bottle with holes pierced in the base. Maya stripped off, laying her clothes over the stool. She lathered herself with a bar of the community's lavender soap, positioned her feet securely on the pebbled ground of the chill water and filled the bottle from the spring before holding it above her head and gasping as the icy cascade hit her skin. Once, on a particularly warm day, she even immersed herself in the rocky pool beside the spring. I could pay a lot of money for a spa treatment like this, she said aloud, into the green lushness of the spring glade. Indeed, spa days which had included icy cold dips had been considered a treat back in her village wife days.

I was on holiday
when I was told there was no work anymore.
Not for me, or my wife, or the rest of my family.
I was given a visa to leave the country,
'Go back' to Yemen.
But I'd never lived there, and the way I speak
is different from the way they speak.
I'd face the same kind of prejudice as in Saudi
Arabia.
So I went to the UK.

45

Daisy

Navengore, end of February 2020

Email from: Daisy_halfcrazy@dmail.com
To: Maya Joy Galen

Subject: The best news ever!!!

Mum, Mum!
I tried to call you, but you must've not had a signal or something. I left a voicemail though. I'll try again later but I've got to tell you somehow, right now. I want to write it down so I can read it back again later and remember it's real. It's REAL.

Ohmygod. I can't believe I'm able to say this at last. I FOUND HIM. Umid. I'm crying as I write this. I found him and I've told him about Avalie. He couldn't believe he has a daughter, Mum. He said he thought I would have forgotten about him a long time ago, that's why he didn't answer the emails I sent him as soon as I knew I was pregnant. He never even read them; he thought it was for the best as he was in such a bad situation.

He was in Calais, Mum! He must have been there when you first went to volunteer! Can you believe that? But he got over to England in a small boat, it was awful for him. But guess where he is now? In Hull, just an hour or so's drive away from me. Isn't that mad?

We FaceTimed; I saw his beautiful face again. I can't believe it. And once we got over the initial awkwardness and his shock over finding out about Avalie, we talked just as easily as we used to on Samos. He said he liked my hair with its pink ends, lol. He also said he thought I'd be married by now, to a nice Englishman. I said I'd been too busy looking after our daughter, and that I'd always hoped I'd find him again. I told him about volunteering in Calais, and he thanked me on behalf of all refugees. I cried, of course. And then he asked to see Avalie, and he cried when she waved at him on the screen, and I told her he was her daddy. She said daddy to him, Mum. For the first time ever. It was so cute. He said he wants to hold her so badly.

He said she looks like his sister, that's who I named her after, remember I told you? He showed me a photo of her once and it's true. He said his mother would love to see Avalie, though not yet as she'll be angry with him when he tells her. I said we could do a FaceTime together with his mother one day. I felt shivery all over when I thought about the future.

So, I'm going to drive over to Hull tomorrow! I'm going to see him again for the first time in two and a half years. I just. Can't. Believe it. All my waiting, all my sorrow at thinking he might be dead, or in prison or something, all over now.

And guess what? He's got his leave to remain, Mum. He only received the official letter recently. He's working in a restaurant and he's going to college. He wants to go to university. I feel so proud of him, even though it's not my place to be so. But he is Avalie's dad. She's finally got a dad, isn't that wonderful?

Oh yeah, I forgot to tell you how I found him! Although I've already told you in the voice message and I'll tell you more about it when I talk to you. But it's a brilliant story, and even more reason for Avalie to be proud of her dad and him to be proud of himself. He was in a TV documentary! Can you believe it? About refugees in Calais. I'd heard it was going to be on Channel 7 and so obviously I wanted to watch it. I got Lola to watch it with me because I wanted her to see some of the locations around Calais where we'd done distributions, and what it was like there. I was trying to see if I recognised any of the refugees they interviewed, and then I saw Umid, right there on the screen, it was the weirdest feeling. To hear his voice again … my heart. He didn't look well on the second interview, I thought. He said he'd been depressed. I felt so sad for him. This woman, the filmmaker, did two interviews with him, you see. It was filmed in 2018. I'm surprised you never came across her, Mum, because she talked to some volunteers, too. But anyway, that's not the point, that's how I found him.

He mentioned me, Mum, in the documentary. Well, he didn't specifically, but the interviewer asked him if he had a girlfriend, or maybe a wife, and he went all shy and embarrassed. He said he didn't but there had been a girl on Samos. That was me! Lola was gobsmacked. I think she'd begun to wonder if Umid really existed, like Avalie was an immaculate conception or something. So, you see, it wasn't just me chasing him after all.

I've sent you a link to the TV programme. And then you'll recognise Umid from Samos. Mum, will you come home? You said you'd come home if I ever needed you, and I think I do now. This is a massive event in my life, even more than Avalie being born, in a way. I don't know what's going to happen with this, but I really need your support now. And if you don't come soon, you might not be allowed to travel, because of that COVID 19. They're talking about lockdowns in Europe. Lockdowns, can you imagine that?

Please come home, Mum.

Lots of love from me, Avalie, Lola and Elijah and hopefully

Daisy checks her speed, over seventy. She still hasn't got used to driving a small car again, after Mum's van, which barely goes over fifty. The car has a habit of running away with her. She slows down.

"All right in the back there?" she calls to Avalie, meeting her eyes in the rear-view mirror, reflected from the mirror suspended over the back seat. Avalie's facing backwards in the expensive car seat system insisted upon by Lola. She'd been shocked that they'd used an old fashioned, second-hand forward-facing car seat held into the van's back seat by an ordinary seatbelt when they were in Calais. Lola thinks she knows so much more than Daisy about being a mother and about childcare in general, since she's done those extra qualifications for the nursery. But nobody knows more about being Avalie's mother than Daisy. And now Daisy's long held wish for her daughter is coming true at last – they're on their way to meet Umid.

"Mam-mam-mam-mam go see Daddy!" yells Avalie. She follows it with a peel of laughter and kicks her feet in their shiny new black boots on the seat back.

Daisy starts shaking as they approach the Humber Bridge. She steadies her hands on the wheel. Breathe, she tells herself. Just breathe. It's Umid, remember him? Remember how easy it was to talk to him? *My darling, my love. I've never stopped thinking about you.* But still the shaking grips her, coming from deep inside her stomach and radiating out into her muscles and bones. She's afraid she's going to be sick. She's sure the car must be juddering all over the road. She holds tight to the steering wheel. The wide river comes into view, a low mist hanging over it. To calm herself, Daisy starts humming, then singing a song about how wide the water is and that she can't get over it. It's a lullaby she's sung to Avalie many times, tears sometimes

302

running down her cheeks as the longing felt as if it was breaking her heart. Avalie joins in from the back, half-words, her high voice a tin whistle note. The water *is* wide, but this time Daisy will get over it. The shaking subsides and warmth spreads through her muscles. On the bridge she feels suspended above clouds. A parting in the mist reveals choppy water far below and a sudden burst of sunlight through a slit in the grey mass choking the sky colours it golden for a moment. Daisy breathes as deeply as she can.

At the tolls she scans her card for the £1.50 fee. Driving off the roundabout she heads into West Hull. She pulls into a car parking space at the edge of the road and taps the meeting place they have agreed on into the Satnav. A city centre carpark where Umid will meet her, then they can go to a café before taking a walk with Avalie if the rain holds off. Umid says they can show her the boats in the harbour. They can get fish and chips by the Marina later, he says. He has never eaten anything as delicious as the fish and chips in Hull. Her hand trembling again, she texts Umid to say they have arrived in Hull, and that she's on her way to the carpark.

"Okay, baby," she leans around her seat to feel the reassuring warmth of Avalie's hair. "We're going to see Daddy very soon now. Last leg of the journey."

"Lap leg, lap leg," Avalie chants as Daisy starts the car again and pulls out into the traffic. The satnav takes her onto a busy road and eventually leads her on a roundabout route into the city centre, where she finds the carpark and drives in carefully through the metal gates. Looking out for a parking space, she's suddenly terrified to search for Umid. What will it be like seeing him in the flesh again after all this time?

She keeps her head down waiting in the queue at the ticket machine, thinking back over how she got in touch with Umid again. Lola had reluctantly settled with her on the sofa in their flat, not having liked to talk much with Daisy about the work she'd been doing in Calais. Lola prefers the things the two of them have in common to the things that make them different. She feels Daisy should concentrate on the life they're living now: bringing up their children and running the nursery together, she thinks Daisy should get on a dating app and try to meet a partner 'more like us'. But she agreed to watch the documentary because Daisy's been so down lately. Perhaps Lola thought it would serve as closure to Daisy's 'obsession' as she calls it, with refugees.

But it was the opposite. The documentary proved to be an opening. There he was, Umid, on the screen. And he admitted to not having read Daisy's emails, to spare her, he'd said. What use could he have been to her in his current circumstances? He *had* been thinking of her, after all. He'd looked so young on the programme, and so gaunt. Her heart had ached for him. Then at the end it gave a written update on each of the refugees interviewed, and it had said Umid was now in the UK, and he'd been granted leave to remain.

She would have tried to contact him anyway, after watching the documentary. Wherever he'd been. First, she phoned the broadcasting company who'd shown the documentary and asked for the contact details of the filmmaker. They were cautious with her, enquiring what her reasons were. When she told them how long she'd been looking for Umid, and that she had important news for him, they asked her to put that information – not the important news itself, just the circumstances she'd outlined – into an email and they would pass it on to Libby. It took a few days for Libby to respond, apparently, she'd been on her honeymoon. Libby was thrilled to hear from her though. She phoned her as soon as she got back from her honeymoon. She told Daisy that Umid was one of her favourite interviewees, and she'd always wondered about the girl he'd mentioned meeting on Samos. What was the news? She wanted to know. But Daisy said she'd prefer to give that directly to Umid himself, and maybe they could share it with Libby later. Sure thing, Libby said. And just like that, she gave Daisy Umid's phone number. And then Daisy texted him, and then he called her, and finally they switched their cameras on so that they could see each other for the first time in two and a half years. His mass of tumbling curls was gone. His hair was neatly shaved at the sides and neatened on top. He looked older than she remembered him, and his face had filled out since he'd been interviewed in Calais. But his eyes, oh, those intelligent dark eyes of his, they were just the same. He said the same about her blue eyes, too.

Daisy's eyes fill up with tears now as she stands in the queue for the ticket machine at the carpark.

"Excuse me," says a voice behind her, and a hand lands on her shoulder. She jumps. Coming to, she sees the spot in front of her is empty.

"Sorry," she says to the man behind. "I was miles away." Miles and years and tears away, she thinks as she punches numbers into the machine.

Turning back to her car with the ticket in her hand, she sees someone standing by the rear passenger door. He's looking down into the window, and he's standing very still. He looks up as she approaches, and she sees that tears are in his eyes as well. Inside the car Avalie is laughing and patting the glass.

"So, you've met her then?" says Daisy as casually as she can. And without even thinking, she throws her arms around Umid, and his arms wind themselves around her in return and he kisses the top of her head.

Her fingers on the back of his neck, the soft hair growing there. The curve of his head in the palm of her hand. The tightness of his arms on her back. Their cheeks pressed together; their bodies pressed together. His quick hard kisses on her neck. Their lips finally meeting. Their eyes drinking each other in.

"Mama!" Avalie calls loudly from the car, and they pull apart, breathless and laughing.

"Hello," Daisy says to him, brushing fronds of hair away from her eyes. "Allow me to introduce you to your daughter."

He opens the car door for her, and she leans in to swivel Avalie's car seat around. Avelie bends her back and kicks her feet as Daisy fumbles with the fastener that holds her straps in place.

"Stop it," Daisy says. "You're hurting me."

"Out, out," shouts Avalie. "Now!"

"I'm trying, baby. But my fingers are acting silly. Hold still, please."

"Let me," Umid says. He moves Daisy's trembling hands gently aside and releases the buckle with one click. "There. That's because you're not kicking *me*, young lady." He stands back. Avalie's gone motionless. She stares up at her father with enormous eyes and a trembling lower lip. Then she blows out a breath and gathers her voice.

"Out, out," she demands imperiously.

"At your service, madam," Umid says. He leans forward to take his small daughter in his hands for the first time.

"Oh my god," he mutters to Daisy under his breath as he moves Avalie oh so carefully out of the car doorway. "I could never have imagined this." He holds her up against his chest, encircling her with one arm, stroking her back reverently with his other hand. He whispers something in his own language into Avalie's ear. Daisy watches in fascination.

"What was that?"

He dips his chin in a way she remembers from Samos, when he felt uncomfortable. "Oh, it's just part of a prayer, we whisper it into the ear of a new-born, but I wasn't there, so . . ."

"That's lovely," Daisy says. "I'm sorry you weren't able to be there."

"It doesn't matter now. I'm not religious, anyway. I am, what do you call it? Agnostic."

"Me too," says Daisy. "I believe in humanity, that's all. Difficult sometimes I know, but . . . "

Avalie shakes her head and rubs at her ear, then she pats Umid's close-shaven beard.

"Tickle," and she lets out a peal of laughter.

Umid rubs noses with her. "You will have to get used to that. Hello my daughter. Hello, sweet Avalie. Your daddy loves you very much."

"Down," demands Avalie, throwing her head back. "Me walk."

"I'm sure you can. You seem like a very independent lady to me." Umid smiles at Daisy over the top of Avalie's head, and she senses his smile is full of the pain of their lost years.

My wife and my boys
were not allowed to leave
and we were forcibly separated.
I send them money from my small allowance
to pay rent and electricity
but there's never enough to go round.

46

Daisy

Hull, end of February 2020

The carpark is opposite the Central Library, so they cross the road and go into the café there. Umid insists on buying them all a cake. He holds Avalie's hand as they walk up the steps.

"What do you eat?" he asks her.

"Cake," she replies. In the café she points to a cream and jam scone at her eye level in the display cabinet.

"Is that okay?" Umid raises an eyebrow at Daisy.

"Mine," Avalie says. "Dat one."

Daisy nods. "If that's what she wants. She might only eat half of it, so I'll share it with her."

"No. Me." Avalie taps hard on the glass.

"Fine, fine." Daisy doesn't want to spoil the day. "I'll have one of those blueberry muffins, please." She's holding all her muscles tense and it's causing her to shiver slightly again.

"Are you okay?" Umid looks at her from under his eyebrows. "Cold? It took me a while to get used to the weather here. Thank you," he says to the girl behind the counter as she places their chosen cakes on the top. "A tea and a coffee, please. What will Avalie drink, Daisy?"

"Milkshake?" It feels too much; everything. Daisy's exhausted already. She crouches down at Avalie's level, seeing the waitress's body through the glass as Avalie does. "Strawberry, you like that one, don't you baby?"

"No!" Avalie pushes Daisy away. Why is she behaving like this? Daisy's embarrassed. The tears that have been behind her eyes all day rush to the surface again. She half-wishes she was already back at home on the sofa with Lola, recounting her day. She's dreamt of all this so long it feels too difficult to do it in real life. What happens now, how do they talk about moving forward from here?

Umid carries the tray over to a table in the corner. There are shallow steps leading up to the seating area. Avalie refuses to allow Daisy to hold her hand, and cries when she trips and bangs her knee. Daisy grabs her and swings her onto her hip, glad Umid hasn't rushed forward to try and take over in comforting their toddler. He waits patiently at the table, stirring sugar into his coffee. Stealing a glance at his downturned face, Daisy suspects he might be finding it as difficult as her to know what to do or say. And yet the hug, when they first met in the carpark, was so easy.

She sits on the chair beside him, settling a calmed-down Avalie onto her lap. Avalie reaches immediately for the scone. Daisy breaks a piece off for her, using a knife to smear it with cream and jam.

"No, no, no!" protests Avalie, shaking her head excessively. She stretches towards the plate. "Me."

Daisy's tempted to shove the whole plateful at her, but she knows Avalie will end up with cream and jam smeared all over her face, and probably drop the scone if she tries to shove it all in her mouth at once. Avalie slams her hand down on the edge of the plate, causing the scone to flip off onto the table.

"Avalie!" She's not usually this difficult. Daisy makes a big effort to control her temper. It's a massive deal, meeting your father for the first time, after all. *It's a massive deal for me too.*

Umid calmly positions the scone back onto the plate, uses a napkin to wipe the excess cream off the table. He takes a knife and cuts the scone into pieces that Avalie will be able to manage. When he places the plate in front of her, she takes one of the pieces, staring at him again with her wide-open eyes that are so like his. She's just trying to take all this in, Daisy thinks. Until now she hasn't had much concept of a father, after all.

Between discovering Umid's whereabouts and this meeting, Daisy found a book to read to Avalie, called *Are you my daddy?* She hopes her daughter makes the connection between the book and the stranger sitting at the table with them. Avalie stares at Umid a moment longer. He smiles at her and her wet lower lip trembles, before stretching into a mirror-smile. They're so alike. Warmth floods Daisy, easing the muscle tension. She feels her own mouth stretch into a grin.

She finds the courage to meet Umid's eyes and the rush of feeling is like a blow to her chest. It almost hurts to look at him, he's so beautiful. And he's solid and real, no longer merely a series of images on her phone, and memories, so many memories.

"This is amazing, isn't it?" she says.

Almost at the same time he says, "I never thought this would happen. Hard to believe she was in the world all along, and I didn't know about her." He touches Avelie's hair with the back of his forefinger. "I'm sorry I didn't get in touch with you before, Daisy. I remembered your email, Daisy-half-crazy, how could I forget? I never forgot you either, I promise you. It just wasn't the right time. I had to let fate run its course."

"It's okay, I understand. I'm sorry you had to go through everything you did. I can't even begin to imagine. You're so brave." Her hand creeps over the table to meet his. Their fingers loosely interlock.

"Don't say that. I'm only one of many. Thousands, hundreds of thousands, as you know. You've been there, Daisy. To Calais."

She nods. "I'm glad I saw. I'm glad I took Avalie to see. One day she'll understand the man her father is."

"So many of us, Daisy. We're not brave, any of us. We were scared and cold and frightened. But we had no choice. We did everything we had to because we had no choice. I'm no different from any of the others."

But you're the one who's mine. The one I care about the most, she wants to say. But she knows it's too early. They need to get to know each other all over again and she needs to be careful, this time. She goes hot at the thought of him knowing she followed him to the border. One day, she'll tell him. Whatever happens between them, they share Avalie, so she knows he'll always be in her life.

She lets go of Umid's hand, feeling the loss of his physical proximity like a gaping hole. She pours tea from the tiny silver pot into her mug and drinks the hot liquid down.

It's dark when she drives back over the Humber Bridge, Avalie asleep in the back of the car. They did all the things Umid had suggested, showed Avalie the boats on the marina and ate chips looking out on the wild grey sludge of the river. They walked down the old High Street and had a brief look around the Street Life Museum. Avalie loved the simulated ride in the stagecoach. Umid said he was happy in Hull and intended to stay there a while, hoping to win a scholarship to the University in September. I want to do a MA in Film Studies, he said. Maybe I'll make films about refugees one day, like Libby does.

Daisy knows that once she's tucked Avalie up in bed back in Navengore, she'll go online and start looking for primary teaching jobs in Hull. She knows she'll start looking at property there as well. She won't be able to help it. Finally, she knows where she wants to be. Lola won't be happy, but

Daisy has to put her daughter's needs before those of her twin now.

Maybe Daisy'll try and call Mum again when she gets home. She'll be on her way back from Portugal, but Daisy can't wait that long to talk to her.

Everyone in my family is an architect,
apart from my sister, who is a doctor.
I can tell you the names of my forefathers or
        mothers,
seven generations back,
all of them architects:
Bavzegar, Fatemah, Shili, Tahmad, Merdas, Hamid,
        Amin.
I come from a family of 12,000: rich in history,
my name means 'all my family'.
We come from Esfahan, an old city, twice the size of
        London —
five times bigger than Tehran.
I worked as an architect by day
and a gymnastics coach after 6 pm.

47

Daisy

Hull, March 2022

Daisy finishes hanging the silver and gold wooden stars Avalie picked out for her birthday decorations.   Avalie insisted on buying something they could reuse on other occasions, like Mama's birthday in May, Papa's in June and then for Christmas and New Year, too. She's been learning about recycling at nursery.

"Are you happy with that?" Daisy asks her daughter, "does it look nice?"

"Hmph.   I wanted stars there, too," Avalie points to the space on the right of the bay window. "We should have bought more, Mama." Her mouth turns down at the corners.

"Right. I'm sorry sweet pea, I miscalculated the area. Can you think of anything else we can hang there?"

"Umm. Let me think." Her daughter's eyes brighten. "I can make some myself. Will you help me?" Avalie turns and runs out of the front room, no doubt heading for the craft drawers in the dining room.

Daisy climbs carefully down from the stepladder. Umid will be mad when he finds out she's done it, he promised to finish the decorating when he gets home from teaching at the college. But Daisy feels edgy. She wishes she'd worked a couple more weeks before beginning her maternity leave. She can't remember feeling this way when she was about to have Avalie but then, she'd been obsessed with trying to find Umid before the birth. Their second daughter is due in three weeks, she and Umid had decided they didn't want a longer age gap.

"Hurry up, Mama," Avalie calls from the dining room, with its window looking out onto Daisy's beloved small garden. There's a rowan tree in the centre, and a fishpond in a wooden barrel beneath it that Tink loves to balance on the edge of. It's too deep for her to catch any of the fish, though. Umid planted a water lily in the barrel, he says it's the national flower of Persia. She and Avalie planted climbers all around the fences on both sides and the wall at the back.

When Daisy lumbers into the room Avalie has already got out card, scissors, felt pens and the gold paint they used for Christmas decorations. "I want to write names on these: one for Elijah, one for Rudi, one for Electra and one for Emil. When are they coming, Mama?"

"Electra and her brothers should be arriving in Lincoln tonight," Daisy says, stretching her back before she settles in the chair next to Avalie. "But we'll see them tomorrow afternoon, along with–" she counts them off on her fingers: "–Gramma, Grandpop, G-Sue, Aunty Lola, Uncle Jake, Elijah, Uncle Jamie, Aunty Leilja, Uncle Joe and Uncle Amar. That's a long list, isn't it? And most exciting of all your new cousin William. So perhaps you should make a star for William, too, as he's new to the family and he's bound to be shy. I'll need a ruler to draw the stars for you. Can you get one from the drawers?"

"Oh yeah, I forgot about William. How old is he again?" she passes the ruler over to Daisy, who starts drawing the stars.

"William is nine years old."

"That means he's the same age as Electra. She won't be the oldest cousin anymore, will she, Mama?"

"No, in fact William's a little bit older than her. Apparently, he loves football too, so they'll have something in common. Uncle Joe's going to have to learn to play, isn't he? Oh dear, he hated sports when he was a kid."

"Maybe Uncle Amar can be the dad who plays football with William. Then Uncle Joe can just watch." Avalie is already plastering gold paint over the first star. She assesses Daisy's progress with the cutting out. "Oh yeah, and don't forget to cut one out for me, Mama. I want my name on one. They can be the cousin stars. Oh yeah, and one for Sara. We can put it on her cot when she's been born can't we, Mama?"

"That's a great idea, sweet pea. Oh look, Sara seems to agree as well, she just gave me a great big kick. Feel that—not with . . . ah, too late. Now look, there's a gold handprint on my dress where your baby sister kicked your hand. Maybe she wants to be a footballer too, hey?"

———

Avalie's fourth birthday party is in full swing when Umid comes into the front room to find Daisy. He takes his wife's hand. He's shaved off his beard again and allowed his hair to grow longer than usual, it makes him look younger. She has a strong recollection of the first time she met him, under an olive tree on Samos. How he smoothed out his blanket for her and wiped his hands clean on his jeans before shaking her hand. She shivers to think she had no idea then how their lives would turn out. The documentary Umid featured in was bought by a bigger broadcasting company last year and is about to be shown all over Europe, with rights sold to the US and Australia. The new company want to make a follow-up programme. Umid has agreed to take part as long as the privacy of his wife and children is respected. Daisy's so proud of him. For everything. He completed his full-time

317

MA course with a grade just short of distinction, despite most of the work having to be done under lockdown conditions due to the pandemic. He was asked to speak at a conference on migration at Hull University, and more speaking dates are in the calendar.

Those lockdown months the year before last were hard on the two of them, trying to get to know each other again but not being able to see or touch. Daisy had begun the process of buying the house before the first lockdown, and then everything had stalled. Umid had become ill with the virus after Christmas, and Daisy hadn't been allowed to care for him. She tightens her grip on his hand. *But we're here now.*

"Where's our sprite?" Umid says, looking around for Avalie. They both scan the hordes of children racing from one part of the room to another. Joe's set up a kind of treasure hunt, but Daisy can't make out the rules. She's not sure if anyone can, but they seem to be having fun. Joe's adopted son, a thin boy with a set expression, sits alone on a stool tucked between the end of the sofa and the wall. Joe confessed to her that William's seeming inability to adapt to his new living circumstances is causing tension between him and Amar.

"William was fine when we had him on visits," Joe said. "But now he's moved in he seems to hate us both. We don't know what to do."

"Oh Joe, you both knew it was going to be difficult, didn't you? William's just testing you. You have to be strong. Falling apart's what he expects, don't prove him right."

Now she sees Amar sitting on the end of the sofa and leaning towards the boy. He makes a comment she can't hear. The boy's mouth twists up at one corner. He's going to be fine; Daisy thinks. *It just takes time, like it did for Umid and me to adapt to co-parenting Avalie. And look at us now.*

Avalie comes bounding into the room, dragging her grandmother by the hand.

"I just showed Gramma my guineapigs," she says. "Gramma makes a good guineapig noise, don't you, Gramma.

Do it, please."

Red-faced, Maya obliges by squeaking from the back of her throat with her lips pressed together. The other grandchildren stop what they're doing and break into a round of applause, led by Electra. Rudi and Elijah join in with the squeaking, scampering around the room on all fours, while two-year-old Emil tries to keep up with them and falls over Grandpop's legs. It's chaos.

Daisy notices 'G-Sue', formerly of the surname Metherington, looking Maya up and down from her perch on the sofa arm next to Con. G-Sue's wearing a blue and silver bodycon dress. Daisy suspects she'd never be able to get up off the couch if she actually sat *on* it.

Daisy and Umid weren't the only couple in the family to get married last year. Con and Susannah have moved into a new build on the outskirts of Navengore. The Cottages is now on the market; Lola has closed the day nursery and she and Elijah are moving into Jake's house in Sleaford. Lola's back in the job she had before Elijah was born. At Christmas, she and Jake announced their engagement. Lola says she wants a long engagement so they can save up for a big wedding. Daisy remembers the joy of her tiny, homemade wedding to Umid last summer, when she was two months pregnant. Only Joe and Amar were able to make it over from Germany at such short notice, which is why Jamie and his family have made the effort for Avalie's birthday, and to visit The Cottages for the last time.

Daisy laughs out loud at the guineapig antics. "Oh Mum, I remember you imitating mine and Lola's guineapigs when we were small. That was one reason I wanted to buy them for Avalie."

"Daisy," Umid presses her hand. "It's time for the call with my mom, we should make sure we're online before she is. You know how stressed she gets. Hang on, Avalie, don't go anywhere, we're about to talk to your *maman bozorg*, she wants to wish you a happy birthday, remember?"

"Oh yeah, *Maman Bozorg*. I'm excited!" but she has a glazed look in her eyes. Over stimulation, maybe. Or too much sugar. "Umm, can Gramma come?"

"Why of course," Umid says graciously. "The two grandmothers can discuss their brilliant granddaughter together. What a great idea. That's if you want to, Maya?"

"I'd be delighted," Maya says, taking Avalie's hand as the four of them head to the wasteland of desecrated food remains in the dining room, where the laptop is set up ready. "It will be wonderful to meet Grandma-Darya at last, I've heard so much about her."

Iran is a Muslim country.
If you change your religion, you are threatened
with persecution.
A friend told me about Christianity.
I studied on the internet,
changed my habits, made my decision –
changed religion.
I miss my wife,
her brown hair and blue eyes.
She's a psychologist,
a friend's wife introduced us, and we fell in love.
We've been married five years.
She encouraged me to try and find
a safer life for us in the UK.

48

Maya

Lincoln, June 2022

The doors of Refuge House opened at 10 am, but when Maya arrived at 9.30 there was already a family standing outside. A father with a thick, untidy beard and a torn tracksuit jacket, a mother wearing a black headscarf and a long grey dress, and four children: three small girls and a boy of about twelve, Maya guessed. The family were accompanied by the social worker who regularly collaborated with Refuge House. The social worker's car was parked on double yellow lines outside the building in the centre of town, so Maya understood the visit to be serious. The social worker, Denise, caught her eye and whispered. "Straight off the boat." They must have been bussed up from the south coast.

Maya hid her shock at the sight of the older of the three girls, a child of nine or ten, maybe? She was so tiny; it was hard to tell. But the resigned expression on her face suggested she was older than she looked. The child wore a pair of adult-size flip-flops. She shuffled around her parents on the pavement. Maya swallowed a lump in her throat, meeting the social worker's eyes again above the girl's head.

"Come inside," unlocking the glass doors, she ushered the children in ahead of her. "Let's get some lights on." She smiled at the boy. "What's your name?"

"Alan," he raised his chin.

"And where have you come from?"

"Kurdistan."

"Okay, well, welcome to Lincoln. I hope you'll come and see us regularly here at Refuge House. We have a room with computers in, you know. You can play games in there or do your homework. I'm sure you'll be going to school soon."

She disabled the alarm and pressed the light switches in the corridor; almost a tunnel that led into a large, bright space with glass panes in the ceiling.

"Come in, everyone," she turned to smile at the father, carrying the second-youngest daughter, aged about four; and the wide-eyed mother, with the two-or-three-year-old in her arms. "I expect there are a lot of things you need. Let me take you through to our supplies room. You can choose clothes and shoes for yourselves and your children, and we also have household items; bedding, curtains, rugs, pots and pans, etcetera."

The father, his eyes downcast, looked to his son. Alan spoke to him in Kurdish and the father said something to his wife. They both nodded at Maya, attempting smiles.

"Thank you," the mother said haltingly, and the father pressed his free hand to his chest.

Maya blinked hard, forcing another bright smile onto her face as she unlocked the door to the supplies room, filled mostly with good clean second-hand items. There were some new donations too, and others like underwear and shoes bought with funding from Maya's list of donors. Something about this family struck her as familiar. It was another family she was thinking of, washed up on the beach at Samos five years ago. Daisy helped them. They also had

323

children around these ages. But they would be much bigger now. She wondered where that other family ended up, hoped they were safe and settled.

Inside the room, the parents got busy searching through boxes and rails of clothes for their youngest children, while the older girl and the boy looked around by themselves.

Maya turned her attention to the girl wearing ridiculously large flip-flops. "What's your name, love?"

The child pressed her lips together and glanced at her brother.

"Landa," he told Maya.

"And how old is she?" asked Maya.

"She's ten."

That girl is a mere sliver of flesh, Maya thought. Her thin shoulders were hunched, but her eyes when the veil of resignation parted were darting, alive and vivid. Maya reached to the rail and selected a few things she thought Landa might like, but the girl shook her head, determinedly sorting through t-shirts, dresses and jeans on her own.

"We need to find you some shoes," Maya said. She and Denise pulled out boxes of shoes together, ranging in various sizes for both the adults and the children.

Once Landa had shoes on her feet her demeanour changed, her face opened in a smile. Maya wanted to scoop her up, make whatever nightmares that haunted her go away.

The parents amassed a pile of t-shirts, leggings, socks and pants for their girls. From another box Maya fished out a t-shirt with a unicorn on the front, which she handed to the smallest child, but when the slightly older one spotted it, she grabbed the t-shirt for herself, and the two little girls fought over it with a crescendo of screams. The four-year-old broke into a bronchitic cough, tears and snot streaming down her face.

The parents tried to comfort their daughters, speaking calmly and stroking their heads and backs with gentle hands. Maya was blown away by their stoicism and dignity.

She couldn't imagine finding the courage to put her family through the kind of hellish journey she'd heard about repeatedly in recent years. She felt a hollow in her chest.

After some searching, she found a jacket for the father and a long dress and a coat for the mother. Alan had equipped himself with jeans, shorts, t-shirts and a hoody. He'd also found some trainers that fit.

"Do you have any football boots?" he asked Maya.

"I don't think so," Maya said, "but we can put out a call for you."

Landa carried her own small bag of clothes. Maya went off to the kitchen to make drinks for everybody, while Denise enlisted Alan's and his father's help to carry boxes of bedding and household items out to the car.

Once she'd locked the supplies room, Maya opened the toy cupboard where the younger children excitedly selected games and soft toys to take away. She showed Alan and Landa the computer room. While Denise drove off with the carload of supplies, Maya encouraged the parents to sit at one of the café tables and drink some coffee before Denise returned to collect the family and take them back to their new temporary home. It was a small, terraced house on a side street off a busy road east of the city centre, Denise had said.

Maya's team of volunteers was beginning to arrive, closely followed by groups of service users. The café area was becoming busy. Maya felt her face breaking into smile after smile as she embraced some of the younger male service users, the ones she called her 'fosters'. She'd never forgotten the feelings of those years when she didn't know where her own sons were, and she considered her nurturing of these young men from Africa and the Middle East a gift to their mothers. Sometimes she even got to be introduced to their mothers on video messages, those who were lucky enough to be able to maintain contact with their families.

Maya repeatedly rejoiced in the fact that she'd found a

place to belong at last, and close enough to her daughters to visit them regularly. Her occupation as manager of Refuge House was everything she'd been looking for. No need to move on anymore, there was a renewable flow of displaced sons to care for, and a stable home for her to return to at the end of each day. Some of her money from The Cottages, along with sizable donations, from often-surprising sources – including Con: the wedding present Daisy had asked for in honour of her new husband, he said – had been put to good use in setting up the place that felt like home from home. A place she could continue to do the work she loved whilst keeping her arthritic joints warm.

Wednesday was men's distribution day. The queues of mainly young men waiting for the clothes rails and boxes to be brought out reminded Maya of the distribution queues in Calais, only at least the volunteers and service users here were not all standing in mud. It never failed to strike Maya that these same young men were only weeks or months earlier the ones standing in that mud or dry dust across the channel, accepting food and clothes from volunteers such as herself. And Bill.

Bill was still in Calais, for a while at least. But he'd visited Lincoln the previous year to help Maya set up Refuge House. He stayed in the spare room of her three-bedroom house near the South common, where there were plenty of walks nearby for a now-ageing Alicia at the end of Maya's long days at work.

When she met Bill at the railway station, she felt dizzy at the sight of him. A sense of comfort and familiarity flowed through her. They were both wearing masks over their noses and mouths, of course, but it was the crinkles around his eyes that got to her. An unexpected realisation that *of course* she liked him 'like that'. She was astonished that she'd never recognised her feelings for him during all the years they worked alongside each other in the camps. Bill was one of the trustees of Refuge House. At their preliminary meetings with the local council, he impressed the decision-makers with his knowledge and understanding of the needs of asylum seekers and refugees and their potential benefits to the city. Maya felt certain it was down to Bill that they were awarded a ten-year tenancy of the building on Silver Street.

Bill and Maya were now 'going out' with each other, albeit from a distance. Bill never had bought his flat in Calais, he'd told her he couldn't bear to commit himself permanently there once Maya had left. He was currently finalising his personal business in France and preparing to make the move back to the UK. He planned to rent a flat in Lincoln to start with, and they would see how their relationship progressed from there.

In my country
fires rise from the ground.
tourists arrive to take selfies amongst the flames.
My land is occupied, my people disenfranchised,
I was tortured for protesting.
I crossed the channel in a small boat.
At first the sea was calm but closer to the UK,
in the shipping lanes, the waves rose higher.
I was afraid.
We were all afraid.

49

Daisy's Diary

September 2022

Hello Diary,

I'm afraid I haven't written in you much lately, or much at all, to be honest. I remember the hopes and plans I had for you, diary, when I first set off with Mum for the mysterious Greek island of Samos. I thought I'd write in you every day. Instead, there are only a few entries from that time. Life got in the way, as they say. Whoever 'they' is. Well, I say it, anyway.

Hard to believe that was five-and-a-half years ago. I've just looked back through your early pages and seen how I was wondering who would read you one day, after I'm gone. I never imagined a few years later I would have two daughters of my own, and such a story to tell. I'm going to try harder now, to tell it. Reading back over those few entries from 2017 - and the ones around the time Avalie was born (I'm sorry, my sweet Sara, that I haven't written about your birth yet) and then the lockdown months, which I recorded avidly because I wanted to write and write about the re-found love between Umid and me – make me realise how important you could be in helping me remember things in the future, diary.

The story of us. Now he's my darling husband. My love.

It's not always easy, you know. To be with the one you love so much it hurts. Sometimes he shuts me out and I feel angry and resentful with him. Sometimes – and it's hard for me to admit this, even to myself – I find myself thinking 'after everything I've done for you'. Awful, I know. I'm trying hard to be a better person. It's understandable that Umid needs to retreat into his own head occasionally. He still has nightmares, about fleeing from Iran, about the boat trips, about the border crossings. Missing his mother. But most of all, he says, about the months in the UK waiting for his Home Office interview and then waiting for a decision, worrying he might be sent back. And on top of all that there are his complicated feelings about not being in Iran now. Probably never being able to go back. He feels he should be a part of the revolution. A friend of his was killed recently for protesting. But that's why Umid had to leave in the first place. I suppose it might sometimes come across to him that I want him to forget all that and just appreciate what we have now, but I don't, truly. Those experiences are part of him and how they've formed him is what made me love him in the first place.

But yeah, as Avalie would say. I need to be more understanding.

Umid's in Birmingham for two nights. Staying with our mutual friend from Samos: Moussa, who's waiting for his wife and daughter to join him in the UK at last. Umid was invited to speak at the University of Birmingham at something called a social geography conference. He's also been offered a position as co-director on a new documentary about refugees, so he'll be away more often from now on. I'll miss him. But I'm so proud of him.

I hope he finds time to call me later.

Avalie is fast asleep in her bed now, clutching the paisley scarf that little boy and his aunt on Samos gave me. Rasan and Farah. I wonder what happened to them. I hemmed the scarf with a gold silk border and placed it in Avalie's crib when she was a baby: I wanted her to have a link with the camp where I met her father.

It was Avalie's first day at big school today. It's a shame Umid wasn't here to see her off. My eyes fill with tears as I think of her tight little smile when she went into the classroom on her own, while I stood in the playground with Sara in her pram. Oh Avalie. what things we've been through together. I go cold now when I think of how I took her to the sites around Calais. When I ask her, she says she doesn't remember anything of that time, but sometimes she'll make a little comment – for example, she mentioned the childcare she used to go to when me and Mum went to the warehouse, she described Juliette's (the woman who looked after her) kitchen perfectly – so I know those memories are inside her. I'm hoping it will help her understand her father's occasional dark moods as she gets older.

I'm sitting in the back bedroom now, at my desk (Umid has a desk in our bedroom). I keep my sewing machine in here and this is where I do my lesson planning – I teach Year 6 now, although I won't be going back to work until Sara turns one – and for now I plan to try to continue these diary sessions.

Sara was born in this room. I'll describe the room and then tell you about her birth, diary. It was the most magical night.

I forgot to mention Sara is asleep on my lap right now. She's such a contented baby when she's kept close to me or Umid. She's also happy to sit in her baby chair and pump her fists at Avalie while she watches her daily allowance of

TV. That's while I get the evening meal prepared.

So, the room. It's small, just big enough for a double sofa bed and my desk and chair. The window looks out onto my back garden. I made curtains for it from a thick flannel sheet which I dyed pale green and stencilled daisies onto. I also sewed the sofa bed cover in the same fabric. The walls are the colour of peaches. I oiled the bare floorboards and laid a thick, fawn rug over them. The room feels cosy and nest like; that's why I wanted to give birth in here.

I expected Sara to look the same as Avalie when she was born, but whereas Avalie was small and had a tiny, elfin face; Sara was plump and round cheeked. Her skin was covered in vernix, even though she was five days late.

Mum came over from Lincoln to look after Avalie, though Sara's big sister was present immediately after the birth. It was a Monday afternoon, I had to call Umid home from work. My labour was quick and triumphant. I felt Sara's feet pushing on the top of my uterus as she helped herself be born. My favourite midwife attended the birth and I'm sure that helped relax me and made it easier.

Oh, my sweet Sara. I'm sure your birth was simple and uncomplicated because I wanted for nothing. Your father was there, that was all that mattered.

When you were born, in a hurry, the midwife encouraged me to pick you up from the floor, but I looked at Umid's face and I said I wanted him to be the one who held you first.

He raised you into his arms, your cord still attached to me, and whispered part of a surah from the Quran into your ear. Even though he's not religious, as he's told me plenty of times. But I was glad he had the opportunity with you. I remembered how he'd whispered to Avalie the first time he met her.

This little one is beginning to stir on my lap. Soon I shall feed and change her before putting her into my bed and hoping she'll sleep on her own for a while. Then I'll ring Lola and see how she's getting on. She's been much sicker during this pregnancy than she was with Elijah. I thought she would want to bring the wedding forward but no; she's still planning on a huge affair in a fancy venue, but she's postponed it for a couple of years.

Before I leave you for tonight, diary, I just want to update you about Mum.

My amazing Mum. You know she came back from Portugal a few weeks before the UK: in fact, before the whole world was plunged into lockdown. That was a scary, confusing time, wasn't it? A world pandemic, the stuff of blockbuster movies. Our family was lucky enough to sail through it, apart from Umid and Dad. But neither had to be admitted to hospital, thankfully. I look back at your pages, diary, and remember the weird feeling of having to write that word, lockdown, for the first time. I never wrote much about Mum then, because I only really wanted to talk about Umid.

Mum stayed at the flat with Lola and me, but she was restless and wanted to do something, she said. While I rushed through viewings of properties in Hull, she decided she was going to buy a house in Lincoln. She'd had money in the bank ever since her divorce from Dad. She found a three-bedroom house with enough space that the boys and their families can stay with her if they want. Good thing now that The Cottages is sold, and Dad and Susannah have moved into a smaller newbuild. At the same time as the paperwork was going through – delayed, like the paperwork for my house – she had the idea to build a centre for refugees and asylum seekers in Lincoln. That's when Bill managed to get over from Calais to help. They had so much bureaucracy to go through, I don't think Mum could have done it alone. Besides Bill, she needed two other trustees for her newly set up charity. One of them is our old family doctor, who Mum used to work for. The other is a solicitor, one of Mum and Dad's dinner party friends from back in the day.

Refuge House is in its second year now. I can't tell you how proud I am of Mum for what she's done. She has a paid position as the overall manager, and she's responsible for balancing the books and applying for funding, but most of the people who help run the centre are volunteers. Now Avalie's at school, I've agreed to drive over once a week with Sara to help. I'd like to become involved in distributions again.

But the main point of this update is that Mum and Bill have got together at last. Bill's given up the flat he was renting, and he's now moved in with Mum. She says it's no big deal, that she was perfectly happy on her own, but there's a light in her eyes now that I think has been missing for the past few years.

Happy endings do exist, only they're really beginnings. All the sorrows and regrets that preceded the endings/beginnings — and I know Mum has plenty of those as does Umid, as do I — run through our blood. They help build us.

I think Mum's grown back into herself. She knows who she is again. From my perspective she's the best mother, and grandmother (of almost eight) but most of all she's a strong and determined woman who's making a difference to the world. She's always making admiring comments about the strength of will of her daughters and granddaughters, but she doesn't seem to realise we all inherited our strengths from her.

Oops, Sara's woken up properly and is starting to cry.

That's all for now.

Goodnight, diary.

Author's note

At the end of *The Vagabond Mother*, Maya decides to invite her daughter Daisy to accompany her on a volunteering expedition to a Greek refugee camp. At the time I had no plan to write a sequel, and I thought it would be a good way to steer Maya's ongoing story in the imagination of the reader and leave it there. It also gave me an opportunity to lift Daisy out of the claustrophobic situation with her twin sister Lola, who had recently given birth.

Since about 2015 I've followed the progress of the ever-increasing world refugee crisis. The theme of refugees featured heavily in my 2019 novel *Sea Babies*. I never thought I would be able to write a novel about refugees as their stories weren't mine to tell, and I didn't know anyone who was a refugee.

But I wanted to incorporate the theme of displacement into a new novel, and I also wanted to turn the premise of *The Vagabond Mother* – that to own nothing is to be free – upside down. To be in a situation of wandering homelessness, carrying everything on your back, can only constitute freedom if you have chosen it.

Because I had left Maya and Daisy on their way to a refugee camp, I decided to take up their story again. It would involve a lot of research and the idea that I would one day volunteer in a refugee camp myself.

Then, in 2021 at the tail-end of Covid 19, I answered a call from Hull Help for Refugees to help at a weekly distribution of clothes and other essentials to people who were asylum seekers and refugees and living in my city.

At the time I had no idea of the impact this would have on my perception of myself and of my place in the world. I have never felt such love, acceptance, and humility as during the past couple of years since I've been involved with the community at Welcome House in Hull, a centre for asylum seekers and refugees. Maya's project, the fictional Refuge House, is inspired by this.

During the early months of 2022 I spent some intense hours at Welcome House, interviewing many asylum seekers and refugees and writing down their testimonies in their own words. These I transcribed into a 16-piece poem, the verses of which now form the chapter and part headings in *The Vagabond Seekers*. The people I interviewed have been happy to have their stories told. I hope to facilitate the telling of a lot more of these stories in my next book.

The story of the refugee character Umid in *The Vagabond Seekers* is amalgamated from the testimonies I've been privileged to be entrusted with.

Tracey Scott-Townsend

Acknowledgements

Where do I start? The Vagabond Seekers is about family, connection, and community. I'd like to thank my birth children, as always: Felix, Ruben, Zak and Faye for helping me develop as a person and being constantly inspirational to my writing with their travels and achievements, and their basic good-human qualities. Also, for making me a granny, Zak and Jacky!

My sons-by-choice, Omid and Mujtaba. Newly arrived, Omid came full of energy into our clothes distribution at Welcome House one day, his black curls bouncing. "I want to help," he said. "I volunteered in Greece and in Calais". We were novices at the job, he proceeded to show us how it was done most effectively. He was also there almost from the beginning of me writing *The Vagabond Seekers*. His extraordinarily vivid personality, sense of humour, creativity and determination won me over straight away: I'm proud and honoured that he calls me Mum and I love him to the moon and back.

My connection with Mujtaba rose through his inexhaustible thirst for knowledge and self-improvement, he asked for books and learning materials. He has strength, fortitude, and only occasionally lets his vulnerability show. He's taught me an enormous amount about cricket! His mother told him on a video call to ask me to look after her son, and I promised I would. I'm proud to be his 'other mum' and I love him, too. I always wanted six children: I have them now.

The contributors to the chapter heading testimonies, and those who helped bring humanity to my attempt to portray the refugees' situations in this book, and those who continue to inspire me as a writer and a human being: Karim, Mohammed, Rawad, Baraka, Elham, Hassan, Fawaz, Yacob, Jafar, Eissa, Hasan, Shakib, Leonel, Joel, Raul, Moussa,

Meysam, Raquel, Eduardo, Amin, Djimet, Amir, Anei, Mohammed M., Iftikhar, Qaderi, Sayed, Suliman, Yelyzaveta, Jasem, Mohammed A. and many others, thank you for sharing your stories with me.

The community at Welcome House who have really made me feel a part of things: the super-strong women Manel and Warda especially for their amazing cooking and organisational skills, Bashir for supporting my book launch(es), lovely Maryam who always has a smile for me, all the reception and hardworking kitchen staff.

The volunteers of Hull Help for Refugees and the many other charity organisations that work together with refugees and asylum seekers in Hull and elsewhere.

The wonderful crew at Care 4 Calais when Phil and I volunteered there, the experience was humbling.

Thanks, as ever, to Sara Jayne Slack for her editorial advice, and to Sarah Carby, my amazing and dedicated beta reader. I always enjoy sharing early drafts of my books with both of you.

Finally, thanks to Phil, for going through this journey with me every time.

About the Author

Tracey Scott-Townsend is the author of eight novels. Her latest, *The Vagabond Seekers* is the sequel to her 2020 novel *The Vagabond Mother*.

Tracey was a practicing visual artist for many years and is a former spoken word poet. She is the mother of four grown children and one grandson, who she spends time with on his family's rural homestead in Portugal every spring and autumn. She also has two 'adopted' sons.

Tracey works as a physical activities facilitator with asylum seekers and refugees in Hull.

She loves writing in her shed, travelling with her husband and dogs in their camper van, and working in her garden. There she grows vegetables and creates a wildlife haven for the multitude of frogs and one minute newt, who have congregated around the tiny tin-bath pond in the neglected lawn.